BOSSY
BODYGUARD

DOMINATING DESIRES
BOOK THREE

MAHI MISTRY

Bossy Bodyguard

Copyright 2023 Mahi Mistry

All rights reserved. No part of this book may be reproduced or transmitted in any form or by any electronic or mechanical means, including information storage and retrieval systems, without written permission from the author, except for the use of brief quotations in a book review.

This book is a piece of fiction. Names, characters, places, and incidents are the product of the author's imagination. Any resemblance to actual events, locales, or persons, living or dead, is coincidental.

This book is licensed for your personal enjoyment only.

This book may not be re-sold or given away to other people. If you are reading this book and did not purchase it, or it was not purchased for your use only, then you should return it to the seller and purchase your own copy. Thank you for respecting the hard work of this author.

Published by Mahi Mistry
Cover Design by GetCovers
Edited by Jeanie Creech
Proofread by Edresa Ramos
ISBN e-Book: 978-93-5526-735-1
ISBN paperback: 978-93-5627-346-7

*Dedicated to all the readers.
You are more than enough.*

PART I

"The only eyes I want on me right now are yours."

1
QUITE A DIRTY LITTLE MOUTH YOU HAVE

EMMA

Turns out, going alone at a sex-club was lonelier than I thought.

My eyes zeroed in on the bar. Many patrons clad in expensive suits and glittering dresses were either seated in the personal booth for more privacy or dancing on the stage. Heads turned towards me, and the awareness of being watched creeped over my skin with a slight shiver.

But I ignored it.

Because I was Emma Moore, and I had been under an eye of surveillance since the day my mother conceived me.

My fingers clammed into a fist and my breath wavered, but I focused on one thing only——the bar. I needed to stop *it*. Stop thinking for a while. Sex was unfortunately out of the question, but thankfully, humankind has created several other ways to give our minds a break. One of them was—

"A Negroni please," I said to Joe, the bartender, who winked at me and started making one of my favorite drinks.

"No more seconds today, Em." Joe slid the pink glass towards me, a scrumptious slice of orange peel garnish bobbing over it. "Or your brother will kill me."

"Or he might skin you alive, sweetheart." I batted my lashes at him, taking a long sip. The strong alcoholic drink with its sweet taste gave a small sting of burn to my throat as I downed it all in two more swigs.

Joe looked horrified.

"One more please," I said just as sweetly, sliding the empty glass back at him.

He sighed, taking it and filling another one for me. Then he served a handsome couple in the corner. Both men were in such awe of one another, whispering in each other's ears and smiling. Something bitter slid into my throat and I quickly looked away from them.

My hands clenched remembering this morning—the funeral of my mother.

Without thinking, I threw my head back and swallowed another gulp of the alcohol, wiping my lips with my hand— chuckling how horrified my mother would be if she saw me right now. I drank another glass and pouted at Joe when he showed me the rule that showed only two drinks were allowed.

Grumbling underneath my breath, I slid off the stool, wobbling in my high heels. I was in a rush, so I had worn my favorite Manolo Blahnik pink heels with a pretty gemstone each. I was so caught up thinking about the afternoon that I didn't see where I was stepping. Seconds stretched by as my eyes slowly blinked at the lights and realized that the world wasn't tripping. I was.

"Motherfuckingshitballs—"

"Quite a dirty little mouth you have."

A hot, deep voice whispered, strong hand keeping me from tripping. My first thought hearing his voice was *sex*. And not the sweet, sensual kind with a lover's clumsy kisses. It was deep, rough, hair-pulling, ass-spanking, knees-and-lips-bruising kind of sex.

Mmm, sexy.

My eyes drifted over to the burly man who was sipping his drink with the stealth of a predator. *Panther.* He looked like a panther in his black shirt and mysterious aura. I tilted my head, my hair falling over my bare shoulders as goosebumps skittered over my entire body, noticing the large palm wrapped around my arm.

"You should see what else this dirty little mouth can do."

I blinked. The slow realization of what I had just drunkenly blurted echoing through my head.

Uh. Oh.

I did not just say that out loud.

"Oh, but you did," the smoky voice said, my eyes drifting from the inked hand on my bare elbow to the arm that was hidden beneath the sleeves of a shirt and an expensive suit hanging from the stool. I was impressed at the size of his biceps, which were probably as big as my thigh, and over to his exposed neck and then his face. *My god, he is one of the hottest men I've ever seen.* "And if that polite but tempting comment was an invitation for me to get you in a room… then my answer is yes. Only if you are sober."

His eyes were on my face when he said those dirty words in his sexy voice. My hands clenched into a fist at the look in his piercing dark eyes. He was too intense. His large frame that dwarfed the stool, his hands, his handsome, sharp face and his eyes. They seemed like they weren't looking at my face… but at my soul.

It unnerved me.

It unnerved me even more when I decided to play with him.

Maybe I was really drunk.

A sly smirk traced my lips, my eyes raking over his broad frame. *Perfect.* So fucking perfect. My mom's tasteless funeral. My boyfriend cheating on me with a guy. And now having this hot specimen falling in my lap was just *perfect*. Because I could really do with some hot, hard and rough one-night stand. Especially in my brother's sex club. I could just imagine the look of anger on his face. *Ha!*

Flipping my hair over my shoulder, I stepped closer, making sure that my bare thigh brushed his silk pants that were so perfectly tailored that I had to stop myself from shamelessly ogling his strong thighs.

"Are you sure you'll be able to handle this mouth?" I asked, my voice dropping to a lower note so I could sound sultrier. My black almond-shaped nail trailed over his arm revealing ink running through his shirt and over his shoulder that was strong and firm. I could just imagine how it would feel to sink my fingers into them. My mouth went dry when he let me touch his neck, his skin soft and warm.

Even his Adam's apple was hot.

A tremor of pleasure ran through my spine when he leaned closer, the tips of his fingers brushing the back of my thigh, making my head buzz with potent heat.

"There's only one way to find out, isn't there, Doll?" he said, taking a sip as ice clunked against each other in his glass.

"I'm Emma," I tried to keep my voice even, but it turned into a small whisper.

He noticed. His lips curling at the corner as he said, "Cillian."

Cillian. It suited him.

His Asian features seemed familiar, yet unique. High cheekbones, a strong nose which seemed a little crooked—maybe from a fall—no, he didn't look like someone who'd just accidentally fall—and hooded brows. His lips seemed soft and lush with a deep yet already healed scar running through them on the left corner. They seemed oddly inviting, but what unnerved me were… those eyes.

I looked away, blood rushing to my cheeks when he noticed me staring. *What the fuck am I doing?* I wasn't someone who got embarrassed staring at someone else. Others get embarrassed and scared when I found them staring at me.

Who is this guy?

No—he was too big to be ever called a guy. He was a *man* through and through.

"Then we should—"

"Are you alone?" His smooth voice purred through my ear and I swallowed down the urge to lean closer and smell his perfume.

Or sit on his lap.

"What?" My voice was high-pitched, and I had to move my hair over my shoulder to fan my neck. I was getting hot. I was feeling hot. "Alone? Yes. I recently broke up with my jerk—"

"Let me rephrase, Doll." He moved closer, so close that I could blink at his chocolaty eyes without craning my neck, so close that I could smell his smoky cologne, so close that his warm breath caressed my lips. "Did you come here alone?"

Doll. I had been called a doll many a time, but mostly it was condescending. When he said it though, it was as if he was making love to that word. Do*ll.* Trailing the l's a little and making my panties damp with just one fucking word. *Doll.* I wanted to hear him call me that again and again and again.

I swallowed the lump in my throat and nodded. "Yes. I came here alone."

I knew what was coming next. He'd ask me for my hand if he's a gentleman, but he didn't look like he was a gentleman despite the expensive fabric of his suit and how polished his shoes were. He'd probably just take my hand or hurl me over his shoulder and lock us both in a room until we were satisfied.

He hummed, a low rumbling sound that felt too intimate and too raw. "Are you into primal kink, then?"

My eyes widened and my lips parted, his eyes flickering to them for a second. "Primal kink?"

"Prey? Predator?" He squinted his eyes as he looked over my body, my skin singing with warmth just by his gaze, and he hadn't even touched me yet. "You seem like a prey."

"I'm not!" I snapped, my hands clenching on my clutch as my heart began racing. Licking my lips, I averted my eyes from his face to his watch. It seemed oddly cheap compared to his entire expensive outfit. It didn't match, but it was vintage. A classic.

I met his stare again and said, "I'm not. Why'd you ask?" *Are you into it?* I added mentally. *If so, then I'm into it too.*

His eyes slid over my shoulder and they sharpened like a blade. "Someone has been watching you, Emma."

My nerves stirred, and I turned to see where he was looking. There were a lot of people in the club. But there was also a staged space where people who had voyeuristic kinks could watch the crowd. I shuddered, hating the feeling of being looked at when I wasn't aware.

Shaking my head, I brushed it off, knowing someone must have recognized me from the thousands of tabloids with my face plastered all over them since my mother's death.

"The only eyes I want on me right now are yours," I whispered, keeping my attention on him, aware of others' eyes turning towards us. Why wouldn't they stare? He was so hot, and I was ready to pull my skirt up and sit on him then and there, giving them a worthy show.

"Is that so?" he grumbled, his voice low and rough. I shivered when the tips of his fingers brushed over my inner thigh before they trailed over my waist, his hold firm. Like he meant business. Like I was *his* for the night.

"Come with me. I'm going to take my time to see what that dirty little mouth does, Doll."

2

SHOW ME

CILLIAN

The girl in the black dress seemed like a nuisance. The kind that gets you in trouble with just one batt of her pretty long lashes or sweet smile full of dirty promises.

I could tell by the relaxed yet confident way she walked with a little sway of her hips which made me and the entire male population in the club clench their fists. She knew exactly what she was doing.

Little vixen.

Her baby blue eyes widened just a fraction when I stood up from the stool, easily towering over her curvy, short frame even when she was donning those sexy pink heels. I could sense the surprise and lust pooling in her panties—if she was wearing any—by the way her breath hitched and the subtle clench of her thighs.

Fuck me. I loved the way she smelled. A sweet, sensual mix of coconut and heady vanilla.

I raised my brow when her eyes peered over my frame for the umpteenth time. For a split second, the urge to just tug down my sleeves and call it a day came bubbling up. The stupid idea of Sean forcing me to go to the new sex club in town would be a failure, and he would set me up on a blind date with one of his paralegals. Again.

I was scary. I knew that. I saw it every day. Full of scars and ugly truths.

But before I could tell Emma to forget about it, she stepped closer, her eyes full of heat. Pink tongue poked out to wet her plump bottom lip as she whispered, her voice breathy, "Show me the way, Cillian."

I wanted to wrap my hand in her hair and make her say my name again. I controlled my desire and thought about this sinful night and how many chances I'd get to make her moan my name. Scream even. It was a good thing it was a sex club and I had read that my suite had soundproof walls.

I wrapped my arm around her waist, noting the small hue of blush pinking her cheeks, and made our way to the private elevators. I didn't notice her being uncomfortable, but I could see that she was nervous. Tucking her hair behind her ear, fidgeting with the hem of her dress that was made for her.

"Are you having cold feet, Emma?" I asked, pausing in the hallway with dim lights. Unfortunately, it wasn't the best time to talk about it, since we could hear the sounds of skin slapping against each other with sounds of pleasure pouring through the open sex rooms on the ground floor.

"I'm…" she paused, peering at me, and said, "I'm excited."

I stared at her. Her dress and the way she was fidgeting. I tilted my head. "Show me."

"What?" Her voice was barely audible.

I kept my eyes on her face and repeated, "Show me how excited you are, Doll."

Her eyes widened, understanding exactly what I meant. She looked around the hallway which had red dim lights and an exotic scent in the air. It was heady.

"Right here?"

"You heard me."

Emma took a shaky breath, staring at me as I slid my hand into my pocket. Mostly because I didn't want to push her back on the wall, tug her dress up and find out myself just how *'excited'* she was.

I waited patiently, keeping my eyes on her when she tugged her dress up a little. Her pupils were dilating and the pulse on her neck was hammering when her other hand followed. I stayed still, holding my breath, when I saw the look of pure lust flashing across her face once her fingers found what she was looking for between her thighs.

She was trying so hard not to let it affect her, trying to play it as if she did it every day, but I knew she didn't. Something about her seemed honest and innocent. I took a step closer when she tucked her dress back and lifted her hand between us, showing me her fingers.

My eyes finally drifted from her pretty face to her glistening fingers. They were coated in her arousal. *Fuck.* I was so close I could smell her.

"Good girl," I whispered. "Now lick them clean."

I didn't have to repeat it.

Emma took her fingers in her mouth and sucked them between her pouty lips, like I had told her.

"Such a good girl," I said in awe, her eyes glazing as her cheeks hollowed before she pulled out her fingers. "Don't swallow. I want a taste of your pretty pussy."

Her eyes widened, and a blush creeped up her neck when I closed the distance between us and cupped her cheek. Her skin was so soft underneath my calloused fingers. I tipped her jaw and waited for her to deny me or say no. Instead, Emma pushed her breasts against my chest, arching her back and planting her soft, luscious body against mine.

"Needy girl," I smirked, closing my eyes and claiming her

lips with mine in a soft, quick kiss. When I pulled back to look at her flushed face, I could smell her arousal.

The taste of her…

I pushed her back against the wall and swallowed her gasp of surprise with my mouth. If the first kiss was gentle, the second kiss was rough and passionate. I wasn't kissing her lips. I was claiming them, devouring her mouth, marking it. I slipped my tongue inside her and groaned when I tasted her.

Fuck. I needed more.

Angling her head, I kissed her harder, growling when her nails ran through my hair to my nape. She tasted so good that I wanted to lose all my inhibitions and kneel on the floor and eat her out in the hallway with her pink heels dangling over my shoulders.

Emma let out a small moan, rubbing herself on my thigh that was between her legs. *Dirty girl.* I pulled back, heaving as I fixed my shirt and hair. Her blonde hair was mussed, dress tucked up to reveal the small glimpse of pink fabric underneath. Pink shoes and pink panties.

"Let's go." I offered her my hand, and she took it, her pale skin glowing with red blush. "I need to have you naked and alone."

"Not a fan of exhibitionism, Cillian?" she asked, her sultry voice taunting me as I showed my membership card to the guard standing outside the private elevator.

After pressing the button on the highest floor, I turned my attention to her. "I don't like to share what's mine," I said in a firm voice and continued, "and you're mine for tonight, Doll."

3
HAPPY BIRTHDAY

EMMA

I don't like possessive men. Period. Nine out of the ten times, they think that I'm their object of desire and a toy to play with when bored. Like a kitten who would hiss at anyone who tries to steal his favorite toy.

But when Cillian said it...

I don't like to share what's mine. And you're mine for tonight, Doll.

It wasn't possessive. It was demanding. An order. A prayer, if you will. And it was just for one night. I was his, and he was mine.

So why not have a little bit of fun?

My eyes ran over his form in the suit, stripping him naked in my head and wondering how hot he'd look with tattoos all over his body. *Did he have them all over his body?* I was willing to find out as soon as I got him alone.

It was different with him standing so close in the elevator but not touching me. My thighs were still a little shaky at what he had told me to do in the hallway, and I had done it without a single thought. Because no one challenged Emma Moore and won. I had done it out of pride. I wasn't afraid if anyone saw me and enjoyed the show, but some small part of me had done it for the approval in his eyes and the soft way he called me *good girl*.

My lips still felt the press of his lips and the bite of his teeth. How he had kissed me… claiming my mouth with his, tasting me and devouring me.

The elevator stopped on the top floor, my nerves twisting in my stomach. I clenched my clutch and walked into the private suite which had high ceilings, spacious marble floors in black, and furniture covered in blood red velvet. My attention stayed on the St. Andrew's Cross with its cuffs and the staged four-poster bed.

"Do you want something to drink?"

I turned around to see him drop his membership card in the bowl by the door containing a key fob. *Was he a regular here? Did he bring all his conquests to the suite?*

"I would like some champagne," I replied, walking towards the sprawling couch in front of the fireplace, throwing my clutch on the armchair.

"It's much better than I thought," Cillian hummed, looking around the suite as if he was seeing it for the first time. "Less dungeon-y."

"Is this your first time here?" I asked because I wanted to know.

How the hell did a man like him enter Vixen, the sex club, and not get laid every time?

He glanced at me, his eyes on my feet where I was fiddling with my heels. "Do they hurt?"

Frowning, I shook my head. "No."

"Good. Keep them on," he said, removing his silver cuff links. My insides warmed, leaving the heels alone. "It is my first time in the club."

I tilted my head, watching him remove his suit jacket and neatly hang it on the coat holder. My mother wasn't a good mother among various other things, but she was good at teaching me how to move gracefully, sit, talk, eat, smile and even move my eyes. I could notice that Cillian's movements were also methodical. Yet clean. He made something as small as removing his suit seem like an art. I could stare at him all day.

I would guess he was in the military or a cop. Or worse… a hitman.

"Then why do you have a premium membership card?" I asked, crossing my legs so the dress hitched just a little over my thighs, but his eyes didn't stray from my face when he walked to the couch holding a bucket of rocks with champagne, and two flutes.

He looked absolutely ravenous and delicious in the dim glow of fire. With his black shirt stretching over his broad shoulders, revealing more tattoos on his neck and rolled-up sleeves, he was sex on legs. Powerful yet sensual.

No one should look that good holding a bucket of champagne and flutes.

That was just illegal.

"Would you believe me if I said my friend gifted me this membership on my fortieth birthday?" he asked, his dark eyes warm.

I nodded, too stunned to speak. He didn't look like he was forty. More like early thirties. *Damn*. He has fine genes.

"W-when was it?" I asked and leaned to pour the bubbly drink in a flute. I needed a drink or two.

"Today."

My eyes snapped at him, seeing him sit so calmly.

He turned forty… *today*.

I parted my lips to speak, but I stopped when the cold drink poured over the glass, spilling over the coffee table. I jumped and moved the bottle on the side, mumbling a small sorry.

"You seem surprised."

"Yeah, um, sorry—happy birthday!" I stuttered, hating myself for being a nervous wreck. "I thought you'd be in your early or mid-thirties, that's all. You look handsome for your age."

Shut. Up. Emma.

A small smirk curled over the ends of his lips and my attention was caught by the scar running across it. It was strangely erotic.

"I'm glad that you think that, Emma. I suppose you are in your early twenties?"

I swallowed the lump in my throat. I'm nineteen. So I guess it counts. "Yes," I said, tucking my hair behind my ear and took a sip of the champagne, humming at the fruity burning taste.

Technically, I shouldn't be even up here in a suite. The sex club had strict over twenty-one policies but there were certain perks of being the sister of the club owner.

"So, how do you want to celebrate your birthday, Cillian?" I asked, taking another sip, keeping my voice sultry and my body angled.

But he wasn't looking anywhere else but my face. I hated that.

"You." His eyes were as dark as his hair when he said the words firmly.

"Me?" I asked, a flush creeping up my neck.

"After I find out what your dirty little mouth can do, I'll fuck your sweet cunt." I took a shaky breath when he leaned his elbows on his knees, clasping his hands together and gazing at me with primal hunger. "Maybe even your little ass if you're into that."

Oh. My. *God.*

4
WATCH ME

EMMA

My cheeks were blazing when he tilted his head, and noticed every little tremble of my body. He was like a predator.

"Give me your panties, Doll."

"What?"

"You won't be needing them anytime soon. So, give them to me before I tear them off of you." Cillian said those filthy, arousing words as if he was talking about weather and not about my fucking panties. "I won't be gentle, Doll," he added, still sitting in that damn armchair and looking smug as hell when I swallowed all the champagne from my glass and kept it on the table.

If he wants me for his birthday, I'll make sure this is one of his best birthdays ever.

"Cillian," I called him, my voice sweet and soft. Moving my hair over my shoulder, I spread my legs and slowly tugged the skirt of the dress up my thighs. "Watch me."

I licked my lips, keeping my eyes on him, watching him watch me as I hooked my fingers through the lacey panties and slowly peeled them over my inner thighs. I let out a sigh as the cold breeze brushed over my slicked pussy, peering at Cillian and biting my lip as I slid my underwear over my calves. I let them pool over one of my heels, stopping at one ankle.

"You want my panties?" I asked him in a sultry voice, lifting my leg so the lace dangled over my ankle and the pink heels he so liked. I wasn't ashamed that they had a wet spot that he could notice. It also offered him a bare view of my pretty pussy, as he liked to call it. "You can have them. Come here and take them."

I knew what I was doing.

I was taunting a beast. A feral, wild beast.

Cillian stood up, and it was my turn to feel smug. His dark hair peppered with the slightest grey made him so attractive. Delicious even, with the tattoos underneath his shirt and silk pants that fit him so well.

The air thickened around us. Full of heat and lust and sexual energy so potent that I could smell it. Taste it.

Somehow, just the way he looked down on me sprawled on the couch made me wetter.

Cillian didn't say anything. He didn't need to.

He prowled towards me and wrapped his long fingers around my lifted ankle. His thumb brushed over my soft skin, making me shiver. I didn't even want to move my leg. I let him tug the panties off of my heel and—

My lips parted when he took them to his face.

"I fucking love how your pussy smells, Doll," he growled, throwing the panties away. "Get on your knees for me. I want to play with your pretty mouth first."

I was moving before he finished his sentence, a small smirk appearing on his handsome face, making me feel heady.

Even though it was uncomfortable with heels on, I knelt on the marble floor and fiddled with his buckle.

"Wait."

I paused, holding back the whine that was climbing up my throat. I *didn't* want to wait. I wanted to use my mouth on the impressive bulge that was in front of me and make him groan. But I waited, reeling in my breath, and watched him place a plush pillow in front of me.

I frowned at him when he said, "Kneel on the pillow. I want to bruise you and mark you... but not your knees."

My eyes widened. Heat spread all over my body when I knelt on the pillow, thankful for the comfort of the cushion, and settled in front of him again. I swallowed the lump in my throat at the sheer size of him. He was tall and broad-shouldered, and some small part of me loved the size difference between us.

I was surprised when his fingers caressed my cheek, cupping my jaw and making me look at his handsome face. His eyes were full of lust but they were soft when he said, "Do you know about safe words and safe gestures, Emma?"

I nodded. Even though Damon was my brother, for as long as I have visited his club with or without my friends, he made sure I knew everything about the rules. He even made me join the beginner's live demonstration. I learned words like *dominant* and *submissive*, *top* and *bottom*, about RACK, and how important consent and communication were. I loved it.

"I know traffic light safe words. Red to stop, yellow to take a break and green to keep going."

"Good girl." His praise warmed something deep inside me, his fingers stroking my cheek lightly. "And which color you are right now, Doll?"

I quickly answered. "Green."

He smiled. "And what would you do if I'm fucking your pretty mouth and you need to stop?"

Heat crept up my face at the erotic image flashing in my head and said, "Safe gesture."

Cillian took my hand and I had to hold back a shiver when he placed it on his strong thigh. *Fuck. Me.* I wanted to sprawl on his thigh. Either to cuddle or grind on it until I cum. "You tap me here twice and everything will stop. Understood?"

"Yes, Cillian." My eyes lit up and I smiled, batting my lashes. "Can I please suck your cock now?"

"Now how can I refuse such a sweet request?"

I took a deep breath before unbuckling his belt. It was leather and the feel of it on my hands made me wary of how he was going to bruise me or mark me. Shaking off those thoughts, I unzipped him. I kept staring at his black boxers and the massive boner inside them.

How the hell am I going to fit him inside my mouth?

I slid down his boxers. When his cock came into view, I exhaled a shuddering breath from my parted lips. My eyes drifted to his thick girth and the glistening metal on the underside of the dripping head. *Wow.* I snapped my eyes to his face.

"You have a piercing…" I trailed off, licking my lips when I eyed it again, wondering how it'd feel inside my mouth or —*fuck me*—inside me.

"And?" He asked, raising his brow and waiting for me and watching my every move with his obsidian eyes, making me squirm on my knees.

"I… n-nothing," I said, heat covering my face, moving my hair over my shoulders.

"Mhmm. Now be a good girl and open your mouth for me, Doll."

5

SHOW ME YOUR TONGUE

CILLIAN

Emma obeyed, parting her pouty pink lips after wetting them with her tongue. I had to ignore the itch to fist her pretty blonde curls and thrust inside her welcoming mouth.

Her soft fingers wrapped around my girth, a deep groan eliciting from my throat when she pumped me slowly before taking me in her mouth. I relished the warmth and wetness, exhaling sharply when she gave small cat licks to the head, playing with the piercing.

Fucking tease.

With a low growl, I wrapped my hand around her hair, tugging her head back and holding her jaw. I leaned down and said, "Stop teasing me. It won't end well, Doll." She trembled, but I continued with my firm voice, "Are you going to suck my cock like a good girl?"

She nodded, her throat bobbing.

"Open your mouth and show me your tongue."

She obeyed and her eyes widened when I spit on her tongue. When she didn't tap my thigh or pulled away, I tightened the hold on her hair, noting the little tremble.

"Good girl. You are going to hold my cum in your mouth like this until I tell you to swallow."

When she nodded, her eyes going hazy, I dipped down and kissed her. It was a messy, rough kiss full of little bites that left us both panting. I pulled back and straightened up, loving the dazed look on her face. As if she couldn't get enough of the kiss and touching me. It was a heady sensation to know that she felt the same way I did. I wanted to kiss and devour her.

Emma's eyes flickered to me when she hollowed her cheeks before swallowing me and the sight of my cock disappearing inside her mouth sent delicious shivers rolling over my body. She wasn't playing around this time by teasing me. Her mouth was fucking heaven, and I loved the little hums of her moans that went straight to my balls.

"So good." I growled, "You are being so good for me, Doll."

Emma moaned, her lids fluttering hearing the praise. Her hand on my thigh was trying to hold on to me as if she was desperate to suck me. Her sharp black nails dug into my thigh and I had to restrain the animalistic need of fucking her mouth. My balls were full and tight, ready to shoot my release inside her, but I held back. I wanted to last longer and watch her, take her in. *But it had been so long...*

She looked so fucking beautiful, her baby blue eyes piercing me with so much heat that it was a miracle I was able to control myself for that long. Her eyes were gleaming with tears and her eye makeup was smudging the corner of her eyes, yet I had never seen anyone with her beauty and... *fuck*—the way she sucked my cock was fucking art.

Emma pulled away, her lips wet and swollen as she took a deep breath, and moving her hair over her shoulder, she dipped down and took me all the way inside her mouth. I sighed her name, feeling the tightness of her throat. Tears trailed down her face, but she was a woman on a mission and I couldn't hold back any longer.

Fuck.

I groaned, throwing my head back when she deep-throated me. My balls were so full and aching. I fucked her mouth, my hips jerking as I held her face close, shooting my seed inside her. Tremors of orgasm exploded through me, my muscles clenching as she kept her hot mouth on me.

"Such a good girl," I grunted, sighing when I was all spent and pulled back, eyeing the pretty mess. Her blonde hair was mussed, mascara running down her face and my cum spilling from the corner of her mouth.

"You can swallow, Doll."

Her throat bobbed, her eyes sparkling with a potent emotion that made my softening dick twitch. I tucked myself in my pants and knelt across her.

"You did so well, pretty girl," I said, dabbing away the tears with my napkin and helping her clean up.

* * *

Emma

I licked my lips, relishing in the musky male taste that was Cillian. He wasn't what I had expected underneath the suit. He had tattoos and a Jacob's ladder on his cock that had felt like heaven and hell when I had deep-throated him. Not to mention the way he had held me, spit on my tongue and then kissed me.

I held back a shiver, squeezing my thighs together when he leaned closer to run the soft cloth over my neck and cleavage. I couldn't believe the man. He had fucked my mouth seconds ago and now he was being so gentle with me, touching me like I was fine China.

And yet, his eyes burned with more lust, way darker than before.

He tucked a lock of my hair behind my ear and tilted my chin to him. "Are you okay, Doll?"

I nodded, my eyes raking over his large frame. Licking my lips, I closed the distance between us and said, "I want you."

His eyes darkened, but he remained silent.

I didn't care. I wanted him. *Now*.

"How do you want me, Doll?" he rumbled, his voice husky. He smelt so good.

I had never wanted a man so badly.

I touched his face, caressing his cheekbone and five o'clock shadow. My cheeks turned hot when I thought about the little stubble grazing against the soft, sensitive skin of my inner thighs. My eyes lowered, so did my hand, and he let me touch him. My thumb grazed over the scar that ran through the corner of his lips.

I shivered under the heat of his gaze, my pussy burning with aching need. I licked my lips. "I..." My voice was too breathy, so I cleared my throat and tried again, "I want your face between my legs. I want you to eat me out."

His onyx eyes flared with lust, and I didn't have a second to gather myself when he pounced on me like a predator finally mauling his prey. *Oh god*. I moaned when he swallowed my gasp, kissing me and biting my lip like he was waiting all night for me to say those words to him.

A whimper tore out of me when my back pressed against something soft, but I was too consumed in the way Cillian devoured me with his rough, passionate kisses. When I was breathless, he pulled back only to torture me with pleasure with his sinful mouth on my neck, biting and licking it.

"C-Cillian!" A broken moan, and he paused, his hot breath fanning over my bare skin. I concluded that I was on the four-poster bed with him hovering above me despite not knowing when and how he moved me here.

His calloused hands brushed over my arms, sensitizing my skin with his hot touch. "Your skin is so fucking soft," he grumbled, his eyes roving over my dressed figure. A scowl etched his handsome face, and he looked like a villain ready to kill anyone who stood in his way. *Good thing I've always had the hots for the villain.* "You are wearing too much."

"Then strip me out of this dress." My voice was sultry and barely audible.

His fingers paused their exploration, and he gave me a dark look. "Remember," he said softly, leaning down when his large hands trailed over my back. I arched my back to him, to give him access to unzip the dress, and he continued, "You asked for this."

I frowned, and the frown turned into a loud gasp when the fabric of the dress ripped, the sound echoing in my ears, and I stared in both horror and awe when Cillian tore my expensive dress into two pieces. Each of his hands had one long piece of fabric that he threw away, ignoring the look on my face and shamelessly staring at my naked body.

"Fucking hell, Doll," he growled, his eyes drinking me in.

"That was Valentino," I said, finding my voice. "You ripped a—"

"I don't fucking care." His blazing eyes pinned me back on the bed. "I'll buy you more expensive dresses if I'm the one tearing them off of your gorgeous body."

My eyes were wide, goosebumps skittering all over my naked body when he licked his lips, a small smile curling on them. "Now... where were we? Something about my face between your pretty thighs, yeah?"

I hummed because my voice had died and I couldn't think when he gazed at me like I was a renaissance art.

Oh Jesus.

6
THERE WE GO

CILLIAN

Emma's baby blue eyes were wide as she stared at me, noting the reaction on my face when I saw her naked on the bed. Her blonde hair splayed on the dark sheets with her gorgeous curvy body spread open for me to devour. Lick, eat, bite, kiss.

"I can smell how turned on you are, Doll," I whispered, my voice low and rough. It was hard to maintain or even give a flying fuck about how starved my voice seemed when I had such a pretty feast in front of me. "I could spend hours touching you."

My hands glided over her pale, creamy skin, squeezing her waist, leaning down to kiss her soft belly before biting it gently. I smirked hearing the sharp intake of her breath and licked the bite mark before kissing her stomach. I loved her body. It was full of softness, silkiness, and warmth.

It seemed that I had lied. I could spend *years* touching her. Which was a very indecent thought, knowing it would last only for a few more hours and we would never see each other again.

Instead of those thoughts, I focused on her, the sweet sounds that poured out of her when I spent minutes playing with her perfect tits. Fondling them, pinching her nipples until they turned bright pink and licking them, kissing them gently and leaving hickies on her. Maybe it was a little possessive of me, but I wanted her to remember this night, her time with me, at least for the next few days.

"Cillian." Her soft moan was a delight to my ears when I spread her legs, my hands squeezing the soft flesh of her thighs. A throaty groan rumbled out of me at the sight of her pretty pussy leaking with pearly juices that I couldn't wait to put my tongue on.

Slow. Take it slow, Cillian.

But it had been years, and I was starving.

"You want me to make you feel good, Doll?" I whispered, brushing light kisses on her sensitive skin and settling between her spread legs, my broad shoulders keeping them wide open.

"Y-yes," she breathed out, gazing at me with her hazy eyes, her heavy breasts heaving with each breath she took. "Please, Cillian. Don't make me wait—*oh*."

Her head fell back when I flattened my tongue over her pussy, tasting her. Emma moaned, and I growled. I pushed her thighs wider before spreading her slicked lips with my thumb, groaning at the sight of her pink and sensitive clit and licking her again when more arousal seeped out for her.

Fucking heaven.

"Your taste—*fuck*, I want to eat your pretty cunt for hours," I groaned, lapping at her wetness. I nudged her clit with my nose and flickered my eyes to her face.

Emma was gasping, small sounds of pleasure pouring out of her when I ate her out, her moans increasing when I teased her opening with a finger. Slowly stroking her pussy and pushing it inside her warmth. My cock stirred at the tight clamp of her walls, gently pulling my finger out before pushing it back in. My mouth was occupied with her sensitive clit, licking it softly and adding another finger to make her comfortable for what was coming next.

* * *

Emma

I WAS IN HEAVEN.

Or I had died and went to hell.

Because there was no way any man was this good at eating pussy. Cillian was taking his time with his expert hands, slowly unfurling me and stretching me with his thick tattooed fingers while his hot mouth played with my clit. I didn't even have to tell him to pay attention to my clit.

He knew what he was doing.

Being gentle and rough in the best ways possible.

"Oh *fuck*," I whimpered, my thighs quivering as pleasure kept growing and growing inside me, ready to explode. I reached down and held on to his soft hair.

His dark eyes flew to my face, and he kept his pace, knowing I was so close, gently stroking his fingers on my G-spot, coaxing me. "Yes, I know you are close, Doll. Cum for me. Cum on my face. *Yes*—there we go."

His deep voice surrounded me and I let go, pleasure bursting out of me, white sparks blinding my vision as I rode the delicious orgasm, groaning his name. I moaned when I found his thick dark hair between my thighs, licking me clean, already preparing me for the next climax.

"Cillian," I said, my voice laced with pleasure. I bit my lip when he pulled away, his nose, lips, and chin covered in my wetness. He licked his lips, and I died at the sight of his scarred, sexy lips tasting me again and again, as if he couldn't get enough of me. "I want you to fill me up."

He smirked, his gaze sliding over my naked body as if he was planning how he was going to fuck me. I shivered, watching him throw away his shirt. I heard a small cling of metal, but I was too occupied with the art that was Cillian. His muscles were strong, with a hint of hair and tattoos all over him in a beautiful, intricate design and swirls.

I didn't even know when I leaned up to touch him, his skin warm and heart beating fast. His jaw was clenched when I slowly raked my nails down his chest, licking at the piercings on his nipples. I touched him there, a hiss of pleasure coming out of his mouth, but he didn't stop my exploration.

I became confident, flicking my gaze at him and kissing his chest. His pupils were so dark and dilated, full of lust and fire. I kissed his wide pectorals, loving how large and strong he was. And yet shivered when I kissed him gently on his nipples, teasing the piercing with my teeth.

"*Emma,*" he grunted in a warning, but I didn't care. I was having fun teasing him like he had all night.

"I like your tattoos," I whispered, running my hands over his back and leaning so close that my breasts squished against his chiseled body. "I love your piercings, Cillian," I said, kissing the line of his abs and slowly made my way down until I found his thick cock bulging in his pants and cupped him.

Peering at him through my lashes, I said, "I want to ride you."

His eyes were burning with heat when I pushed him back on the bed, unzipping him and making a quick work to get rid of his pants. I swallowed the lump in my throat at the sexy sight of him leaning against the headboard, covered in tattoos and piercings, with his hard shaft bobbing on his stomach, already leaking with pre-cum.

My throat dried up when he lazily stroked himself, eyeing me and crooking a finger in a come-hither motion. "Crawl here, Doll," he said, his voice hoarse with pleasure. "Ride your pretty cunt on my cock and make yourself cum."

7
GOOD GIRL

EMMA

"Ride your pretty cunt on my cock and make yourself cum."

I crawled to him, a small smile playing on my lips as I straddled him, gasping at the hot sensation of his dick rubbing against my clit. My gasp was swallowed by his lips and I melted in his arms when he kissed me gently, our tongues dancing together, building the anticipation of our union as I greedily rubbed over him, only to have him spank my ass and squeeze it before pulling away.

I whined at the loss, but he only chuckled, his chest rumbling with the small laughter. "Hurry up," I said, watching him tear a foil.

How he made opening a condom wrapper with his teeth sexy was beyond me. It should definitely be illegal.

"You can ride me as much as you want, Doll," he said when I watched him roll down the latex, my pussy yearning to feel his piercing inside me. "Now sit on my cock."

"My pleasure," I said, leaning forward on my knees and looking down at his impressive length. Biting the inside of my cheek, I held the base and slowly rubbed myself on the tip, sighing at the pleasure.

"Quit being a tease," he growled, holding my waist and threatening me with a gentle squeeze. "Put me inside your pussy before I fuck you."

I smirked at him and licked the scar on his lips before kissing him. "Don't threaten me with good time."

I held back my moan when he pulled me against him, holding my waist and claiming my mouth with his. I would never tire of his soft lips and spicy male scent. *Which wasn't a good thought considering the age gap and this being a one-night stand.* I was pulled out of those thoughts when his thick tip pressed against my entrance, waiting and pulsing for me to move.

Holding his shoulders, I braced myself and slowly sank down on his length. I was whimpering, and he was groaning. His fingers dug into my waist as he slid inside me inch by delicious inch, creating a burning sensation as he filled me up.

"Cillian," I whispered in a broken moan when the stretch of his thick girth filled me up, my walls squeezing him when I settled on top of him. My thighs quivered at the pleasure of being so full that I was on the edge of an orgasm.

"So good," he growled. His hands ran from my hips to my back, caressing me and holding me close when I shivered. "You feel so fucking good, Doll. So perfect on my cock."

I bit my lip at the dark, hot look on his face. His hair was long enough to cover his furrowed brow, and the delicious clench of his jaw with that scar on his lips made him look ethereal. His thumb pulled at my bottom lip and I took it in my mouth, biting it gently, moaning when he pulsed inside me.

"You okay, Doll?" He asked, kissing my cheek and trailing

his lips to my neck, squeezing my breasts and licking my peaked nipples.

I didn't have any words, so I nodded, slowly rocking myself on him and gasping at the sensation of his metal piercing rubbing inside of me.

Holy shhittt.

"You feel so big—*fuck*," I cried out when he filled me up, my pussy clamping him in a tight fist.

Cillian let out a hiss of pleasure, squeezing my ass in an almost a painful grip that was definitely going to leave a mark. But he let me pick the pace, letting me use him for my pleasure, as he had said earlier. His hands played with my breasts and so did his lips, and teeth, leaving marks all over my body, and I let him because the bite of his teeth on my hardened nipple sent a shot of pleasure each time I fucked into him.

"I want you to cum again, Doll," he commanded, licking his thumb and sliding it between our bodies to my clit. When I bucked with a soundless moan, he rubbed it, his expression going darker. "Cum on my cock like a good girl you are, hm?"

I was close and the fact that he noticed, increasing the pleasure by touching my clit, sent me spiraling over the edge as I came. My lips parted in an O and entire body trembled when the orgasm rolled over my body, fire licking my spine as climax gushed out of me.

My head was on his shoulder when I came to, blinking my heavy-lidded eyes and humming at the soft caress of his large hand on my back. I could have snuggled and fallen asleep on the comfort of his enormous body, especially when he raked his hand through my hair, but he was still hard as a rock inside me and I wanted to please him.

Before I could voice it out, he rolled us so that my back was on the bed while he hovered over me. I licked my lips at the sexy view of his broad shoulders and tattoos in front of me. He didn't even have to tell me to spread my legs.

"Fuck me, Cillian," I said, my voice hoarse with pleasure as I slid my hand between my legs and rubbed my sensitive clit. He watched me, his cock throbbing inside me, and I wanted nothing more than that man to ravish me at that moment. Even if it meant walking funny for a few days, I wanted him to have his fill.

"Scream for me when you cum this time," he said, and his voice was all sex. My eyes widened when he spread my legs wider, throwing them over his shoulders and leaning close so I felt him go deeper, making me whimper. "What's your safe word?"

Biting my lip, I said, "Don't stop."

He narrowed his eyes at me and closed a hand around my throat, choking me gently with a warning. "Try again, Doll."

"Go harder?"

He pulled back and slammed inside me, rocking my entire body on the bed with his powerful thrust.

I cried out, holding on to his arm. "It's red," I trailed the word red when spikes of pleasure burned through me.

"Good girl." He cupped my cheek and said, "Don't forget it."

8
ARE YOU SORE?

CILLIAN

"Yes, Cillian—*ah!*"

Emma moaned, her voice soft and sultry, full of pleasure when I dragged my dick out to slam inside her perfect pussy. I had to clench my teeth and hold on to her pretty body to keep myself from coming. She was fucking perfect. Her breasts jiggling with each thrust, her warm, curvy body perfect against mine, and her pouty pink lips parted in a soundless gasp.

I kissed her calf on my shoulder, biting the soft skin. I wanted to mark her everywhere. Claim her.

"Touch yourself," I grunted, filling her up, her walls clamping me. "Rub your pretty clit and make yourself cum again, Doll."

She obeyed, gliding her hand down her body, but she stopped when I pounded inside her. She was gasping and panting, a thin sheet of sweat glistening on her.

"I—I can't." She twisted her face into the sheets, her hands fisting them. "Cillian!"

"Yes, Doll, I got you," I whispered, leaning down and

spreading her legs wider. "I'll make you cum again, yeah. I know you can."

Her reply was a muffled groan when I kissed her, slowly rocking my cock inside her as our tongues danced against each other. I was so close, but I wanted to make her orgasm one more time.

Sliding a hand between us, I rubbed her clit and increased my speed. Her eyes widened and her thighs were shaking. I knew she was on the edge as well, so I rolled my hips and kept my pace, making sure to rub my piercing over her G-spot, knowing how much she loved it.

Just when I felt her pussy spasming around me with her orgasm, I climaxed as well, filling her up with my cock and groaning her name as my body shook with white hot pleasure. I stroked her shaking legs, letting her ride out the aftershocks, and slowly pulled out before dropping beside her, panting at the ceiling.

Fuck. That was one of the best sex of my life.

My body tensed when her hand landed on my chest and I looked at her, her eyes closed as she tried to catch her breath, one golden lock falling on her face. Relaxing under her touch, I pulled her limp body closer and tucked her hair behind her ear. I rubbed her back, gently soothing her trembling body.

I was proud that she enjoyed it as much as I did, if not more.

"Are you okay?" I asked once our breathing had calmed down. I would have loved to cuddle her after a warm shower, spending each precious second to clean her up by touching every nook and cranny of her sexy body. But I was too content to keep lying with her in my post-coital bliss.

"I think you broke me," Emma whispered, her blue eyes clear as they peered at me.

I chuckled, kissing her hair and smelling sweet vanilla.

Fuck, I had to keep calm, or I was sure I would take her again. I leaned up on my elbow, marveling at her pink nipples and the hickies all over her body before pinning my stare between her legs.

"Are you sure?" I teased, running my hand over her waist, "I can check if your pussy is—"

"No." She hid her face in my chest, her cheeks red. "Don't tease me or I will ask you to fuck me again."

My cock stirred.

"I don't see any problem. Just give me a couple of minutes—"

"Are you kidding me?" Her wide eyes looked at my face and lowered below my hips. "*Jesus*. I won't be able to walk for a few days."

I sat up, my brows furrowing and spread her legs against her protest. "Are you sore? Does it hurt?" I asked, concern lacing my voice. "Do you want me to call a doctor? I think they have a medical team—"

"Cillian." Her hand wrapped around my arm as she sat up with a little wince, and I wanted to call downstairs and ask someone for a doctor. "I'm okay, I promise. It's… it's been a few months, that's all."

"Are you sure, Emma?"

She nodded, a small smile playing on her lips as she stood up, my eyes dropping to her marvelous breasts. "Take a shower with me."

Emma turned and walked into the adjacent washroom without an answer. I closed my eyes and took a deep breath after staring at her juicy ass. The room smelled like sex and vanilla. I reached the washroom just when she started the shower. I pushed her against the cold wall, wrapping her legs around my waist as steam covered the both of us.

Just a few hours and I was addicted to her.

Later. I would think about those thoughts later.

***

I bit back a smirk when she walked out of the shower, her hair damp and body covered in hickies, with a small hiss escaping her lips. She had a small towel that barely covered her, water droplets falling on the floor as she made her way to the dresser.

I picked up the fresh clothes I had ordered from downstairs and kept them on the bed, and took the towel from her, turning her chair around to help her pat her body dry. It was also an excuse to gaze at her.

"You don't have to. I can dress up on my own."

I hummed in agreement and picked up the body lotion, her eyes raking over my chest and hips. I had worn my pants when she had walked out of the washroom but I loved how hungry she looked even after all the sex and orgasms.

"But I want to do it," I said, warming the lotion in my hands before applying it on her arms. I knelt in front of her, her eyes watching my every move as I spent a bit more time than was necessary moisturizing her breasts.

Emma squirmed on the chair, her little sighs going straight to my dick, and I was about to ask her for round four when I noticed the little mark on her hip.

"What's this?" I asked, tracing it with my finger, her spine straightening and body tensing.

She barely glanced at it. "Must be a bruise from all the sex."

I kept my hand on her thigh when she tried to stand up, and looked at her. She was avoiding my gaze.

"No. This is not a sex bruise." *It's something else.*

"Y-you must have held me—"

"Emma." I kept my voice soft and continued when her eyes met mine, "If I held you tight enough to bruise you, there would be four more marks here. What happened?"

Did someone hurt you?

I bit back the urge to demand an answer from her, but I knew she wouldn't have a mark like that without falling really badly or someone...

Who dared to touch her like that?

9
CALL ME

EMMA

I stood up, not meeting his eyes, and looked for anything to cover myself with.

"Emma, if it's some—"

"It's nothing. Leave it," I said, keeping my voice steady, but it was difficult when he genuinely seemed concerned about me. I found the clothes he had ordered and donned the comfortable long-sleeved dress over a black bra and underwear. They were definitely expensive, and he had gotten my size perfect.

Why couldn't he be mean and leave me after the sex? *No.* He just had to cuddle me, shower me, give me more orgasms, rub lotion on me, ask about that damn bruise and buy me the similar style of black dress that was more comfortable than the one I was wearing before.

"Emma—"

I was saved by the ring of a phone. He let out a sigh and picked it up, turning his back on me, and I *definitely* didn't watch the muscles of his back clenching as he moved, or even his mysterious tattoos and definitely *not* the low hanging pants that revealed two back dimples and a tight ass.

I can't believe I was staring him with an open mouth.

What's worse was that I wanted to ask for his number and ask him to meet me again. *Just* for sex. Nothing much.

But I knew that couldn't be possible. He was forty, and I was nineteen. The age gap didn't matter to me, but we met in the sex club that my brother owns, and that was definitely not a good start for a relationship—

What the hell am I thinking? It *was* just sex. It was *just* sex. It was just *sex*.

"You got dressed...," he trailed off, his eyes falling to my hips before flickering to my face. I crossed my arms when he continued, "Do you want me to drop you home?"

"You're leaving?" I sounded too eager. *Damn it.* "I... I don't want to go home. *Yet.*" I added when he frowned at me.

Even though Cillian might have treated me with utmost respect like a gentleman, I wasn't going to tell him the reason why I was in a sex club in the first place.

He wore his shirt, and I had to look away because he looked too handsome even while covering his beautiful tattoos and piercings. If I had been more confident—no, if he hadn't brought up that bruise, I would have demanded him to fuck me on the floor before he left.

It was very, very stupid and petty, but I hated the person who had called him. I didn't want him to leave just yet.

"Are you sure, Emma?" His voice sounded much closer, and I lifted my eyes from the floor to his face when he walked towards me. "I can order you a cab—"

"I'm fine." My voice was clipped and my smile was fake.

He tilted his head and touched my chin, rubbing the pad of his thumb on my jaw. It was just a small caress, but it sent warm flutters to my belly. "You don't have to lie to me, Doll. You can stay here as long as you want. I can book it for you for a week if you want me to."

My mouth parted, and I remembered something. Shaking

my head, I said, "But that would be over fifty grand for a week…"

"I don't mind, as long as you feel safe here." He leaned down, his hot breath whispering in my ear, "Besides, it will be a treat to have a pretty Doll using this suite however she wants."

"Even if I bring other men in here?" I asked, raising my brow when his burning gaze met mine.

He smirked, raking his eyes over my body, and shrugged. "As long as you remember to call me first when you want someone to fill you up, I don't mind." His hand trailed from my waist to back, lowering to my ass and giving it a light squeeze, his dark eyes twinkling in delight. "I haven't fucked you here yet, anyway. And something tells me that you'd love to have all your pretty holes used, hm?"

My eyes widened and before I could agree or disagree or worse—kiss him. He dipped down and kissed the corner of my lips.

His stare was intense when he pulled away, taking a step back. "Call me."

I stared at his back when he picked up his suit and walked out of the door, leaving me alone in the suite with my thoughts and soaked pussy.

"Ughhhh, fuck him!" I ran a hand through my hair, sighing at my reflection in the mirror. My cheeks were flushed pink and eyes were gleamed.

I jumped when there was a knock on the door of the suite and frowned. *Did he come back?* I definitely did not rush to open the door or anything. I was just curious about what brought him back—

"Oh, hello," I said to the hotel staff and hid my disappointment.

"T-this is for you." He pushed a bottle in front of me and I raised my brow at the name of the champagne.

"But I didn't order any—"

"The man ordered it for you," he said, his mask hiding most of his features. Masks were not mandatory for the hotel staff, but most of the people wore it anyway to remain anonymous. "He asked me to tell you that you should enjoy it."

I took the bottle, staring at the alcohol, and wondered why he didn't share it with me. Maybe he had an emergency after all.

"Thank you," I offered a small smile and closed the door.

Staring at the ceiling, I muttered, "Might as well enjoy the drink."

I was sitting on the couch where Cillian had asked me to remove my panties and sipping my second glass of the cold bubbly drink. I never realized I'd feel so alone after having sex so many times that it made me sore. I wanted him to stay with me. Even some cuddling would have been nice.

Shaking my head, I downed the drink and stood up, stumbling towards the bed to sleep with the sadness that crept over me. I had loved Caleb for so long that I had forgotten how it felt without it. His betrayal stung deep, not because he liked guys, too, but more because we were best friends before we got in a relationship.

He grew up alone in his huge bungalow because his dad worked abroad a lot and sent him an allowance every week. Just how I grew up alone in my mansion with a blockbuster star as a mom who shouldn't have conceived me in the first place.

"Oh fuck, there was something in the champagne." *No doubt it was making me sadder.*

I groaned, falling on the bed and groaned again because it had the lingering scent of Cillian and his sexy cologne. I rolled away and my eyes fell on the small, glinting metal on the floor.

With my heart in my mouth, I knelt on the floor and picked it up, turning it around in my hand as my vision burned. My head throbbed. My heart was pounding so loudly that my ears were ringing.

I didn't know when I dropped the golden band and it fell when I tried to pick it up again.

No. Something didn't feel right.

My eyes were feeling heavy. I forced them to stay open and find my phone. I needed to call someone... *anyone*.

"H... elp." My voice was groggy and words were slurred even though I had—

Somewhere from a distance, I heard the click of the door unlocking.

Oh god. This was not good.

10

DRUNK?

CILLIAN

I called my son, hearing it ring for a few seconds before I heard his slurred voice. "What's up?"

I paused, looking at the screen, and sighed. "Where are you?"

"Who's this?"

"Caleb—" I nodded at the hotel staff wearing a mask to cover their features and continued, "You called me earlier. Where are you? I'll come pick you up."

I patted my suit to grab my key fob and froze. I didn't have my ring with me. Where the fuck was it?

"It's okay, *Cillian*," he hissed out the words and laughed, his friends calling him. "I can take care of myself."

Pinching the bridge of my nose, I kept my phone away and checked my pockets, but I couldn't find the ring. It was my wedding band and I couldn't lose it. Because if I lost it, then it would mean…

No. I didn't have time for those thoughts.

I must have dropped it in the room—*shit*. A curse flew out of me as I kept pressing the button to my suite in the private elevator. If Emma found the ring, she'd think I was cheating on my wife. I didn't know why, but her opinion of me mattered a lot, despite knowing her for only a few hours. I didn't want her to think I was having an affair.

"Emma?" I knocked on the door and didn't hear a sound. I looked at the corner of my eyes seeing a hotel staff rolling a trolly at the end of the hallway and disappearing. "Emma? I forgot something. I'm coming in."

I heard a clatter and a thud from inside of the room and unlocked the door, stepping inside.

My steps faltered when I found her lying on the floor. In the blink of an eye, I was kneeling in front of her, cupping her cold cheek and seeing her dilated eyes as they peered at me with a dazed look.

"Can you hear me?" I asked, trying to calm my hammering heart. "Emma? What happened?"

With as much gentleness as I could muster, I picked her up and laid her down on the bed. She couldn't be drunk, but there was a bottle of champagne. *Did she order it?* I kept the empty bucket aside after tucking her in bed.

"Where the hell is your purse?" I grumbled, raking a hand through my hair when I didn't find it. "Fucking great."

I glanced from her unconscious body to the bottle. It wasn't even empty. *Then how the fuck did she get so wrecked by just two drinks?*

My knuckles brushed over her forehead, noting the high temperature. I checked my watch and cursed. I have to call the police—

Without another thought, I opened the main door of the suite and halted when I came face to face with a man in shirt and pants, his expression furious.

"Is Emma here?" he asked, but by the tone of it, he could have put a knife on my neck and said it with a disgusting rasp.

"Yes, but she needs—"

His face twisted. "Emma, are you decent?" he called out and muttered underneath his breath, "Since when did you start sleeping with silver foxes?"

My jaw clenched, knowing well what he meant. "Emma is decent and in bed. Who the fuck are you?"

I didn't have to waste my time with the jerk. I needed to call an ambulance and get her checked soon.

"I'm Damon Grant. *Move.*" He tried to intimidate me, but it was hard since I loomed over him without any effort.

I stopped him when he tried to enter the room. The man may have looked decent, but the way he was acting was suspicious. *Like hell I'd let him enter when she was unconscious.*

"I don't care who you are." My jaw clenched when he went past me and I followed him, ready to tackle him down if he tried anything funny. "I need to call an ambulance. She's unconscious."

"What the fuck did you do to her?"

I was taken aback by the rawness on his face when he glared at me before leaning down and checking her pulse.

"I found her like this. If she was drunk, she'd be slurring right now, but she didn't have enough alcohol to get piss drunk. If I suspect something else, then it could mean a loss of motor control." I checked my watch and then the man, who was clearly more concerned about Emma's health than who she slept with. "She either ingested rohypnol, GHB or ketamine. So, we need to get her to hospital ASAP."

"*Wait.*" The man stood up, his eyes flickering to me and the unconscious woman on the bed. "You mean she was roofied?"

My jaw clenched, hating that I wasn't there for her for a few more minutes.

"Yes. If you care about her, get the manager and check the cameras. I'll call emergency—"

"I'm the manager and her brother." He swallowed the lump in his throat when I gave him a poker face. I figured he was either a jealous ex or an over-protective brother or relative, but what I didn't understand was how he could watch his unconscious sister and not panic. It was odd. "Can you hold on to calling nine-one-one? I'll ask our personal doctor to come right—"

I crossed my arms and stared at his cold grey eyes. "Do you know that high doses of these drugs may cause death? I'm not waiting around for you to call your personal doctor."

"I won't let her die too," he snapped, his eyes sharp and challenging me to see if I'd argue. Good for him. He was saved by his phone ringing and he gave me a hard stare when he walked to the corner of the room to take the call.

Let her die, *too*?

I eyed his back and the unconscious woman on the bed. Was she Emma Grant? I knew he was Damon Grant, CEO of the sex club I was standing in, but I didn't know he had a sister. I titled my head, taking a step closer to see if her breathing had changed.

It was normal.

My hands clenched in fists. I wanted to do terrible, terrible things to the person who dared drug her for God knows what—

If I wasn't there, what could have happened? If I hadn't decided to come back upstairs, something... someone could have—the thought made bile rise to my throat.

My fingers brushed over my bottom lip, on the scar that I despised, reminding me of my ruin.

As Damon had promised, their private doctor arrived with a couple of nurses and checked on Emma. I watched everything with a sharp eye, knowing I couldn't sit still. My fingers were itching to check the surveillance camera, interrogate the bartender and especially her brother, who looked both furious and guilty, pacing in the room.

My phone trilled, and I only stepped back to check my screen and sighed. He told me he'd take care of himself only to call me back again. I was used to it now. He only ever called when he needed something from me and most of the time it was money, even though I gave him more than enough allowance. Flickering my eyes to Emma, I made sure she was being cared for before picking up the call.

"Hey... uh, can you pick me up?" His voice was casual, but I knew my son enough to know that he was nervous. He seemed sober too.

"What happened?"

I could hear loud people in the background, and I knew he was still at the party.

"I—not right now Tania—can you just pick me up?" He seemed annoyed, by me or Tania, I didn't know. "I'll text you the location."

"*Caleb.*" I tightened my hand on the phone as I looked at the unconscious woman on the bed. "You told me specifically that you will take care of yourself when I asked where were you. Can't you call a cab? If you are hurt, I'll be there in ten—"

I heard him laugh, making me frown. "I shouldn't have fucking called you. My bad. Sorry to disturb you from your work, *Dad.*"

The call ended before I could say another word. He said the word *Dad* as if it was a curse. Maybe he thought it was ever since...

Shaking my head, I glanced at Emma. Her golden hair was splayed on the bed, and she looked much better than how I had found her. Her brother was looking after her. I could get the ring later. It seemed little matter when Emma was unconscious and my son had called me twice.

Swallowing the lump in my throat, I told Damon I was leaving, promising him I would be back to ask if they caught the person who roofied her.

For now, I needed to go pick up my son and make sure he was okay.

11
MALEFICENT VIBE

EMMA

Before

The day my mom died was one of the happiest days of the eighteen years of my life. Oops, nineteen. It was my birthday, after all.

It started with me waking up to Caleb's phone call, demanding me to open the curtain of my bedroom window and looking over the vast backyard towards his parked Jeep. My boyfriend was waving at me with white balloons and shouting, 'Happy Birthday, Emma fucking Moore!' Despite how it could have angered Mother (when one of her maids updated about my life), I was grinning.

I was happy.

"Miss Moore, are you listening to me?" the sweet voice of Mrs. Karen cranked through the phone, making me snap out of my head and shiver. I looked around at the dinner table, Mia and Summer laughing at Caleb's dad joke.

My head felt heavy and tongue felt like lead. "Can you hear me, Miss Moore?"

"Yes." I stood up, briskly walking out of the restaurant

and breathing in a lungful of crisp night air. It was such a good weather. "I can hear you, Mrs. Karen. Can you please repeat what you just said?"

The door behind me opened. I turned around to see Caleb's small smirk and a raised eyebrow that clearly meant, 'Are you done? Can we go have amazing, raunchy birthday sex now?' It had been a while, after all. *Months.*

I blinked.

"*No.*" The slight pause was the only sign of my disbelief. "It can't be."

"I'm sorry, dear." Mrs. Karen, bless her, really sounded apologetic and sincere. "It'll be all over the news in a few hours and Mr. Grant told me to have you at home... or those reporters will hound you."

"Damon called you?" I asked, walking away from Caleb's narrowed eyes. I didn't want to explain to him about everything. I couldn't even look at him right now.

"Yes, Miss Moore."

I clenched the phone in my hand. *Of course, he did.* He couldn't call his own sister to wish her happy birthday or... break the news of our mother's death.

"Okay," I said softly. "Okay. I'll be back soon."

"You going somewhere?" Caleb asked, holding my arm. Mia and Summer stepped out of the diner.

"Em? Is everything okay?"

I glanced between Caleb, my friends, and the floor before looking at them again.

"My mother... she's dead."

* * *

"It's not black enough," I said, examining my nails. The nail salon artist paused and looked at me with wide eyes. I smiled tightly and stood up from the stool. "It's fine. You can leave."

Turns out even the blackest of the black nail polish didn't suit the 'It's my mom's funereal and I really need to seem sad and pathetic' look.

She nodded, scampering to pack the nail paint, filer and acrylics. The scent of acetone was too stifling in the room. I left one of the many sitting rooms, my heels clicking against the marble floor.

The house didn't look different. There was an air of grief and caution. I had to clench my hands in a fist to stop myself from snapping at any house staff who kept staring at me with concerned looks. *Why were they concerned about me?* They shouldn't be concerned. I was fine. I was perfectly... *fine*.

"Emma."

I sighed in relief when Mia walked through the main door in a black dress. Her hands were cold when they touched mine. "How are you doing?" Her hazel-green eyes were full of worry. Her dad and James gave me a solemn look before disappearing into the house.

Mother's funeral included people like her. Her co-stars, directors she worked and slept with, and their rich sons and daughters crying over the casket. It made me sick that the people who barely knew her for months were crying over the loss that only I and Damon could feel.

But I wouldn't put it past my brother to feel anything but a sense of relief, now that he was half the owner of her will, which would be announced later that day.

"She looks like she needs some Jell-O shots or six large cups of coffee," Summer drawled, walking over and pursing her lips as she looked over my attire.

I glanced down at the tight-fitting black dress. "What?" I asked her, "Is Valentino too much for my mother's funeral?"

Summer and Mia picked up a stem of wine glass. "You look stunning. Those red lips, winged eyeliner and dress are giving serious Maleficent vibes…" Mia gave her a look, so she added, "Only if your hair wasn't blonde."

"Thank you." I flicked my hair over my shoulder and took a deep breath before walking into the main hall where everything was cleared up to place the coffin with mom's large photo.

Everyone glanced at me as I walked to the front, clenching my hand to keep my poker face. My heels echoed in the silent room and I knew if mom was here, she would have loved it, with one of her rare smirks as she took a sip of wine.

My eyes met hers in the frame as I sat down on the plush chair with my back straight. Her hair was blonde and short, curled in soft waves as her sultry green eyes looked at the camera, fluttering her lashes. Even from a picture, I was awed by her beauty. Her act and elegance. I could never be like her. I knew that since the day I was born.

Somehow, even she knew that.

The only things I got from my mother were the blonde hair, symmetrical face, and stubbornness. While she was thin and lithe, like a bird, I was curved with wider hips and an ample chest. I never wanted to be like her. I should be glad. I should be glad… but my heart ached because Dorothy Moore didn't deserve to die all alone in her private plane.

"That was quite an entrance." My spine straightened when Damon sat beside me. I flickered my eyes at his sharp profile. Dark blond hair and grey eyes.

"You're late," I replied when the pastor started speaking, nerves making my stomach clench.

I looked ahead when he turned towards me. "We need to talk to lawyers after the funeral," he murmured, crossing his arms and leaning back on the chair as my chest tightened with a rare emotion I never felt.

A need to be comforted.

I mentally scoffed at the thought. As if Damon Grant had any emotion in his tall body. He was more of a stranger than my own brother. We had never gotten along. He had kept our father's last name because he despised mother for the same reason he despised me... my existence. And he never missed a chance to let me forget about my mistake of being born into the family.

I swallowed the lump in my throat when the prayer was over. I had to step up and speak a few words about mother. I looked at her pale face in the coffin and bile rose in my throat.

My lips felt numb. I couldn't do it. Her chest wasn't moving... she wasn't breathing. My eyes blurred, and I didn't know what I would speak about.

How she starved me? Locked me up? Pinched me? Hit me? Dug her nails in my skin and scolded me with her sly grin until I sat straight and never cried again? How she pretended I didn't exist?

"*Emma.*"

The sharp voice of my brother pulled me out of my inner turmoil. I met his eyes and saw my own mother glaring at me.

I hated it.

I took a step back from the coffin, my feet stumbling when the heel I wore came off. Mia stood up, but I bent down and fixed it back on my feet. I could feel people take a sharp intake of breath as I kept my chin high and walked out of the hall without saying anything at my mother's funeral.

I needed to distract myself. I needed to forget about cold green eyes, and get lost. I needed, I needed.... I needed *comfort*.

And I could only think of one person who could give that to me.

I checked my phone and frowned when I saw no message

from him. He could be waiting for me in my room. I walked upstairs, my hands clammy and shoulders slumped, ready to bury myself in his chest—

My steps faltered when I heard the gasps from the inside of my bedroom. Staring hard at the white double doors, I listened to the familiar male grunt echoed by more gasps. I took a wavering breath and straightened my shoulders, marching towards my room and pushing the doors open.

My lips fell apart when I saw my boyfriend, Caleb Chang, on my king-sized bed with Aaron. Both of their cheeks were flushed and lips red, swollen as they pulled away from each other and stared back at me with wide eyes.

"What the fuck?"

12

A PRESENT

EMMA

Before

"What the fuck?"

I didn't know if I uttered those words, or if Caleb or Aaron did. I blinked. Confused, hurt, sad, and raw. I felt like I was split open from my heart. Well, at least Caleb had succeeded in giving me what I needed.

He had officially distracted me from my mother's funeral.

I turned, ready to leave—

"Em, wait!"

I glared at him, not caring that he was doing his zip up. "If either of you ruined my Egyptian cotton sheets, I'll sue you. Clean up your own mess and get out."

I left the room and locked myself in the nearest washroom.

My knuckles turned white at how hard I was clutching the sink. I ignored the pleading voice of Caleb, squeezing my eyes shut and lowering on the floor, covering my face.

This wasn't how my mom's funeral was supposed to go.

This wasn't perfect.

I should've been able to give a speech about how sweet, nice and caring she was, lying with my tears and fake smile. Nod prettily and accept the handkerchief from creepy old directors and wipe my tears, hug my friends and lock myself in my room with Caleb, get drunk and fall asleep, cuddling him until every emotion for my mother washed away.

Bile rose in my throat, images of Caleb with someone else other than me flashing in my head. I scrambled towards the toilet and threw up my morning smoothie into the bowl. Tears burned my eyes as I cleaned myself up, making sure my dress wasn't ruined, and retouched my makeup after brushing my teeth.

I needed to be alone right now. I needed to stay alone.

Just like my mother.

* * *

Now

My head was throbbing. It felt like someone was hammering away at the back of my skull, my lids feeling heavy as I tried to open them. My entire body hurt and limbs felt sore. Maybe I was run over by a truck. At least three times.

I heard sounds and my name being called.

"Emma! I think she's waking up."

"We can all see that, Sherlock."

I groaned, twisting on the bed that felt too soft and fuck—my arms hurt. With much effort, I opened my lids, flinching at the headache, and looked around the unknown room—

"Are those chains?" I asked, my voice groggy, staring at

the heavy chains dangling from the wall. "Why are there chains on the walls?"

"How are you feeling?"

My eyes averted from the chains to the person I least expected to ever be concerned about me, ask me that question. I giggled, covering my mouth and looking away from him.

"Like you care." I met Mia's and Summer's worried eyes. They were both still in their black dresses. "What happened?"

I frowned at the bedroom I was in and knew that this was definitely *not* my room. I was still wearing my black dress. My heels were missing from my feet and placed on the side of the bed with an empty bucket. My pink Manolo Blahnik heels.

"Did I get drunk?" I muttered, scratching my head. I remembered getting in a car, asking my car driver to take me to the Vixen Club. I talked with Joe, had drinks and then... *Panther!* I remembered that man. Asian, tattoos, all black hair with a very light sprinkle of grey, his hands holding me upright. I remembered him. Cillian. Piercings. Sex. Lots of orgasms.

Quite a dirty little mouth you have.

"Where's that man?" I asked, noticing his large frame was absent. "H-he was with me. Where did Cillian go?"

"He saved you," Damon said, his face poker.

"He did? But I remember he was with me and then—"

"You were roofied, Emma," Damon gritted, my eyes snapping at his face. My palms felt clammy all of a sudden. I knew I didn't feel right. "Someone slipped a rohypnol in the champagne bottle and that man saved you."

I shook my head, the curled ends of my hair brushing my shoulder and making me shiver. "N-no, I wasn't. I'm sure." My voice was shaky, and I didn't believe that I was roofied. Someone tried to...

"*Em...*"

I didn't like the sound of pity from Mia. Flaring my nose, I stood up and glared at all three of them. "I wasn't roofied. I was just drunk. Ask Joe, I drank a lot of glasses of negroni. Then I had champagne with Cillian, but..." My feet still felt wobbly, but I took my heels and my purse, ignoring their burning stares on me. "I've a headache. I'm gonna go home."

"*Emma.*" Damon wrapped his hand around my wrist, stopping me. His gaze was concerned, and it made me feel like shit. *Who was he to care about me? No one.* "We already talked with Joe. Maybe you should—"

"Nothing. Happened," I said, yanking my hand from his hold. "I'm fine."

I didn't wait to hear any more fake concerns from someone who had ignored my existence for the past nineteen years. My friends didn't deserve my anger, but they were being too anxious about some stupid little thing. I wasn't roofied. I was just drunk.

Because I remember Cillian entering the room after I had found his ring. Holding me when I wasn't feeling well and laying me down on a bed. Yes, he cursed a lot, but he took care of me.

I would feel better once I sleep it off.

My driver didn't ask me questions as I settled in the car's backseat. I sighed, closing my eyes and massaging my temples. It was a long fucking day.

My phone pinged with a text. I checked it and froze, uneasiness spreading over my body, stiffening my hands.

Unknown: *It's okay, don't be sad. I'll take care of you. I left you a nice present. See you at home soon, love.*

It was an unknown number, and I didn't know what the sender meant. *A present?*

Shaking off the stupid thought, I rubbed the goosebumps on my arms and asked the driver to hurry. I wanted to shower again or maybe take a warm bath and sleep for a week straight.

I went to my room as soon as I got home, ignoring how empty it felt compared to that morning. Throwing my phone on the bed, I stripped out of the dress and ran a hand through my hair before entering the washroom—

A gasp left my mouth. This time fear with uneasiness rolled over me, buckling my knees. On the white marble sink were my panties covered in—

Bile rose in my mouth as I averted my eyes to read the message on the mirror written with a red lipstick.

'I bought a new pair, don't worry. Hope you like the present.'

There was a heart, too, and true to the words, there was a pastel box placed beside the bath. I didn't want to open it.

I rushed out of the washroom and covered myself in a robe, eyeing my room, the closed closets, and quickly I dialed nine-one-one.

Maybe... just maybe, Damon was right. I was roofied.

13
SHE NEEDS YOUR HELP

CILLIAN

"So, whose party was it?" I asked, changing the gear and taking a turn while Caleb kept looking out of the window. I could smell the weed and beer on him. His eyes were bloodshot, hair ruffled, and he was still wearing the suit he had worn that morning.

"Don't know." He shrugged, not sparing me a glance. "I just went there to get high."

My jaw clenched. "And where's your car?"

"At E—" He stopped whatever he was saying and straightened up. "It's safe. I'll pick it up tomorrow."

God, how fucking hard is it to have a conversation with my own son?

"Where were you?" he asked, flickering his eyes at me for a moment. "You shaved and dressed up. Date?"

"No," I scoffed, tugging at the collar of my shirt. "I was at a club. I'm too old to date someone." *Definitely too old for someone like Emma.* I thought bitterly.

He stayed quiet for a moment, staring at his lap before whispering, "Mom would've liked you to be happy."

My hand loosened on the steering wheel as I blinked at the road. Clearing my throat, I said, "I'm happy."

"Sure. Whatever you say."

He just had to bring Olivia up.

Swallowing the lump in my throat, I changed the subject. "How's your girlfriend doing?" I asked. "I'm sorry I couldn't come to the funeral this morning."

Caleb scoffed, running a hand through his dark hair. "She's not my girlfriend."

I frowned, knowing that he was in a relationship with her for the longest time. Even though he never told me her name or brought her home for dinner, even after I asked him several times, I knew he liked her. Maybe even more than like. "What happened? Did you guys break up?"

"Yeah, kind of," he shrugged. "I fucked up, and she'd rather skin me alive than talk to me."

I winced. "Sounds sweet."

Glancing at him, I noticed how his shoulders were slumped, his eyes glazed. I clearly didn't want to talk to him about his recent breakup while he was high as a kite, but these days, we rarely saw each other.

"Do you want to talk about it?"

His brown eyes slid towards me and he let out a bitter laugh. "*Right.* Now you want to play Dad. It's a bit too late, don't you think so?"

His tone made me furious yet guilty, remorse making me feel shittier than I already was. I knew I wasn't there when he needed me, but I had tried. I have been trying for the past few years.

Caleb couldn't wait to get out of the car as soon as we reached home, leaving me alone as I glared at the garage. I had achieved everything I wanted, but my son hated me and my wife was six feet under the ground.

I got out of the car and checked my phone, thinking

about the golden blonde hair and warm skin that smelt like vanilla. Her soft warm fingers holding my scarred hand. I hoped she was okay and her brother was looking after her.

* * *

"I told you already, I'm done." I took a deep breath before clenching my fingers on the deadlift rod and pushed, its weight burning my arms and chest as I did ten more reps.

"This client is old money, Cillian," Elena, my ex-boss and also a Sheikha of Azmia, spoke through the phone on speaker. "And the case is worth looking at. They'd really appreciate your help."

I grunted when I placed the rod back on the support, glaring at the ceiling light of my home gym. "You know how I feel about rich clients, Elena."

She was quiet for a moment and said, "What if I told you she really needs your help?"

"She?"

"Yes. Her mom just died, and this is too serious to pass it on to someone else. Besides, she lives in Coral Springs to —*Zayed!* Put that thing down. Now." Her voice was sharp and I could hear her husband saying something in a taunting voice. My heart clenched at the sound of their teasing banter. "I'm sorry, Cillian. As I was saying, she lives in Coral Springs."

I ran a hand across my face and couldn't believe myself when I said, "Fine, I'll check the case. I'm not agreeing to it, but if you think it's worth looking at, then I'll go meet her."

"Thank you, C—I'm sorry, I've got to cut our call short." I heard someone shriek before her phone hung up.

Dammit. I just had to agree to another case when I said the previous one was my last one. I didn't need any more money than I already had. Raking a hand through my hair, I sighed, knowing I would probably take the case if Elena thought it was worth helping the client.

In half an hour, I had showered, got dressed in my usual dark pants and shirt, and had breakfast sitting on the kitchen island. I had knocked on Caleb's door, but he didn't respond even though I had made haejang-guk soup to cure him from his hangover.

I looked up the address of the house, sighing when it showed a vast vintage mansion. Driving there didn't take much time. The weather was slowly cooling up in the morning, but the sunlight still felt warm and airy. It was a beautiful day. In another era, I'd have liked to take someone on a brunch date. But I neither had any companion, nor did my son want to see me.

My car came to a halt as I saw the huge black iron gate topped with spikes. I lowered my sunglasses when a man who looked like a guard knocked on my tinted window.

"You can't go in. The owner has specified that only cops and the house staff are allowed."

"I'm Cillian." I showed him my ID. "The detective Elena Hill Al Fasih sent."

His eyes were wide when he passed me back my ID and bowed his head. "You can go in, Sir."

I pushed the glasses back over the bridge of my nose and drove towards the driveway, circling the sculptured fountain. My polished shoes scrunched when I stepped out of the car, buttoning my suit and straightening my cufflinks. The mansion was bigger than I had anticipated. Despite the security at the front gate, there were no cameras or security measures taken if someone—a robber, for example—decided to climb through the low levelled floors and get in through any open windows on the first floor.

I had to wait for exactly twenty-two seconds after pressing the doorbell. My glasses were hanging on my shirt, my eyes drifting from the black roses in the vase to the person who opened the double doors.

It was an old woman, dressed in black, with a low bun and a small smile.

"I'm Cillian. Elena asked me—"

She stepped aside, welcoming me in. "We are glad you could come. Both of them have been waiting for you." There was a huge chandelier on the ceiling, two staircases dividing the mansion into two wings. "Please, Mr. Cillian, follow me."

Sliding a hand in my pocket, I followed the woman, noticing the emptiness of pictures. There was lots of art—huge paintings framed on the walls, sculptures, expensive decorations, but there were no photos of any pets or children. Even though the interior was sleek and vintage, it felt like it was copied from a yearly architectural magazine that only rich people read.

It didn't feel human.

"You have to talk to them—"

My feet didn't slow down when I heard a familiar voice coming from a guest room near the kitchen.

"I told you, I don't want to talk to anyone." The same soft feminine voice. "I want to go to Mia's house. Or Summer's. I'm fine."

"Sir, Ma'am," the woman announced, walking into the room, my eyes going from the annoyed look of Damon to the scared, nervous look of Emma. "This is the detective Miss Elena sent. His na—"

I took a step closer, eyeing the siblings and how Emma shook underneath the blanket she was curled in. "I'm Cillian. Nice to see you again, Emma."

PART II

"Why did my ex's dad have to be so hot?"

14
MISTER CILLIAN

EMMA

I didn't expect to see the handsome man again. In my house out of all places. My eyes drifted from his thick hair to the exposed skin of his neck. I could see a hint of more tattoos. The suit he was wearing was different from before. It was much darker and fitted his large frame perfectly.

He extended his hand, introducing himself. "I'm Cillian. Nice to see you again, Emma."

Cillian. My throat felt a bit sore from screaming his name all night.

"Damon Grant," my brother said, shaking his hand while I was still processing that Cillian was in front of me. "You met at the club?"

"Y-yes," I muttered, pulling the blanket closer and glancing at Cillian, looking away when his deep eyes were still on me. They made me wary and nervous. I shivered, for a completely different reason, and continued, "He saved me. *Twice.*"

Meeting his eyes, I whispered, "Thank you, Cillian."

He nodded at me and looked at Damon. "What happened?"

My body froze, remembering the events from last night as sleeplessness and exhaustion tugged at me. I was going to be late for school, but I just... *couldn't*.

Damon sighed and showed him my phone. "There's more. Upstairs, in her room. I'll be right back, okay? I can ask Mis—"

"No." I stood up, scrunching the blanket around me. "I'll come with you. I'm fine."

Cillian's eyes were burning the side of my face, but I didn't dare look at him. Because if I did, I would break. He would know how truly shaken I was. How scared and anxious I was.

"Someone sent her this text when she was coming back home."

Cillian looked over his shoulder at me. "Were you alone, or was there someone with you?"

"No. My driver was driving."

He nodded, looking at the paintings hung by the wall as we climbed upstairs. My knees buckled, but I was more furious than scared. I didn't care about anything else right now than to know who had the audacity to play with me, Emma fucking Moore.

If mom was alive, she'd threaten, torture and even kill that person by herself. Not because I'm her daughter, but because someone decided to scare a Moore. She wouldn't stand by in a blanket if it was her.

Damon paused just before my room. The white double doors were open from when I had rushed downstairs in the middle of the night and called nine-one-one.

Another reason I was mad at Damon was that he had talked with the cops before they could investigate the scene and scolded me for calling them. Giving me yet another lecture on how it'd look bad in the paper and tabloids. That private security would be better than cops.

"Are you sure—"

I glared at Damon. "I am sure. This is my room."

I walked past the two men even though my body hated going into the room. Everything was still the same. My lilac, pink, and white comforter on the enormous bed, the dresses I had tried on the day before still scattered on the floor, my strewn makeup and perfume collection with my heels placed neatly on the white shelves.

"When I came back home, I-I wanted to shower and when I entered the bathroom, I saw… this."

The door was open so all of us could see the words written on the mirror above the sink.

I bought a new pair, don't worry. Hope you like the present.

With a heart in the end in my red Chanel lipstick. I couldn't look at myself in the mirror or the sink. It made bile rise in my throat.

Even Damon averted his eyes.

But Cillian didn't care. He walked right inside the washroom, his polished shoes silent on the soft white rug. He was hard to read when he inspected my underwear. I covered my arms, trying to rub off the goosebumps and watched him kneel and tilt his head at the pastel box near the bath.

"Is this yours?" he asked, his voice deep.

I shook my head. "I-it's not. Someone… I don't know how it got there. O-or who put it there."

"Interesting," Cillian whispered, standing up and pulling out his phone. I took a step back when he moved from the washroom back to my room, speaking to someone on the phone.

"What do you think this is?" Damon asked, his phone trilling in his pants, but he ignored it. "Intruder?"

Cillian ended the call and glanced at us. Like before, I

couldn't stand the intensity in his eyes and looked away. I don't know why they made me so uncomfortable though they seemed familiar. It was odd. And very infuriating.

"I've called forensic to take your underwear and that box, and to check your room. I need to talk—"

"Wait," my brother interrupted. "I didn't agree to have more people involved in this. Can't you find who did it?"

Cillian hummed and slid his hands in his pockets. He looked so out of place in my white and pink room with his dark clothes and large frame. Even though my room was as big as that suite, Cillian made it look tiny by just standing in it.

"Let me ask you this, Damon, would you ever let a twelve-year-old kid drive your McLaren GT?"

I raised my brows and turned to Damon.

"Of course not. He's a kid."

"So, I'm sure you'll understand why I need a team to look over her room. I don't specialize in lab work, but they do. Now, do you mind if I talk to your sister alone?"

"I do min—" Damon stopped when his phone rang for the umpteenth time. He glanced at me and I rolled my eyes at him.

"We can talk in the guest room, Mister Cillian," I said, not waiting for his answer when I saw the dark glint in his eyes.

It ran through my entire body, making me very aware of what I was wearing—absolutely nothing, underneath the blanket.

"Sure, Emma," he whispered, his voice smooth and soft and making me feel unsteady on my feet.

This man is starting to feel like trouble.

Could I really talk to him alone in a room with a closed door after what happened?

15
I'LL STAY

CILLIAN

"Why do you have a blanket?" I asked Emma, following her to the guest room and eyeing the way her manicured black nails were clutching the damn thing so tightly.

I had known her for a few hours and in that time, I knew she wasn't the type to get scared easily. My hand tightened into a fist, seeing her let out a small sigh of relief when we walked out of her room.

She looked over her shoulder, a wavy lock of blonde hair brushing her cheekbone. "I might be traumatized. This is just a precaution."

My lips twitched. "Of course."

Her brother was reluctant to leave me alone with his sister, which I understood. If I was in his shoes, I wouldn't let any man close to her.

My jaw clenched remembering the white release on her pink underwear. Someone was either playing a sick joke or it was something much more serious. Unfortunately, my guess was the latter.

The text, the writing on her mirror, the spilling on her

underwear, giving her a present, and all that time, directly addressing her.

"Actually…" She halted when we entered a room smaller than hers with white and grey sheets and none of her girly shit like makeup, dresses or the sweet vanilla scent that lingered in her room. The room was musty, most likely because it hasn't been used a lot. She must have slept here after what had happened. The sheets were mussed up and there was no bedspread; most likely that was the blanket draped over her body. Was she afraid of going back to her room alone?

Her cheeks were dusted with pink when I closed the door behind me, keeping it unlocked. I didn't want to make her feel unsafe or crowded because I was tall and broad in front of her tiny frame. She could be still under the shock. I stood at a safe distance and raised my brow, waiting for her continue.

"Do you mind if I take a quick shower and change?" Her voice was small and she couldn't meet my eyes as she spoke. *Huh.* I tilted my head, watching her body language, but unfortunately, she was covered in a blanket, and I could only see her face and bare feet, her cute toes painted in pink. *Adorable.*

Her pretty feet wrapped around my waist when I slammed inside her—I forced myself to look away, hoping she wouldn't notice my red ears.

"I-I mean, I can do it later if you're in a hurry and have to be somewhere else, and we can talk—"

"*Emma,*" I said her name, clenching my hand in a fist because I hated myself for liking—*no*, loving the way it voiced out. Her name was soft and angelic. Like her. "I don't mind."

If it was possible, her cheeks tinted more and she nodded, turning around and letting go of the blanket. My fist unfurled and lips fell apart. My eyes trailed from her soft golden locks to the barely-there robe that covered her curves. My cock twitched and *fuck fuck fuck, this is not the time—*

I turned away from her, squeezing my eyes shut and biting my fist. *This is terrible.* All the blood had run south and it was so fucking wrong. I shouldn't be twitching in my pants just at the sight of my possible client in her perfectly normal robe. I shouldn't. I especially shouldn't reminisce about the night before, when I was on the job her brother hired me for.

But fuck, I was getting hard.

I pressed my teeth harder on my fist and exhaled sharply.

Order me to take a bullet and I could do it, but standing guard when Emma has to shower? Not a chance. I couldn't do it.

"I'll wait outside," I bit out, wincing at myself, because my voice was all rough and deep. I was about to open the door when I felt a pull on my suit.

I stopped.

"P-please don't leave."

I stiffened and turned around to see her face. Her fingers were clutching my suit, not pulling on it, just holding it, stopping me from leaving the room. Her face was hidden by her hair, but her voice was trembling. She was afraid of being left alone.

Terrified.

"I... I'll be quick. I promise," Emma whispered, and I heard her swallow a lump in her throat. "Please, Mister Cillian."

My throat went dry. I didn't mean to... I really didn't. But I couldn't stop myself, couldn't stop the urge to protect her. Bury her in my arms and keep her safe. With me. *Forever.*

I cupped her cheek and looked at her blue doe eyes which

were glistening with tears. "I won't leave you. I'll stay, Emma."

Her lush lips parted as she blinked up at me. *Fuck*. I hadn't noticed how close we were. How soft her skin felt underneath my calloused hands, how beautiful she looked. She smelt so fucking good and her sweet vanilla scent was everywhere.

"Okay. Thank you, Mister Cillian," she said, my self-control threatening to break.

"Cillian," I said, my voice rougher than before. *You called me Cillian—no, screamed my name all night. You can call me Cillian on the job.* "Call me Cillian."

She licked her lips, my eyes flickering to them. "Okay, Mi—Cillian."

I pulled away before I could do something extremely terrible. Like lean down and kiss her. Pin her hands over her head, ravish her pouty lips and feel her curves with my hands and mouth, checking if she was wearing anything underneath the thin robe and then punishing her if she wasn't.

You're going too far, Cillian.

I clenched my fists watching her walk into the en-suite washroom, keeping the door ajar. My eyes burned and skin felt hot hearing the whisper of the cloth pooling around her ankles. Her cute pink-colored toes. Then the shower started.

Fuck.

Coming here was a terrible mistake.

What the fuck did I agree to?

Emma

My skin shivered as warm water cascaded over it. I wasn't trembling just because of the water. The other reason was the burly man waiting for me in the room.

Cillian.

I let out another shuddering sigh and cupped my burning cheeks, remembering how he had touched me, his calloused hand gentle as if he was holding fragile China.

I was still sore from the night before and already my body wanted another round.

"You're overthinking, Emma," I said to myself, quickly washing off the body wash. I was glad that he was in the room. Despite his large frame, he made me feel protected. I felt safe in his presence.

And I know he agreed to stay because I was about to burst in tears. Even though I pretended that the thing with my underwear and unknown messages didn't affect me, I couldn't stop shaking with fear and uneasiness when I had to shower alone without anyone looking out for me. I was too much of a coward to ask Mrs. Karen and too proud to ask Damon. He'd probably just scoff and roll his eyes at me, tell me that I was wasting his precious time.

But Cillian hadn't said anything. He just promised me that he'd stay in the room.

I wrapped myself in a towel and looked for some clothes in the bathroom closet. But, of course, I was stupid and forgetful. That guest room didn't have any clean clothes.

Covering my face with my hand, I kept mumbling 'Oh, God' until the panic set in and I couldn't stop myself from unlocking the door.

Before Cillian could look away or get horrified, I blurted, "I forgot my clothes."

I had never moved faster towards a door but a strong arm wrapped around my elbow before I could turn the cold knob.

16
MEET THE EX

EMMA

"Stay. You'll get cold. I'll go get them," Cillian bit out, pulling me back and not looking at me as he opened the door. "Which drawer or... closet?"

My cheeks scorched with embarrassment as I crossed my arms. "Just some pajamas in the second closet and... there are undergarments in the drawers." *Color coded*, I added mentally.

He didn't spare me a glance and left to fetch my clothes. I shivered from the cold and caught my reflection in the mirror.

I looked red. My cheeks, ears and neck were blushing red. I jumped when there was a sharp knock on the door.

"Y-yes?"

Instead of answering, the door opened and I stared at the broad chest in dark shirt that belonged to Cillian. I took my clothes in a hurry when he handed them to me and the door closed on my face before I could thank him.

I was a mess. I was never a mess. But I was becoming a mess just because of him.

Sighing, I let go of my towel and glanced at the clothes he had picked out for me. I pursed my lips seeing the bra and resisted the intense urge to open the nearest window and scream.

"Barbie. Seriously? What the fuck?" I whispered to myself, angrily clasping the hooks of the bra. "Out of all the expensive bras—he had to pick this one!"

I whispered out more curses because I knew he was waiting outside and I didn't want him to hear me.

A humorless chuckle escaped my lips when I saw the underwear. I dangled it in front of me, my entire body burning with anger and embarrassment. I had underpants from La Perla, Agent Provocateur, but no, he picked out the ones that Summer and Mia had given me on my birthday to prank me. A freaking Teletubby underwear and a Barbie bra.

Either Cillian had a sense of humor in his big, stoic body, or he was punishing me for making him wait in a room while I was too scared to shower alone.

I knew it was the latter.

At least the underwear was pure cotton and comfortable. I thanked the Fashion Gods (whoever they may be), as I donned the full-sleeved tee shirt and plain sweatpants.

He must have not found the secret stash of embarrassing clothes in the back of my drawer.

"I'm decent!" I yelled after pulling the socks on my feet and hand-combing my damp hair.

I had to miss school today, and even though no one would mind because of my mother's death, I didn't want to miss it. I wanted to be around my friends, study, mix chemicals and note their reactions. I wanted to be around people, but I wondered why I was shaking at the idea of being out in public where anyone could—

"*Emma.*"

I blinked out of my thoughts and raked my graze from the carpeted floor to Cillian. I hadn't noticed he had entered the room and was staring at me with a concerned look on his face.

"Are you okay?" he asked, crossing his arms.

I nodded, tucking my hair behind my ear and asking, "I'm sorry for making you wait. What did you want to talk about?"

"How's your romantic relationship?" he said, his voice sharp and authoritative. "Any breakup recently?"

I let out a loud laugh. I was about to snort too when I noticed his serious expression. "Oh? I thought you were joking..." I rubbed my neck.

Cillian hummed and kept staring at me with a look that screamed 'I don't joke.'

"I broke up with my boyfriend of one year and three months yesterday," I said, clearing my throat and twiddled with my thumbs on my lap. "No other romantic relationship before that."

"I don't want to prod, but... was it a bad breakup?" His voice had turned softer and I hated that he was giving me pity. I wasn't someone to be pitied, so I raised my chin and met his gaze. "Was he violent?"

My mouth fell apart, "Violent? He'd never... Cal would never do that." Caleb could be a player, and he was sometimes dumb about people's feelings, but he was never violent towards me or anyone. Heck, he was the one who'd cry every time a pet died in movies, and I had to console him. "Why are you asking me that question? You think my boy—ex-boyfriend did this?"

He was rubbing his chin and I was finding it a bit hard to focus. "Well, most of the stalking cases are committed by exes. And women are most likely to be stalked by a current or former intimate partner during the rela—"

"Stalking?" I stood up, cutting him off, "You think I'm being stalked?"

"There's a thirty percent chance that you are. For now."

"What do you mean, *for now*?"

"This person sent you a text, gave you a so-called present, invading your privacy. And there is a huge chance that they would do this again." Cillian looked at me and I didn't like the way he sighed and added, "This is why I asked you about your ex—"

"*Emma!*"

I jumped hearing my name called and relaxed knowing who it was. "You want to talk to my ex? He's here. You can interrogate him all you want."

"Emma! Where the fuck are my car keys?" Caleb yelled, storming upstairs and I could hear his heavy footsteps going past the guest room towards my room.

I opened the door and called him, "Caleb, come here. Someone wants to talk to you."

I heard Cillian mutter, "Caleb?"

Caleb looked haggard in our school's uniform, his shirt half untucked, tie rumpled and eyes red. He looked like he had partied all night with drugs and alcohol. Yet I couldn't stop the feeling of sharp pain between my ribs. I had seen him with someone else on my bed.

I looked away and let him enter the room, crossing my arms. "This is my ex, Caleb Chang. Cal, this is—"

"*Dad?* What the fuck are you doing here?"

My mouth fell apart when I looked between the two men. Caleb looked angry and guilty while Cillian looked shocked. And it was the first time I saw his cool and calm expression break.

What the fuck?

I don't know if you're keeping a count, but that's twice I've been surprised in less than twenty-four hours.

17
WHAT DID I MISS?

CILLIAN

There have been a few times in forty years of life that I wished I wasn't present in a particular situation and instead lock myself in a room, bury myself in huge blankets, and never ever meet another person again. Most of the time, it was during a life-threatening situation where I had to save a comrade who had been shot, when Olivia went into labor, and when I found her dead.

Apparently, standing in the guest room of my son's ex-girlfriend, whose damp hair was wetting her tee shirt, was one of those situations. Mostly because I was the one between her soft thighs last entire night.

Jesus Christ. Did I fucking sleep with...

"Dad? What the fuck are you doing here?"

My eyes twitched—which was never a good sign—looking at Caleb and Emma. He looked like he was ready for school in his very rumpled uniform and tousled hair.

"This is work," I said, trying to keep my voice emotionless. Because I had slept with my son's ex. *Emma.* "I thought you were Emma Grant," I added, tilting my head at her, who looked equally shocked, if not more, by the entire ordeal.

"She's Emma Moore. She kept her mom's last name," Caleb said, his eyes narrowing on me and turning towards his ex. "Why is my dad in your guest room, Em?"

She looked like she was having a hard time processing all of it. Her brows were scrunched and she wasn't meeting either of our eyes. "W-why are you here?" she asked, diverting the topic, clearly not ready to share to her ex that he could be a suspect.

Fucking great. I'd need an alibi for Caleb, because I knew he'd never do something like that. Even if he could... *no*. He was out of the suspect list if I was handling her case. Emma herself said he'd never do something like that, and I was with him.

"My car's here," Caleb mumbled, his cheeks turning pink. "I parked it in your garage."

I sighed and pinched the bridge of my nose.

"Why did you park it in the garage?" Emma asked, crossing her arms.

"Because I thought you'd need me after... after everything."

My brows raised, seeing Caleb look nervous and flustered.

Emma's eyes flickered to me before she looked at Caleb and said, "Ask Mrs. Karen for the keys. You can leave. I need to talk with Cillian."

"About what?"

"It's personal, Caleb." I tried the stern dad-look, but it hadn't worked a single time. "It's a private case. If you want in, you have to sign an NDA and follow all the security protocols."

His eyes widened, pinning on Emma and stepping towards her. She looked away, her hair covering the sides of her face, and Caleb's face dropped before he took his hand back. *Hm, interesting.* She wasn't afraid of him. If he had been violent towards her in the past, she'd have retreated, but she didn't even flinch. That meant whatever Caleb had done broke her emotionally.

Yet it still made me mad that Caleb dared to hurt her.

"Can't I know as a friend?"

"Leave, Caleb."

I kept my mouth shut, seeing him leave with slumped shoulders. He clearly didn't want to leave and wanted to talk to her about something.

I just hope I can survive this last case.

Emma

Fuck. Me.

The hot, muscular, stoic man with hidden tattoos and barely a few wisps of grey in his thick dark hair was none other than Caleb's father. *Dad*. He was a dad. And I had made a move on him last night... after breaking up with his son. Then I had fucked him. I was still sore because of him.

I move real fast, don't I?

"I didn't peg you as a single dad," I said, after a few moments of silence. Cillian was leaning on the wall beside the window.

I knew Caleb's mom had passed away and his dad was not home most of the time, because I had visited him a lot. A pretty suburban house. I never thought his father was *that* hot—a literal sex on legs, as my friends would say.

Must be his fantastic Asian genes.

"I know Caleb did something really terrible," Cillian started. *Oh, boy, you have no idea.* I looked away, swallowing a lump in my throat when he continued, "He's stupid sometimes about his feelings, clearly got that from his dad, so I apologize for that."

"It's okay," I muttered, rubbing my arms and closed my

eyes. "He—Caleb isn't stalking me. He'd never do that. You know that, too."

He straightened up and buttoned his suit, his expensive watch catching a glint in the light. "My opinion is biased as his father." His eyes drifted to the door as Damon walked in, typing on his phone before looking at both of us.

"What did I miss?"

Oh, I just took a shower, teared up while asking Cillian to stay in the room, wore a Barbie bra and a Teletubby underwear that he brought for me from my room, talked about stalking, got interrupted by my ex who, by the way, also happens to be Cillian's son and had a fun chat about it.

Nothing much.

Cillian said, "We will gather the evidence and I've to talk to Elena about the case." He glanced at me. "Do you feel safe in the house? In your room?"

I froze up when they both looked at me. I didn't know why I was breaking into cold sweats all of a sudden and why the fuck my palms were getting so sweaty—

"I'll take that as a no." Cillian looked at Damon and said, "She needs security around her. And possibly another place to live. There's an eighty percent chance that that person might try to leave another gift or try an attempt to meet you. That attempt could either be forceful or violent."

"What?"

"You mean to tell me my sister is not safe in her own house?"

"What?" I asked again, my voice smaller this time.

"I am not telling you. I'm stating the facts. She's being stalked. Chances are, this was not the first attempt. This person already succeeded in scaring her if she's shaking on her feet going to her room."

"What the fuck is that supposed to mean?"

"*Guys...*" I was feeling parched and seeing black spots.

"I think you heard me the first time, Mister Grant. This was the reason Elena wanted me to take this case, because Emma is being stalked and she needs our help."

"Our mother just died, okay? What she needs is some space and therapy and she'll—"

"Emma." I heard Cillian's voice first. My knees gave as I fell on the floor. "Emma!"

18

BANGING YOUR EX'S DAD?

CILLIAN

Stupid.

I was too fucking stupid.

If only I hadn't prioritized arguing with Damon and looked at Emma just for a damn second. She wouldn't have fainted. But of course, I just had to prove my point.

"She fainted because of the sudden drop in her blood pressure. She'll wake up in a couple of hours. If she doesn't, you have my number."

I thanked the doctor and watched him leave with Mrs. Karen, Emma's personal maid and one of the main house staff, from the doorframe. I gave her a polite nod and wondered how the heck I was going to explain all this to Elena.

Damon had to work, so he had to leave and demanded me to keep him updated. But first, I needed to call Elena.

"Let me guess," she started, her voice husky. I checked the time and mentally winced. It must be four in the morning in Azmia. "You're taking the case."

Flickering my eyes at Emma, I heard myself say, "Yes, I

might." Before she could cheer, I continued, "But this is more serious than the usual."

I told her everything. The mysterious man at the club I had noticed watching her, getting roofied, her room being intruded by someone and leaving her a message and a present. Everything was a mess, but it made sense that the person who had tried to roofie Emma at the club might be the same person who invaded her room.

"Fuck," Elena sighed, and I heard some shuffling in the background with some clicking noises.

Ah, of course. Cleaning her guns. I could relate. Cleaning them gave me a sense of comfort and made me think.

"Did you call the forensics team to gather the evidence?"

"They left an hour ago. We should get a report from them in the morning." I rubbed my forehead, looking out of the window. "I don't like how she's the only one in the house besides the staff, Elena. Her brother doesn't think it's too concerning for her to leave her house. They don't have surveillance cameras, so no one was caught. Even the two guards at the front gate don't know shit."

"Calm down, Big Bear," she joked and turned the phone to speaker when I heard her whisper 'I hate you' to her husband. "Cillian, if you think she needs guards around her, I'll start looking right away—"

"But isn't Cillian the father of her ex?" Her husband, Zayed, asked, his voice rich and serious yet playful.

"Yes, Caleb is her ex."

"How did they break up?"

"*Zayed!*"

"What? It's just a question."

I pursed my lips. "Neither of them has told me the reason yet. But I'm guessing that after her mother's funereal, they both broke up. Caleb left to party and Emma went to the club where I met her." *And took her to my private suite.*

Zayed made a humming noise and asked, "Well, why don't you guard her, then?" He cackled, and I stared at my phone. *How the hell did Elena Hill end up with this guy?*

"That is juicy! Staying at your ex's dad's house. Forced proximity? *Check.* Bodyguard romance? *Check.* Banging your ex's dad? On its way—*ah*, little witch! That fucking hurt."

I heard more yelping and shrieking sounds before Elena was back on the call, this time without the speaker turned on. *Thank God.*

"Please ignore whatever Zayed said. I do most of the time," Elena said, her voice sharp as she continued, "But he made a good point. You have guarded celebrities and politicians before. How about Emma Moore?"

My palms felt clammy thinking about the afternoon where I had to stay in the room while she showered. Going through her color-coded undergarments and choosing the least sexy one (because they were all so goddamn sexy, and I didn't want to make a wrong expression) and give it to her, waiting for her to wear them and hearing her curse me for choosing the one with Barbie while she thought I couldn't hear.

Could I let anyone else other than me guard her? Twenty-four seven? Being so close to her and catching her sweet vanilla scent.

The answer was simple.

Hell no. There was no fucking way I'd let another man or woman guard Emma when I could perfectly do it by myself.

"I'll do it," I said, my voice firm, seeing the sleeping figure of Emma. "I'll be her bodyguard until we catch the bastard who is behind this."

"I knew you'd agree." I could hear Elena's smile through the phone. "What about her living conditions?"

"She can stay here. I'm guarding her, so I will monitor

everything, and besides, this might be the place she feels the most comfortable."

"Good. I'll arrange everything and talk to Damon. If he is an ass, I'll hand the phone to Zayed."

"Good idea." I had talked to her husband for a few seconds and I felt overwhelmed. I didn't know how she lived with that devil.

"Oh, before I go, you know that she's in school, right? Senior in high school. So you have to guard her there as well."

"*Oh, fuck.*"

* * *

Emma

I HATED FAINTING AND WAKING UP WITH A THROBBING headache. Groaning, I forced my lids open and looked around me. I rubbed my eyes, surprised to see the familiar chandelier on the ceiling, and slowly sat up. It was odd to be in the same comfortable mattress and satin sheets and feel my heartbeat increase, shivers of uneasiness and nervousness rolling through my spine and all over my body.

The last time I had woken up in this bed, it was my birthday and everything was perfect. Caleb was my loving and doting boyfriend, my mother was alive, and some would even say that my life was perfect.

Now? I had dumped Caleb, my mother was buried six feet beneath the ground and someone was stalking me.

Rolling out of bed, I looked around the room, hugging myself. My windows were closed and the curtains were drawn, yet I still felt like I was being stared at. That I was being watched, and it infuriated me that I was letting someone ruin my life just because they were delusional.

Shaking my head, I checked the time and decided on my options. It was half past seven in the evening. I could either call Mia and ask her about school, any gossips about me, get ahead of my syllabus or I could dress up and go out, stop thinking so damn hard for once.

"Mrs. Karen?" I called out, opening my closet and racking through my dresses. I needed to dress up, go out, maybe get drunk and forget all about it. I could ask Summer. She always knows the right place to party.

"Mrs. Karen!" I called her again, throwing a skirt and a top on the bed. When I heard a knock on my door, I said, "Come in. Can you please tell the driver to ready the car? I'm going out. Which one do you like the best?"

I turned around, holding two skirts. One was black and white stripped pencil skirt with thick fabric from Chanel and the other was a flirty dark red number with thin, light fabric.

My eyes widened seeing Cillian leaning on the door frame, his arms crossed. My mouth suddenly went dry, noticing his suit jacket was missing and the sleeves of his dark shirt were rolled over his elbows, giving me the shameless and delicious view of his black ink. I licked my lips, eyeing the dark swirls running through his veiny, corded arms and underneath the sleeves.

Oh, God... *why did my ex's dad have to be so hot?*

19

CUTE

CILLIAN

Two things I noticed after being Emma's bodyguard for forty minutes.

One. She looked adorable with bedhead hair. Her blonde wavy locks tangled up and framing her face.

Two. She most likely drools in her sleep.

"I'd say neither of them as you're not going out, but if I had to choose, I'd pick the red one. It suits your flushed cheeks."

Her cheeks turned a cute shade of pink and she dropped the skirts on her bed. She didn't meet my eyes as she asked, "What are you doing here?" She was going through her clothes, hiding from me in her closet. "And what do you mean by I'm not going out?"

I straightened up to my full height and entered her room. Since the forensics had done their job, it was back to normal as it was. I had asked the house staff to clean up her room once again, so she won't ever remember that someone had invaded her privacy.

"I'm your bodyguard, Doll," I said, picking up the red skirt from the bed and feeling the soft fabric. I dropped it and looked over at her when I heard her take a sharp breath "I can't let you go out if it means endangering yourself to others... especially your stalker."

"What?" Emma shook her head. "That can't be right. I-I don't need a bodyguard. I just... just find the stalker so I can—"

She stopped and looked back at her closet, hiding her face. She clearly wanted to say more but was holding herself back.

"I don't want a bodyguard."

"I, too, don't want to guard a nineteen-year-old rich kid, but tough luck." My voice had an edge to it. "You should have told me you were nineteen before... everything—*fuck*."

Her blue eyes were sharp as a razor when she looked at me, crossing her arms. I had to force myself to keep my eyes above her chin level because crossing her arms in front of me did nothing to intimidate me. It did the opposite of intimidation.

"All I did was hide the truth." My eyes narrowed at her when she continued, "Besides, if you're my bodyguard, then that means I'm your boss. So, I can fire you right away."

I smiled, prowling towards her. I leaned down to her height and said, "*Cute*." Being this close, I could see the small freckles splattered across her cheeks and nose. "You're my client, Doll. My boss is Elena and don't worry about firing me, this is my last job. So, you can't get rid of me easily until you're safe."

"I *am* safe!"

I trailed my eyes over her bare arms and she subtly moved her hands back, pushing her chest—*fucking hell, Cillian, focus!*

"If you feel safe, then why are your hands shaking, Emma?" I asked, trailing my eyes over her face. Her pupils dilated as she stared back at me with equal ferocity. I pulled back and continued, "You're not safe until we know who's doing this and catch him or... her."

"You think it's a woman?" Her voice was shaky. Even talking about the stalker made her this nervous. Then how the fuck would she survive without a guard? No. I did the right thing choosing to be her bodyguard.

"I think it's a man, but we can't vote out woman." I tilted my head and smirked. "You're a pretty girl after all."

Emma's cheeks were flaming red. I walked towards the door and paused, turning back. "I have your number and don't worry about the driver. He'll be following my commands for a while, so you can go anywhere you want with my permission." I flashed her a small smile, her face growing irritated by each second and I didn't know why, but it made me feel really good. "I'll be staying here, so I need to fetch some things from my house. Behave and I'll come with you."

I was ready to leave her room when I remembered something. "You look adorable with drool, Doll."

When I closed the door behind me, something struck the wood. My smile widened, knowing full well she was going to be a difficult client.

Emma

What an asshole!

A sexy asshole?

I grumbled more curses underneath my breath, curling my hands into fists. How dare he—*ugh!*

Glad that my washroom was finally clear, I splashed cold water on my face. *You look adorable with drool, Doll.*

Eat my ass! Groaning at myself, I washed my face with the electronic scrubber, wondering why the hell Damon agreed to him being my bodyguard all of a sudden?

It didn't matter that Cillian was Caleb's dad. I didn't care that he was some hotshot, the strongest and smartest guard or security out there. He was having fun teasing me and telling me what I should and shouldn't do. Where I should and shouldn't go. So much so that he put my driver under his command. *Who does that?*

Assholes. That's who.

With fresh, moisturized and drool-free face, I strategized my plan. Picking up my phone, I called my friend who knew ins and outs of all the parties and... how to sneak out of a mansion without getting caught.

It shouldn't be that hard.

Right?

* * *

Turns out, I can be wrong sometimes.

"Can you just catch me?" I asked, groaning and struggling to keep myself upright on the wall as I looked over my shoulder at Summer's dark curls.

"Babe, I would if I could. But I'm built like a stick," she said, her hands on her hips. My Louboutin beside her. "Nice underwear, by the way. Really brings out your... cheeks."

"Thanks," I said dryly, my upper body hurting when I slowly lowered myself from the wall. I didn't care that I was flashing my friend. What I cared more about was not to ruin my expensive skirt.

It was easier than I had imagined sneaking out of the front door, but harder to get past the two guards at the front gate; so I had to go to my backyard, over to the pool house while sneaking like a vigilante, and ask Summer to park her car over the tall wall, which I had climbed just because there was a ladder for me to use.

I yipped when my butt landed on the ground, my legs

splayed and hands dirty. It didn't hurt too badly and gave me more adrenaline boost than I had expected.

"So how do you feel sneaking out of your house at ten?" Summer asked, giving me a hand.

My answering grin must be glorious since we giggled. I could easily imagine the look on Cillian's face and it made me really, really happy.

20

I CALLED REINFORCEMENTS

EMMA

I was grinning from ear to ear, rubbing off the dust from my skirt and blouse, fixing my hair. "It's very thrilling. I wish I had done that sooner!"

We both sat in her car, strapping the seat belts on. "Between you and me, if you ever sneak out again, park your car blocks away and start pushing it before you start it so that no one knows you are sneaking out."

I clicked my tongue. "That seems clever. Then why did you start the car right here?" I asked, as she drove past the driveway to my house and towards the road, with overgrown trees on the side, that leads to the town.

"Because I thought you were kidding about having a curfew," Summer said, tapping her fingers on the wheel, giving me a small smile. "First of all, you're Emma Moore and second of all, you kind of deserve a break after yesterday…"

Her soft voice trailed off into the sound of wind and night. I looked out of the window, my mind going to the day before. She was right. I hadn't really coped with anything that had been happening since my birthday.

A warm hand closed over mine. I squeezed her hand back and thanked her for being there with me. Even though my mom was dead, I had dumped my boyfriend, and I had a stalker… at least my friends were with me.

"Is Mia going to join us?" I asked, knowing well that her older boyfriend was a stubborn piece of shit.

"What do you think?"

"If James can pick her up or have a tattoo of his name on her forehead, he might let her off his leash," I said, ending my sentence in a singsong voice.

Summer giggled. "He's not *that* bad."

"Excuse me? Not that bad?" I asked. "Do you remember when he threw her over his shoulder like a freaking cave man at the club?"

"Ahh, yes, I remember. That was kind of hot, huh?"

"What?"

"Yeah," she shrugged, fiddling with the knob of her radio player. The car was vintage, so it didn't have a working radio. "I mean, he's not overly possessive of her and lets her do her own thing. I bet they have nasty, kinky sex afterwards. I kind of like that. I wish I had that."

I remembered the look on Mia's face when they had opened the door of the private room at the club months ago. She had tears gleaming in her eyes, but she didn't look like she was crying from sadness. She looked like she had seen heaven and danced in the clouds. And the way James looked at her every time they both were in the same room made me both want to puke and yell at them to get a room. Like they couldn't have enough of each other.

"Yeah," I whispered, my voice seeming far away. "I wish I had that, too."

I realized too late what I had just spilled.

"What? You have Caleb fucking Chang wrapped around your pinkie. You already have that, bab—"

"I dumped him, Summer," I blurted, fiddling with my fingers. "I found him kissing Aaron on my bed. I broke up with him."

I didn't know why but saying that aloud made my heart ache and throat burn.

"What the hell?" Her voice had gone soft, and she was driving slow as if she was processing what she was hearing. "When did this happen?"

I chuckled humorlessly, tucking my hair behind my ear. "Yesterday. At my mom's funereal. Can you fucking believe it?"

"Yes. No. I... I can't."

We were both silent for a while and I jumped in my seat when Summer suddenly slammed her hand on the wheel, blaring the horn. "That asshole! He cheated on you at your mom's funeral with a fucking guy? Jesus Christ."

"I know, right?" I sniffed, wiping the tear that escaped my eyes. *Traitor.* "I was so furious and sad and done that I went to the club to get wasted and... you know, the rest." *I slept with his hot dad, who is now my bodyguard.*

"Why didn't you tell us, Em?" Summer asked, turning to a neighborhood I wasn't familiar with. It was near our school and even though we were far from reaching the party, I could hear the bass of some pop song.

"I know, I'm sorry. I just wanted to get wasted and forget all about it."

"Well, we are getting you wasted and make you forget all about it tonight!"

"We?"

"I called reinforcements."

I stared at her and her smug grin. "Whenever you have that smile on your face, things never go well, Summer."

"Chill, it's just me, Mia, and a few guys from our school.

Who are single and ready to mingle? Shelter your jerky, then nab that turkey."

"*Stop*. Don't call it jerky."

"Cage that snake, then shake and bake?"

"*Jesus*."

"You're going to be fine!"

I was, in fact, not fine.

As Cillian had to come get me when I almost got naked at the party...

* * *

Cillian

"Why the fuck are you here?" I stared at the black-haired man, sitting on my couch with crossed legs, flashy watch and glasses perched on his nose.

"Nice to see you too, brother," Sean smiled at me with a small wave.

I threw my keys in the bowl, removing my shoes and wearing slippers, and walking inside. "We are not brothers," I reminded him for the umpteenth time, grabbing a glass and pouring cold water from the fridge.

"That's not how Mrs. Chang treats me," he said, talking about my mother and opening the fridge. "She treats me like her own son." He emphasized the last part, grabbing a jar of kimchi and leftover noodles.

I sighed, knowing full well where the conversation was headed. "Let me guess, she put my profile on some dating site and wants me to go on a date? So, you're here to prod me into going to one?"

He leaned back on the island after putting the noodles in the microwave to heat it up. "You're almost right. She threatened me using her secret soup recipe if I didn't give you this letter." He pulled out a plain letter from his pocket and opened it for me. "It's a list of Asian women who are single moms and looking for a suitable, handsome—"

Before he could finish, I picked it up and tore it into tiny pieces and threw it into the bin. Sean smiled at me and pulled a plate from one of the cupboards, pausing and looking over me with a raised brow.

"No, I already had dinner. It's all yours." I sat down on the stool and opened the iPad to look over Emma's school schedule with all the events. "Have you seen Caleb today?"

"Not really. I bought him some beer, but I haven't seen him since I arrived. Must be with his girlfriend or out partying."

I stiffened. "He got dumped by her."

Sean laughed and sat across from me with a steaming bowl of noodles, kimchi, and two glasses of soju. Smart man.

"Remind you of someone?" he asked, wriggling his brow. "You and Olivia broke up every couple of months. Don't give me that look. He'll be with her before this month ends."

I poured another glass of drink and threw it down my throat. "I don't think so," I said, slamming my lips and clearing my throat at the burn. "He told me he fucked up and—"

I shook my head, looking down at her schedule and marking my calendar according to it.

"You'll get stomachache if you won't tell me." He said in a singsong voice, annoying me by playing with the chopsticks in front of me.

Sean Tae was one of my only friends who stuck around me after the death of my wife. We grew up in the same neighborhood, went to the same school, military, and he was the best man at my wedding. He was the one I called when she passed away, and he was standing beside me at her funeral.

He was also a damn good lawyer and knew me too well.

Sighing, I pushed the tablet towards him. "Emma Moore. Nineteen years old and ex-girlfriend of Caleb."

"Why do you have a file on her?"

"She's being stalked and I'm her bodyguard until we catch who's harassing her."

He stopped eating and frowned at me. "Caleb should be the leading suspect?"

"He is." I clasped my fingers together, leaning on the marble. "But I know he is not."

"True. He's too emotional to ever pull this off."

I stared at him.

He swallowed his food and blinked at me. "What? We both know he's lazy, too. He won't do that."

"Yeah... but he still hasn't told me why she dumped him. I don't want to—so you know, that's how I made the stir-fry sauce. Just a bit of oyster sauce does the magic." I pursed my lips, changing the topic abruptly when I heard the door of Caleb's room slam open, the sounds of his footsteps running downstairs.

Sean subtly closed the tablet and stuffed his mouth with noodles so he wouldn't have to speak as my son looked at both of us with suspicious eyes.

"Hey Sean." He nodded at him. He was wearing a clean shirt, and I caught a whiff of cologne in the air. "What's up?"

"Are you going out?" I checked the time again on my watch. "It's way past ten."

"There's a party, so..." He shrugged, scrolling down his phone.

I stared at him. "It's a school night, Caleb."

I didn't want to be a dad right now, but I had to.

He scoffed, looking at me, "Right. Yeah, it is. And are you going to tell me why were you discussing Emma with him? And what were you doing in her room this morning?"

My fists clenched when I felt the burning stare of Sean on the side of my face. "I was in her guest room, and we were talking about *her*. It's confidential. I already told you this morning."

"So tell him you are her bodyguard," Sean said, scooping more food into his mouth as I glared at him.

I closed my eyes, holding my head when Caleb yelled, "What?"

Fucking great.

21

HER BODYGUARD

CILLIAN

"Really. I can't thank you enough for this." Sarcasm poured out of me as I glared at Sean, who was proudly smirking at both of us.

"So, so, so, you mean Em is like being stalked? And this is all... serious?" Caleb asked, his eyes wide, staring at both of us and the screen.

"You're signing the NDA," I told him in my Dad-voice and added, "*Yes*. This is serious adult stuff, so don't go around telling your friends for fun."

"But someone will guess something's wrong when you'll follow her everywhere around the campus. Rumors will—"

"I don't care. You're not telling anyone."

"Okay," he sulked and shook his head as if he couldn't believe it. "Why didn't she tell me?"

I lifted my hand and gently patted his shoulder. "I don't think she's ready to tell anyone yet. She will tell you when she's comfortable."

"And now you know, so this way you can monitor her—"

I glared at Sean. "Don't listen to him. You don't need to do anything. Just focus on your life and studies and forget this conversation ever happened."

"I'll keep an eye on her," he said, standing up and straightening his shoulders. "Even if we are not in a relationship anymore, she's still my friend. I will keep—hold on, I've got to take this."

We both watched him take the phone call and heard the loud music coming from the caller. Sean sighed, stretching his arms. "Kids these days. They can't stay away from their phone for ten minutes."

I stood up. "I need to pack my bag and go keep an eye on her."

I didn't like the way Sean smirked at me, so I paused. "What?"

"What *what*?" He blinked innocently, grinning at me.

"Spit it out."

"Well," he said, his grin widening and continued, "You were in her guest room, alone, and you're looking after your son's ex. Lots of forced proximity and—"

I took the tablet and glared at him. "Don't say another word if you want to explain to everyone why you have a bruise on your right cheek for two weeks. I bet your little girlfriend won't like that."

"Aw, big bad wolf is angy!"

I flipped him off as I walked out of the kitchen and yelled at him, "Clean the dishes before you leave!"

I was about to head upstairs and pack my bag for a couple of days when I overheard the conversation of Caleb on the phone call. I only stopped because I heard her voice and her name being chanted repeatedly.

"Can't you just throw water at her or something and get her down?" Caleb was pacing around the living room, running a hand through his hair, and his eyes only widened when I loomed over him.

He didn't question me when I opened my palm. He handed me his phone and I turned the speaker on. It was a guy's voice who was laughing. "Dude! Why the fuck would anyone stop her? She's looking banging in her bra—*boooo!* Her friends are trying to get her down or something, but I'm telling you, she's ten on ten. I can't believe you got to tap that, you son of a bit—"

"I wouldn't finish that sentence if I were you," I said, keeping the mic of the phone near my mouth and speaking slowly. "What's your name? Doesn't matter. I'm coming there and if I see a single guy having the balls to touch Emma, I'm breaking their fingers one by one and then their tiny little toes until they fucking apologize. Am I clear?"

I didn't wait for him to reply and ended the call when I heard a small gasp. I handed the phone back to Caleb, who was gaping at me. Marching towards the door, I grabbed my keys and barked over my shoulder,

"Come with me. I am attending this party." *And someone is getting into huge trouble tonight*, I added mentally.

It only took a few minutes to reach the house where the party was going on. I slammed my car door shut, glaring at anyone and everyone who dared to stand in my way. I had ordered Caleb to look for Emma or her friends and call me when he finds her. I was going to look from the backyard, but I didn't have to search for her.

Because she was standing half-naked, wet and dancing on the roof. I didn't care. There were a bunch of other girls and guys with her, equally half-naked. but...

My nose was flaring as I stormed past the hooting crowd of drunk teens. Most of them were wasted or high or both. I had given her one simple command before I left. *Behave*. And look how *well* she was behaving.

"Get out of my fucking way," I gritted through my teeth when I reached upstairs. The hallway was so crowded that I had to push past a few people before I could enter the room. There was a tiny pool on the balcony and half-naked people grinding on each other.

I found a fully dressed brunette and dark-skinned girl speaking something in Emma's ears, thrusting her clothes towards her, but she was so fucking wasted that her voice was slurring.

"Emma," I called her, shooting daggers at the guy who was trying to slip his hand over her butt. "What the fuck are you doing here?" I grabbed her arm, taking her from the crowd. Her friends followed me.

"Hey mister, leave our friend alone!"

"Who are you?"

I shot her friends a dark look. "I'm Cillian. Her bodyguard who told her to stay at her house tonight, and an hour later I find her inebriated, half-naked, ready to get naked with anyone who'd give her attention."

She was so fucking limp in my hand that I wondered what the fuck she had been drinking to get so wasted in an hour. Finding a corner, I leaned her against a wall, pushing her hands through the armholes of my suit and covering her up. I didn't think twice before buttoning it up, ignoring the swell of cleavage or how hot her bra and underwear were.

Her hair was all wet, and she kept mumbling something underneath her breath.

"I didn't know she had a bodyguard," the girl in bright clothes said.

I exhaled sharply and showed her my ID. "You can call her brother and ask about me. Look, I know you are concerned about Emma right now, but I'll take it from here."

The brunette narrowed her green eyes at me. "If you are her bodyguard, where were you when Em started sobbing and stripping out of her clothes?"

I stared at her and slowly moved my gaze to Emma. Her

eyes were swollen and there were streaks of tears on her cheeks.

"She was sobbing?"

"Yes. Which was very unlike the Emma I know," her friend said. "I've never seen her shed a tear. Maybe her mother's death and the breakup took a toll on her."

She slurred something and raised her hand in the air, flailing around. "Burn... Caleb! He's a witch."

She hiccupped, her feet giving out and ready to fall on the floor. I straightened her and looked around the crowd to see if Caleb was there. Muttering a curse under my breath, I leaned down and picked her up in my arms.

I ignored the way her soft, warm breath brushed over my neck as she kept mumbling something against my chest. Her hair was tickling my arm and her thighs felt soft to my touch. My scowl only increased when drunk people started cheering her name, seeing her.

"Where are you taking her?" Her friend had to yell even when we stepped out of the house.

I marched towards my car, opening the door and lying down the drunk doll on the seat, holding her shoulders and strapping her up in a seatbelt.

"Her home, where she should have been all this fucking time," I said, turning around and looking at both of them. They didn't look drunk, but their pupils were dilated, and I could smell beer on them. "Do I need to drop you off?"

"There'll be no need for that," a smooth, deep voice said.

22

SERIOUS KINKS

CILLIAN

My eyes drifted to the man in shirt and pants, who had his arm possessively wrapped around the girl with green eyes. His smile was forced and eyes were sharp.

I understood the message well. 'Back off, she's taken.'

"James, I told you I was fine," the girl whispered. She turned towards me and glanced at her friend strapped in my car seat. "Can I come with you? I think she'd feel better if she saw us when she wakes up."

"It's a school night," James, the overprotective boyfriend who seemed much older than the girl, said to her. "Don't you all have a swim meet tomorrow?"

"That's why we are partying. Or were." Summer said, "Let me ask her brother real quick if you are her bodyguard."

I closed the door and called Caleb. "I found her and I'm taking her home. Don't stay out too late."

"But Dad—" his voice blurred out with the loud music. I knew he'd text me later, so I pocketed it and took a swift glance around the party goers. So many possibilities of dangers and suspects.

"Do you remember who gave her a drink in the first place?"

"Maybe Summer knows? But I found her clutching a Jack Daniel's to her dear life. I really hope she can make it to school tomorrow."

Her boyfriend ran a soothing hand over her back and narrowed his eyes at me. "I'm James Fox. I didn't get your name?"

I crossed my arms, keeping my back straight. Even though he was tall and lean, I had both muscles and height on him, even a few inches. "Because I didn't. I'm her bodyguard. Cillian Chang."

"Wait—*Chang?* You're Caleb's brother?" The girl in yellow looked at me with wide eyes. "Damn, Caleb never told me—"

"I'm his father," I bit out, checking my watch. "All clear?"

Both girls were gaping at me. "Y-yeah, sure. All clear. Mister Chang. I... huh? *Wow.*"

I nodded, walking towards the driver's side and opening the door.

"Wait, are you sure you will be with her when she wakes up? She is a sad drunk."

I chuckled, and there was nothing humorous about it. "Oh, don't you worry. I'll be with her when she wakes up with a hangover. She'll also be at school. I'll take care of it."

I'll take care of her.

But I'll do more than just take care of her.

* * *

Emma

WAKING UP WITH A THROBBING HEADACHE THE THIRD TIME IN a row *really* sucked. But I was so used to it by now that I rolled into my bed, opening the drawer and finding—

A small screech of a chair made me shriek. "What? What the fuck?" I scrambled to sit, my head throbbing more than before. "Who's there?"

"Your lovely bodyguard." A gruff sound came from somewhere in the room and I had to squint my eyes at the sudden light and blinked at him through my foggy vision.

"Cillian?" I scratched my head, fighting back a yawn as my stiff fingers ran over my arms... that were bare? I didn't remember wearing a sleeveless top to the party.

Party? Oh no.

"What did I do?" I asked, straightening up and instantly hating the decision of sitting up when I caught the dark look in his eyes.

I held my breath when he walked over to my nightstand and handed me a glass of water and an aspirin. He was still wearing the clothes from before, a dark shirt with top button open, revealing a hint of tan skin underneath and snaking black tattoos, and pants.

"You snuck out of the house when I told you not to. You were utterly wasted, crying like a fucking baby, holding a bottle of Jack's, and started stripping and dancing half-naked in a pool full of horny teenagers." He spoke as soon as I took the medicine, grateful to have something inside my body to relieve the hangover.

Somehow, he seemed a lot closer than before and... *angrier.*

"My memory is a bit funky, but you forgot that I almost jumped from the roof... which I'm glad I didn't."

Maybe it was a terrible idea to add oil to the fire.

"Oh, you have some nerve, little Doll." Maybe I was still drunk because the way he said it with a hot vein popping on his neck made me feel something between my legs.

"You're grounded. No more parties or sneaking out with your friends until you're out of danger. And forget about your privacy. You want to shower? I'm there. You want to change? I'm holding the curtain for you. You want to pee? I'll be with you in the fucking washroom. You want to sleep alone? No fucking more. I will be breathing down your cute little neck until you realize how serious this shit is."

I blinked up at him. He was so close that I could smell his aftershave. And he smelled delicious. Like musk and pine.

"You think I've a cute neck?" I asked, raising my brow.

I loved that it infuriated him. He pulled away and gave me a seething look. I continued, "You have some serious kinks, Mister Cillian. It seems that you're very much into being a voyeur. It's okay, that works for me." I flashed him my most innocent smile. "I'm somewhat an exhibitionist myself."

If it was possible, his eyes turned darker, his obsidian orbs watching me with such precision like he was seeing the real me and not whatever was coming out of my mouth.

He tilted his head, raking his eyes over my body. I shivered, very aware of the fact that I was only wearing a bra and underwear underneath my blanket. *Did he catch me like that? Making a fool of myself in nothing but my underwear?* It was an awfully dirty thought, but I wanted to know what he thought about me...

"Why did you get drunk, Emma?"

Not Doll.

I pursed my lips. "I'm a nineteen-year-old. You know well enough why I'd get drunk at a party."

"I asked you why."

"And I told you the reason!"

I took a sharp breath when he leaned closer. His voice was soft and deep at the same time. "You know what I think? You're fucking sad. You're grieving your mother's death—"

"Stop."

"You dumped your boyfriend and went to a sex club to

blur out everything else that's been keeping you up at night. That's the—"

"Stop it."

"*No*. That's the only reason you sneaked out, because even though your life is in danger because of a potential stalker, you don't care about yourself unless you can forget—"

"*Stop!*" Tears burned through my eyes, threatening to spill over. He didn't pull away, but looked more furious when a tear slipped out. "Stop it. I don't want to hear it," I whispered, swallowing the lump in my burning throat.

"Emma—"

"What do you want to hear? That you're right? Well, good for you, you are! I'm sad that my mom died, leaving me with everything, and that my brother hates my existence, and my ex-boyfriend was lying to me for the entirety of our relationship, and that I'm feeling so fucking alone!" Tears were pouring out of my eyes like a broken dam. "I can't even tell my friends that I'm being stalked or tell anyone that I'm so scared of staying here cooped up in my room alone and waiting for the stalker to come find me and I won't be able to do anything!"

My chest was heaving by the time I stopped speaking. God, I was such a fucking mess. I was sniffling and crying in my *La Perla* bra set and being so pathetic.

I shivered when he leaned close enough to wipe the tears from my cheeks with his thumb. "You are not alone," Cillian said. His voice wasn't soft, but firm. As if he was scolding me.

"I feel alone." I peered at him, his clenched jaw and intense eyes. "I keep overthinking about her death, Caleb, the stalker, and everything. I don't want to think anymore."

He pulled his hand away, his eyes softened a little, surprising me by asking, "Do you want to feel, Doll?"

"Feel what, Cillian?"

"My tongue inside your pretty pussy."

23
DID I STUTTER?

EMMA

"My tongue inside your pretty pussy."

My mouth parted and a different type of warm feeling burst through me when his eyes flickered to my parted lips. "I can help you not think for a while. What do you say?"

"W-what?"

"I'm asking you if I can fuck your pussy with my mouth, Doll."

"What will you have me do in return?"

He chuckled and *oh fuck, oh fuck, oh fuck*, I was in ruin because there was no coming back after hearing Cillian fucking Chang chuckle like that. I wanted to capture that sound and drown in it.

"I'm not asking you to get my dick wet, Doll. I'm asking you as your... concerned bodyguard. To help you not think."

"Oral sex to help me not think?" I pursed my lips and nodded. *"Right."*

"Mhmm," he hummed, a sparkle in his eyes that I've never seen before.

"Are you playing with me right now?"

"If I was playing with you, you'd know."

What the hell is that supposed to mean?

His eyes were challenging and there was one thing that a Moore never backed out of. A challenge.

I kept my eyes on him and tugged off the blanket. "Fine, Cillian." I spread my legs, his eyes still on my face. "I dare you to stop making me think, with your mouth."

His gaze lowered, slowly raking over my bobbing throat to my heaving chest. I didn't know why, but I was nervous. I wanted to know if he enjoyed seeing my body or found it not attractive enough. I had stomach rolls and stretch marks, but I had learned to embrace them after years of bullying from my mom. But somehow, Cillian liking my body or not made me nervous… which was pretty stupid.

Tension thickened in the room. I felt my heartbeat increasing when his gaze stopped short between my legs, pinning on my panties. I ignored the sudden urge to close my legs and shy away from his intense look. My hands scrunched the sheets, waiting in anticipation… what would he do? *Will he spread my legs and eat me out like that night? Will he? I hope he does.*

I took a sharp breath when he leaned closer, ignoring how he was so close to my burning sex. His face neared me, my lips parting. I was too nervous to keep my eyes open and closed them.

"Sweet little Doll," he whispered, his lips brushing over the shell of my ear and making me shiver. "You really think I take dares from others, *hm?*"

Confused and shocked, I opened my eyes, staring at him. "W-what?"

Cillian smiled, his finger trailing over the curve of my cheek. My skin burned where he touched me, and I wished he would touch me more.

He pulled back and said, "You'll be late. Go take a shower."

Huh?

I blinked at him. "What do you mean?"

"Go take a shower," he said slowly, as if he was talking to a kid. "Wear your uniform. Eat your breakfast. You'll be late."

I gaped at him when he stood up from the bed, walking towards the door, leaving me wet and needy. "Are you fucking serious?" I asked, glaring at him. "You suggested oral sex and now—"

He turned back and gave me a look that made me stop myself. "Go take a shower. *Now*."

I flipped him a bird when he left the room, grumbling curses underneath my breath. *Stupid!* I just had to be desperate enough to ask him to eat me out. *Jesus Christ, what the fuck is wrong with me?*

Cillian

I hated being a bodyguard more than anything at that moment.

I should be in the bed with Emma's legs over my shoulder and my tongue mapping out the feel of her sweet pussy. But...

"Make it higher," I said, eyeing the employee at one of Elena's firms who had arrived to install surveillance cameras. "I need to capture the entire backyard from there."

I walked back to the pool and checked if they were making any progress and tried one of the motion sensors, turning it off when it started blaring. I had seen someone in the backyard when I was in the room with Emma. It was such a bad fucking timing. I couldn't think about the dark silhouette of someone standing in her yard, just below her bedroom, when she had dared me to eat her out.

I needed an excuse to get away from her, despite my raging hard on at seeing the wet spot in her pretty lace panties. Before I could find the person, who could possibly be the stalker, the van of the staff to install cameras and sensors had arrived.

My hand turned into a fist. The stalker had a nerve to try and sneak into her room in broad daylight. Especially when I was with her.

I didn't tell her because if I did, she'd get scared again. But I needed to talk to her after school. Maybe I'd tell her then.

"Who are all these people?"

I looked at her uniform and curled hair.

"Is that your uniform?" I asked, trying to rein in the urge to haul her over my shoulder and take her back upstairs and make her change. If that's what she was wearing to school, then God help me, but someone was going to sit in their class with a red fucking ass.

"Why?" she asked, twirling her hair and looking down at her open shirt that showed her ample cleavage and the skirt that barely covered her ass. "If you have a problem with it, you can talk it out with our Dean—or not, since she was arrested—*hey!* I was watching the pe—*ouch.*"

I had closed my hand around her tiny wrist and took her to the nearest room with a door and pinned her against the wall.

"If you don't straighten your uniform in the next thirty seconds, I swear to God, you'll call your brother begging him to fire me."

Her brown eyes were practically twinkling at my suggestion. She smiled, jutting out her hips, and asked, "Or what?"

I pulled back, crossing my arms and glaring at her. "Wear your uniform properly."

"Why should I?"

"Because you're going to a school and not a fucking sex club."

"What if I want to go to school like this? It's not like it's bothering you personally, Mister Cillian, is it?"

This fucking girl...

"You've ten seconds, Emma."

"And?"

"I won't ask you again. Straighten your clothes," I said, my voice stern, but her smile was turning into a sly smirk with each passing second. "*Now*."

"Make me."

Oh wow.

"What did you just say?" I asked, just to be sure—if she wanted to change her answer.

"Did I stutter?" she said and leaned closer to add, "I said make me. *Make. Me.* Mister Cillian."

I uncrossed my arms and smiled at her. "When you feel like crying, remember who started acting like a spoiled little brat, Doll."

"Crying?"

I turned her around, keeping my hand on the back of her neck, and whispered in her ear, "Yes, Doll. Now don't tell me I didn't warn you."

24

SPOILED BRAT

EMMA

I held my breath when his hand tightened on the back of my neck, goosebumps erupting all over my body—

"*Oh,*" I gasped, the burn of the pain against my skin registering before it spread between my legs. I looked over my shoulder, "Cillian, what the fuck are—*mm.*"

I had to bite my lip when he spanked my ass again on the same spot, my legs trembling. His hold on my neck was firm. I couldn't escape or pull away if I wanted to.

"Are you going to be a spoiled brat or listen to me, Doll?" Cillian asked, his hot breath fanning over my ear, making me shiver.

My hands turned into a fist hearing his deep voice. He was so close that I could smell his sexy cologne. I pushed my hips back, smiling over my shoulder as I met his clouded dark eyes.

"Why should I listen to you?" I whispered, slowly rubbing my burning ass over his crotch.

"You are trouble, aren't you, Doll?" he murmured, his large hand squeezing my ass cheek before it inched closer to where I wanted. He chuckled when I spread my legs for him, pushing him closer to my wet pussy. "Greedy. So fucking greedy."

"Shut up and touch me."

I gasped when he held my hair and tugged at it. My lids were heavy lidded when he cupped my pussy through the panties, squeezing it. "Be a good girl and maybe I will," he said, his voice stern and him being so serious and scary only turned me on more.

"Will you fuck me if I behave?" I asked, batting my lashes and continued, lowering my hand, "If you don't, I can just use my hands…"

I gasped when he flipped me around, pinning my wrists above my head with his one hand. His other hand slid underneath my skirt.

"I'll think about fucking your sweet cunt if you behave," he said, his voice hot and deep, making me arch towards him. "Until then… be good."

I had to hold back my gasp when his hand tightened over the lace of my panties and ripped it. My eyes widened when he pulled away, tucking my skirt down as if nothing had happened.

"You'll go to school without panties and my red handprint on your ass," he said casually, as if we were talking about the weather. "If you want to show off your pretty pussy, then by all means, keep your skirt inched high."

"What…"

Cillian looked at his wristwatch and opened the door, not even baring me another glance. "Be out in five or we will be late. If you are not, I will throw you over my shoulder and drag you to school if I have to."

He closed the door shut before I could utter a single word, leaving me seething in an empty room. *What an ass.* I couldn't even wear other underwear since it wasn't my room.

God, I hate him so fucking much.

* * *

"Is he really your bodyguard?" Summer asked when I slammed my locker shut, still pissed off about the morning.

"Unfortunately," I said, gritting my teeth and rolling my eyes at Cillian's large frame following me and Summer to yet another class. He had been keeping his distance to give me privacy, but he wasn't lying about being everywhere I went. He even followed me to the washroom and glared at me when I locked him out of the stall.

I guess he wasn't kidding this morning about being every*fucking*where.

The school board had agreed to let Cillian do whatever he wanted as long as I was safe, since my brother must have donated a large sum to the school for my so-called protection.

"Why the long face?" Mia asked when we joined her in chemistry lab. Her green eyes flickered over my shoulder, glancing up and nodding at me with pursed lips. "I didn't think he was really her bodyguard," she whispered, keeping her notes at our usual seat.

"I wish I could get rid of him," I muttered underneath my breath, tying the plastic apron for the experiments we have to do.

"I'd like to see you try, Doll," a deep voice said over my shoulder, making me freeze. His hot breath brushed over my nape when his fingers secured the apron.

Blood rushed my cheeks, and I cleared my throat when Summer and Mia stared at me with an open mouth.

"You are red, Em," Summer said, flickering her eyes in the corner where I knew who was leaning on the wall with crossed arms and glaring at anyone who looked suspicious.

"*Very* red," Mia added, wrangling her brows.

"It's cold, that's why," I snapped and opened my notes. "I'd love it if you both could focus on our experiment."

"Girl, if you look around, you'll see how everyone's focus is occupied by someone who is tall, dark and handsome with eyes for just one—"

"Summer Hayes."

She mimicked zipping her lips and swallowing the key. I rolled my eyes and straightened up when our teacher entered the room, blushing at the sight of Cillian before stuttering through the experiment.

Jesus fucking Christ. He was just a handsome man! A tall, handsome man.

Cillian

Her chemistry teacher was definitely not the stalker, because she couldn't even focus on her class and kept glancing at me. Did I really pay a huge fucking fee to send my son to such an academy where they had excellent teachers like these?

I sighed once again, keeping my eyes on Emma, who was doing her experiment with determination and taking notes with her friends. I was relieved to see her focused on her studies and not worried about the situation she was in.

My phone vibrated in my pants and I walked to the back of the class, tapping my earbud. "Yes?"

"Is she good?"

"She is in her chemistry class."

Her brother stayed quiet for a moment. "I don't know how you can stand through such boring lectures."

It's because I want to protect her. Even if you don't pay me, I will protect her and keep her safe.

"It's a job," I said, keeping my voice even.

"Sure, the night with her at my sex club has nothing to do with it."

I clenched my phone and gritted out, "Is this why you called me?"

"No," he took a deep breath, and I heard a sound of pen clicking. "Bring her to the club after school. I'll need her when the lawyers arrive."

"Is it important?"

"Yes. They are discussing our mother's will."

"Then bring your lawyers and yourself to the house. She's not coming to the club." I was about to end the call when he continued,

"I am paying you."

I chuckled and said, "Sure, you are. To protect Emma. She's not coming to the club," I repeated. "Bring your rich ass to the house. I don't fucking care."

I hung up before he could utter another word and went back to monitoring her blonde hair. I took a deep breath when I found her smiling with her friends and unclenched my fist.

She is trouble if I'm caring this much about her on the first day of the job. I should have called Elena and ended it, passed it on to someone else since I was emotionally invested.

But I was too fucking selfish.

I would take care of Emma.

25
COME HERE

CILLIAN

I sat in silence, going through the list of people who had attended Dorothy Moore's funeral. The list was long and full of rich, popular models, actors, actresses, and directors. As if it was her birthday party and not her funeral. I was looking for someone with a motive. Past relationship was out of the question. Wait. What about Dorothy's ex? Did she—

"Hi!"

My eyes flickered from the iPad screen to the owner of the high-pitched voice. "Hello," I said, eyeing three girls in the academy's uniform, twirling their hair and batting their lashes at me.

"Hi!" one of them repeated, leaning down. I quickly averted my gaze to my screen. "Do you mind if we sit here for lunch?"

I could feel the stares from the entire cafeteria since I was sitting at the corner table and there were a lot of empty spaces.

"I do m—"

"Oh, great! Thank you so much!"

I held back my sigh when they were about to sit down, but I was saved when Emma and her two friends, Mia and Summer, came in to save me by sitting down on the empty chairs.

Emma flicked her hair over her shoulder and managed to look down at the girl even when she was sitting. "Thanks, Carla."

"So Mister Cillian, did you have lunch?" Mia asked when the three girls left, glaring at Emma and her friends.

"I did." I looked at Emma's plate and noticed the lack of protein. I would bring two lunches tomorrow.

"'Sup Dad!"

I raised my brow when Caleb joined our little coterie. Everyone was staring at him when he dropped his plate and sat on the other side of Emma, sandwiching her between us.

"Why are you here?" Emma asked in the dullest sound without even looking at him.

I didn't want to prod, but I was interested in knowing the reason behind their breakup. I straightened up when Caleb flickered his eyes at me and took a bite of apple before replying to Emma, "If you have a problem, you can sit somewhere else. I'm sitting here to bond with my lovely dad."

I sighed, going back to reviewing my notes. If he thought he was being sneaky by being around Emma to protect her, then he was looking stupid.

Circling Dorothy's name in red, I leaned back in the chair. If I was a stalker, I would do anything to get close to her.

* * *

Emma

"You are an ass," I said to Cillian, my cheeks red when he opened the door of the car for me. He didn't even glance at me when I sat down, tucking my skirt carefully because the sexy piece of ass had made sure I was going commando for the entire school day. I couldn't even attend the swim meet after school since he had something important that he wouldn't tell me.

"I know," he said in a clipped voice when the driver started the car. There was a divider between the front and back seat and Cillian closed it shut, leaning back on the plush leather and pinning his dark eyes on me.

I raised my brow and crossed my arms when he patted his thigh. My pussy clenched at the sight of him in a shirt that was rolled over his strong forearms and revealing tattoos. I had to curb my jealous thoughts when everyone from my class, girls and boys, eyed Cillian and tried to do anything to talk to him.

"What?" I asked, still angry that he had taken away my panties and stayed stoic the entire day without ever looking at me. His job was to protect me, for fuck's sake!

His eyes narrowed and a small smirk tugged over his sexy scarred lips. I hated that I wanted to kiss it. "You're mad, Doll."

"I-I'm not mad or a doll!" I sputtered, looking away from him.

"Do you want to wear panties or not?" he asked, his voice deep and rumbly.

I stiffened, glaring at him through my lashes. "I don't need your permission to wear them, Cillian," I said firmly, clenching my fingers.

"Oh, really?" He leaned closer. Close enough for me to smell his musky male cologne with a hint of spice. I swallowed the lump in my throat at his closeness. "Then why is your pussy wet at the idea of me controlling when you should wear panties... or not?"

"I-it's not."

We both knew I was lying.

Cillian leaned back and patted his thigh. "Come here and sit on my lap if you're not aroused."

My jaw clenched as he tilted his head, waiting for me to make a move. This was such a bad idea. But he was challenging me.

Flicking my hair over one shoulder, I crawled onto his lap like it was my throne and sat on his thigh. Even though it turned me on, I stayed still, keeping my eyes on his handsome face.

"Mhmm. You're right, Doll." His large hands glided over my thighs in a soft caress, making me shiver. "Your pussy is not wet."

I licked my lips, waiting.

His hand slid underneath my skirt as he whispered, "You are *soaking* wet, Doll."

My mouth parted in a soundless gasp when he spread my legs wider and pulled me closer, making my clit rub against the fabric of his pants.

"Does that feel good?" he asked softly, squeezing my ass as I leaned on him.

I nodded, staring at his lips when he moved me over his thigh again. "C-Cillian," I scrunched my fingers in his shirt.

"I know, good girl," he rumbled, running his hand through my hair. "Ride my thigh and make yourself feel good, yeah?"

My cheeks turned warm when I noticed the bulge in his pants. He tilted my chin up, making me look at him.

"I want you to make yourself orgasm. Right here. If you cum before we reach home, I'll reward you. Can you do that, Doll?"

"What reward?" I asked, my voice breathy.

"Any-fucking-thing you want, Doll," he answered, his hands squeezing my thigh. "Go ahead. Ride my thigh and cum for me. I know you want to."

26

BE QUIET

EMMA

I wanted to. I needed to. I had been walking around with bare pussy all day, knowing that he was right behind me. The reason of my dripping wet arousal.

"Will you finger me too?" I whispered, biting my lip when I grew bolder and started slowly rubbing my clit on his thigh.

The pulse on his neck was beating fast, so I leaned down and kissed it. Hearing his sigh, I licked his neck and sucked the skin, biting it. I smirked when he tugged at my hair, glaring at my mouth.

I kept my pace riding his thigh slowly when he rubbed the smudged lip gloss on my bottom lip.

"You're trouble, Doll. Trying to give me hickeys while you are rubbing your greedy little wet cunt on my thigh like a fucking vixen, hm?"

"Your cock loves it," I said sweetly, sliding my hand down his pants.

I let out a sharp breath when he flipped me around, my back on his chest, his hot breath brushing on my cheek when he spread my legs, hooking them over his thighs so I couldn't move them unless he let me.

"Be a good girl and hold your skirt up for me," he said darkly, my hands trying to find support other than his thighs, but it was useless. He was too big. So big that he made the expensive car seem small.

When I didn't obey, he wrapped his hand around my throat, holding it in a gentle but firm grip. "Don't make a sound and hold your skirt up for me, Doll. Show me how wet your pussy is."

I eyed the closed divider and slowly held the hem of the skirt, lifting it over my inner thighs and baring myself to him. Thank God we had tinted windows in the car or anyone who passed by would see us.

"Good girl," he said, his praise flowing from my ears to my entire body, making me shiver in his arms. His hand on my throat slid between my legs. "I wish we could do this in front of a mirror. You'd love how sexy you look right now, Doll."

I dug my fingers into his forearm when his fingers touched me, and he let out a low groan. "T-touch me more, Cillian," I said, my voice sultry.

"Of course, Doll," he said. "I'll touch you as much as you want."

His fingers felt so good on my swollen clit that I had to cover my mouth from letting out whimpers of pleasure. Especially when he increased his pace and stopped completely when I was ready to burst with orgasm.

Instead of letting me whine, he lowered his wet fingers and slid them inside me. My thighs shook, and I was completely slumped on his lap, rocking my hips on his hard shaft while he finger-fucked my pussy.

"Fuck Doll. Hear how hot your pussy sounds when you're so fucking drenched," Cillian grumbled, rubbing my clit with his thumb while sliding his two digits in and out of me.

I could hear it. The wet squelching sound when he fucked

me. The entire back seat smelled like my arousal, and it was so embarrassing yet hot that I couldn't stop myself from moaning.

"Shh, Doll," he shushed me, cupping my mouth. "Be quiet."

"I'm guffa mmm." I was trying to say 'I'm gonna cum' but it came out muffled, and somehow, Cillian knew that I was close and kept his pace steady.

I eyed his thick tattooed fingers sliding in and out of me, his hand clenching with its hot veins. My eyes rolled back in my head when he started doing the come-hither motion inside my pussy. I clenched his fingers as white fiery lust poured out of me, my moans muffled by his hand. My hips kept bucking as his fingers kept rubbing over my sensitive clit, making me come again in his lap.

"Such a good fucking girl," he whispered, his lips pressing against my temple. "Keep coming for me. Let it all out, Doll. I got you."

I opened my eyes, surprised to see that my vision was blurry and that his hands were now caressing my trembling thighs and running over my body.

"You okay, Doll?" he asked, his hands freezing on my body before he turned me around. It was annoying how easily he could lift me up and throw me around. I avoided looking at him when he gently held my chin with his thumb and index finger.

"Do you want to cum again?" he asked, wiping away the streaks of tears from my face and cupping my cheek. "I can make you come again, Doll. Tell me."

"I…" I paused, frustrated at being so confused about what I was feeling. My fingers tightened on his shirt and, taking a deep breath, I met his eyes and said, "Kiss me, Cillian. Please."

I closed my eyes when his lips pressed against mine and I was so frustrated yet overwhelmed at the feel of his soft lips moving against mine. This was unlike any kiss I had ever gotten. It was gentle, exploratory, and full of softness that made my heart calm down.

"You were so good, Emma," he whispered between the kisses, angling his head to deepen it. "Such a good girl for me."

I moaned, opening my mouth to him. His sigh shouldn't have felt so good when I feathered my fingers through his hair. Nor his lips, his tongue, his teeth, biting into my lip and pulling me so close that we were pressed against each other.

His heart was beating as fast as mine, and I wanted nothing more than to stay on his lap and stay in his powerful arms.

"Ma'am, we have reached your home."

Reality came crashing down on me like a bucket of cold water and we quickly pulled away from each other. Panting for breath with flushed cheeks and swollen lips, I realized I could never have Cillian. He was just a bodyguard and his job was to protect me. Nothing else.

"I-I'll be out in a minute," I stuttered, replying to the driver and looking out of the window to see the other two cars parked in the manor's driveway.

Fuck no.

27

SMOOTHIE

CILLIAN

My hands tightened on her still trembling body when it froze. I followed her gaze. Two expensive cars parked in the driveway. I knew the lawyers would be here, but that must mean she knew them and didn't want to meet them judging by her physical reaction.

"Are you okay, Emma?" I asked, turning her face to me, tucking her hair behind her ears. Her cheeks were warm pink and blue eyes gleamed with tears. I didn't know what I had done to make her cry, but from my experience, I knew it wasn't a pain-cry, she needed that release. She needed to let it all out.

"I'm fine." Her voice was clipped when she tried to get up from my lap. But I held onto her.

"You don't know how to lie, Doll," I said, rubbing small circles on the exposed skin of her thigh. "Even if you are not fine, I want to know. I won't prod. Just... let me know." Because someone died because of me when I didn't know about their lies.

She nodded, blinking at me. She was definitely surprised by how serious I was.

Lighten up, Cillian. Emma is just your client. Don't get too attached.

Too fucking late.

"Wear this," I dangled her little pink underwear in front of her, and she quickly snatched it, getting off of my lap and glaring at me. Her cheeks were blooming red. "Wow, not even a thank you. I know your pussy has been bare for me for the entire day, so the least you could do is thank me."

She didn't meet my eyes when I watched her shamelessly as she shimmied up the tiny piece of clothing underneath her skirt, flaunting her pretty thighs and ass to me.

Fuck me, I was still hard as a rock.

"Suck my tits, Cillian," she said, flicking her hair behind her shoulder and dabbed some powder on her face.

I smirked, flicking her nose. "I plan to, Doll."

Tensing up the muscles on my inner thigh, I forced my boner down and got out of the car. The driver bowed at me and shot me a weird look when I crossed my arms, leaning on the car.

"Miss Emma?" he questioned.

"She's applying girly shit," I deadpanned.

He seemed a little younger than me and straightened up at my harsh tone.

"Forgive me for asking, Sir, but what's that on your thigh?"

Emma stepped out of the car and her eyes widened when she heard the question of her driver. I resisted to smirk and reply, 'Oh this? It's how good pussy leaks like when humped on a thigh.'

Instead, I was a complete gentleman and said, "I dropped my smoothie. Come on, Emma."

I dragged her away because she seemed stunned. When

we entered the house, she tugged her hand off me and I let her.

"You are so…" she huffed, walking past me.

"Filthy. I know, Doll." I followed her, leaning down to whisper in her ear, "But it gets your cute little cunt creamy for me."

She growled at me, her cheeks burning.

I stopped her before she could go upstairs to her room. "Your brother called me. He is here with lawyers. You have to talk to—"

"No." She glared at me, her eyes accusing as if I had done some terrible mistake and betrayed her. "Why didn't you tell me?"

"They are already here, Emma," I said, not understanding what she was so upset about. She'd probably get a lot of inheritance after reading her mother's will.

"I don't want to talk—" She was leaving when a voice stopped her.

"Well, if it isn't it Emma Moore…" The voice was deep and snarly, as if the man in the shiny suit who looked like he was in his sixties was dying to meet her for years. His gray hair was dull and sticky. Despite being handsome decades ago, he had lines over his face.

And Emma was fucking shaking seeing him walk towards her.

My jaw clenched, and I stood in front of her, crossing my arms, trying to hide her. This asshole wasn't going anywhere near my Doll.

"You must be the bodyguard Damon told me about." He looked at me from up and down, his lips twisting in disgust at my revealing tattoos. "You are late. The reading was going to start—"

"When Emma wants it to start," I said, my voice stern. "I'll bring her when she's ready."

The grimy asshole tried to look over my shoulder towards Emma, who was definitely trying to hide behind my back. I could feel her warmth and how her fingers were clutching on to my shirt. Fuck. I just wanted to push away the jerk and haul her over my shoulder and hide her in a room, keeping her safe.

"You better be ready soon, little Emma, or I'll be mad."

I leaned closer to him and had to inch down to his height. He looked taken aback when I gritted through my teeth, "Say that to my face. I fucking dare you."

Sweat gathered on his temple, sliding down his face, making me chuckle. "Go take a fucking seat before I kick you out myself."

"What did you just say?" the man sputtered, his face turning pink.

Emma's fingers tightened on my shirt as if she wanted me close to her. I scoffed at the man and turned around, hiding her from his sight, and took her upstairs, her legs wobbly as she clutched to my shirt.

I locked the door of her room and pulled her onto my lap. I let her be, wondering what the fuck had caused her to shake so much just by his presence. I tightened my hold on her, raking my hand through her hair and rubbing her back.

"You are safe, Emma," I whispered. You are always safe with me.

"I'm not... I'm not okay, Cillian," She pulled back and looked at me, her eyes were teary. "I can't do this."

I cupped her cheek. "It's okay. You don't have to. No one is forcing you, okay?" Her trembles were slowing down. "But that asshole will know that he affects you if you don't go meet him head-on. And the Emma I know doesn't back down from assholes like him, right?"

She peered at me from under her lashes and said in a small voice, "Will you stay close?"

My heart hammered in my chest as I nodded, too surprised to speak.

"Attend the reading with me?" she asked again, her fingers fumbling with the collar of my shirt, her eyes looking anywhere but at my face.

"Of course, Doll. I will stay close," I promised her. "I'm not going anywhere. I'm here."

I meant every word I had said.

28
KEEP IT A SECRET

EMMA

"**O**kay." I took a deep breath, trusting Cillian. "I'll go down and meet them."

"Good girl," he praised me, a soft smile curling on his lips.

"Only if you promise to fuck me later," I added, knowing I'd need him to forget about it all later.

His eyes widened, his cock bulging at my words underneath me. "Emma…"

"Yes Cillian?"

"Your brother asked me to—"

"Oh, good idea!" I said, smiling brightly. "If I attend the reading, you have to fuck me in the sex club."

His eyes narrowed. "You are nineteen."

"And I have my own VIP card because it's my brother's club."

"He will be mad if he knows and he'll fire me."

I stiffened. No. I didn't want Cillian to get fired because of me. "Then we will keep it a secret… please?"

He put me on the bed and stood up, his bulge still prominent behind his sexy slacks. "We can't have sex with each other, Emma. You're too fucking young and have a stalker who knows where you live. It's dangerous."

"But you said you'd protect me, Cillian," I said. I didn't care that I was whining. "Please."

"Get ready and meet me outside. Go to the meeting first." His voice was clipped when he stepped out of the room.

Sighing, I flopped on the bed, staring at the small chandelier hanging from the ceiling. It was so hard to tease him and get him to agree. If it was someone else, they'd be on their knees pleasing me, but not Cillian.

He was right. Emma Moore never backs down from a challenge, and I'll take him to bed tonight no matter what.

Even if the meeting goes bad, I will fuck Cillian tonight.

Wearing a white dress that was like a second skin on me, I donned a dark red lipstick on my lips. Leaving my hair down and wearing YSL heels, I was ready. I felt confident despite the nerves churning in my stomach.

"I can do this," I said to myself, shaking off the disgusting memories from before. "I can do this. Cillian will keep me safe."

Taking a deep breath, I opened the door to find Cillian leaning on the wall of the dim hallway. His eyes raked over my body as I stared at him shamelessly. He had taken a shower by the look of his damp hair that made his hair look darker and thicker, and his black shirt and pants that fit him like a glove. With revealing neck and forearm tattoos, he looked so fucking delicious. I wanted to have a quickie with him. *Right now.*

"Come on, Emma," he drawled, running a hand through his hair. I licked my lips at the sight of very few gray hairs lining his dark hair. I wanted to cling to them when he eats me out.

I didn't utter a word as I followed him down the stairs to

the main hallway. My heart was beating so loudly I could hear it hammering in my ears.

Just for a while. Keep it together, Emma.

I eyed Cillian's broad back when he opened the double doors of one of the many study rooms, but it made my gut churn because it was the same study…

Stay calm. You are safe, Em. Cillian is here. Damon too, and even if he is an asshole, he won't let anything happen to you.

"You took your time," my brother said, taking a seat on the couch. My eyes averted to the empty shelves and closed windows. The musty smell of dust and something dark clung to the air.

I took a deep breath, and it seeped into my body, slowly at first, then all at once. I couldn't walk. Couldn't move. I felt frozen and bound by invisible hands that had once, many years ago, touched me without my consent. Made me feel uncomfortable with their exploration and coaxing gnarly voice with and twisted laughter when I couldn't escape.

"Doll," a soft whisper on my right made me snap out of my thoughts, and I blinked at Cillian's piercing eyes. Unlike other times, they seemed soft and concerned.

"Take a seat, Emma," the same gnarly voice, now deeper and more twisted, rang in my ears as I met his disgusting dull eyes. They were roving over my body, and I let him have his fill. He patted the empty seat beside him as his assistant, a young girl in her early twenties, shifted on the armchair. I noticed her lipstick was smudged and her stocking had a hole on one knee.

"Start the reading. I don't have much time," I said, my voice cold as I sat on another armchair. No one had dared to sit at the desk and chair where our mother used to sit, looking out to the floor to ceiling French doors that led to a private garden.

"Still such a hasty child," he laughed, his teeth, some yellow, gleaming in the dim light.

"She's nineteen," Cillian said, sitting beside my brother. "Not a child."

Damon flickered his gray eyes from him to our private, dirty lawyer and motioned him to go on.

My hand tightened on my dress, and I held my breath.

The lawyer, Lincoln, cleared his throat and said, "You should leave. This is a private will—"

"Cillian is staying," I said, raising my voice a little. "Just tell us about the will."

"He is not a family—"

Damon sighed, pinching the bridge of his nose. "Neither is your assistant. We don't care. I've a meeting with an architect after this, so hurry."

For once, I agreed with Damon. I didn't know why mom would give her will to such a lousy lawyer, anyway.

He opened the briefcase his assistant handed to him, and tension hovered in the air when he leafed out a paper and started speaking.

Each word rang through the study, echoing in my ears. As seconds passed, my breathing increased, and tears burned my eyes. Damon's face was devoid of any emotion, but I could see his jaw tick as he flicked his eyes at me.

"Likewise, the manor in Coral Springs and all belongings therein I leave to my daughter, Emma Moore." He finished reading the will and looked at me and Damon.

"A-are you sure it's…" I stood up, snatching the paper from him and reading it. "It can't be."

I felt another presence close to me and a hand on my back, making me stiffen. "But it is." The voice was scratchy, and I scrunched the paper in my hand. "You own Dorothy's entire makeup company, the royalties from all her films, her shares and all her properties, little Emma."

Little Emma...

"Of course she does," Damon chuckled, standing up. "I knew she wouldn't leave me anything."

The hand on my back started lowering, and I wanted to move. Wanted to fight. But I stayed frozen. I couldn't do anything. Even though my eyes burned.

"Take your hand off of her before I fucking break it," a deep, warm voice said, the hand on my back leaving and the sound of Lincoln yelping in pain flowing in my ears.

I watched with cold distant eyes when Cillian twisted it, the lawyer's assistant scrambling away when his face turned red and he started screaming.

"What the fuck are you doing, Cillian?" Damon asked, his eyes wide with surprise and shock.

"What the fuck am I doing?" he asked, staring at my brother and pinning his eyes on me. "Look at your own fucking sister for a moment, you dumb fuck. She has been shaking since she saw this asshole. Her eyes are wet with tears, not because her mom left her everything, but because of this jerk—Did I tell you to move? *No*. I didn't." I covered my mouth when Cillian kicked him, painfully twisting his hand over his back.

"Where was I? Oh, yes, this perv has been trying to grope your sister and you want to throw a fit because your rich mommy didn't leave you any money." His face was full of anger when he pulled away from Lincoln, his chest heaving and nose flaring. His hand closed around my wrist. "Rich people like you disgust me, Damon. If this asshole comes near her again, I'll do more than just break a few ribs or his hand."

He dragged me out of the chaotic study room, his long strides making me stumble in my heels.

I had never seen Cillian so angry. Or seen anyone so angry *for* me.

PART III

"I own you and all your pretty holes."

29
I'LL DO ANYTHING

CILLIAN

Red coated my vision and with each stride, my grip tightened on Emma's wrist. I didn't want to hurt her damnit, but I couldn't think.

The images of that perv's hand on her back and frozen body kept flashing in my head, and it was enough for me to want to break something. Or someone.

"Give me the keys," I barked at the driver and he scrambled from leaning on the car to giving me the keys.

"I can drive you—"

"You can leave," I said, opening the passenger door for Emma. I couldn't meet her eyes when she sat down, and I closed the door.

Exhaling sharply, I sat in the driver's seat and started the engine. I didn't tell her where we were going when I drove out of the driveway, away from her brother and the creep.

"Cillian," her voice was even, but there was a hint of nervousness. My hand tightened on the steering wheel to stop myself from hauling her over my lap and make sure she's okay. "Where are we going?"

"Why didn't you tell me that asshole has harassed you before?" I asked, trying to keep the anger out of my voice.

"It's not important," she replied, looking out of the window.

"Right. So if he does it again you'll—"

"I don't want to talk about it, Cillian," she snapped, her blue eyes sharp. "I'm thankful that you stopped it, but you didn't have to kick him."

Oh, that's what she was mad about?

"I'm your bodyguard and if I see you harmed, I will resort to violence if I fucking have to." My knuckles turned white, and I tried to focus on my breathing, but it was all useless after what had happened in the past thirty minutes. Taking a deep breath, I asked, "Are you okay?"

I could feel her gaze on me, and it made my stomach clench with nerves. I didn't want her to fear what I had done. I didn't want her to fear me.

"I'm okay." Her voice was small, and she was looking at her lap, her blonde hair hiding her face. "No one has ever stood up for me like that, so it was odd seeing it. Thank you."

No one...

"You shouldn't be thanking me, Doll." I slowed down the car and kept my hand on her thigh, tracing the soft skin of her hand. "You didn't tell your mother, Mrs. Karen, or your friends?"

I sighed in relief when she entwined her small hand with mine, her black nails tracing my hand tattoos.

"I told my mom when he touched my shoulder in her study. Saying creepy things that made me uncomfortable." She shrugged, her smile sad when she glanced at me. "But she said it was normal. That if I didn't want unwanted attention from old men like that, I should go on a diet so that these wouldn't be so big and in their way." Her tone was very self-deprecating when she pointed at her perfect breasts.

My jaw clenched, and I squeezed her hand. "I'm sorry your mother didn't help you, Emma."

"It's alright. I-it could have been worse... but Mrs. Karen stayed with me when I begged her to sleep in my room that night." She smiled, but it didn't reach her eyes. "I never told Mia or Summer because I didn't want them to worry about me."

"Is there..." I paused and flickered my eyes at her. "Is there any way I can help you?"

I would do anything she wanted me to. I would listen to her, let her cry on my lap if she wanted, and hold her as long as she wanted me to.

But I had guessed it all wrong about Emma. She wasn't weak, and she definitely didn't need my shoulder to cry on.

"Yes, there is," she replied, her fingers brushing over my knuckles and I had to keep myself in check from sporting a bulge.

"I'll do anything, Doll—"

"Fuck me."

"What?" My eyes were wide, and I had to hold on to the steering wheel so I wouldn't drive the car into a tree. "What the fuck are you asking, Emma?"

"You said you'd do anything, Cillian. I want you to take me to the club and fuck me."

I untangled our hands and looked straight ahead on the road. "I am not going to have sex with you," I said, my voice stern and final. "If you want something else, then tell me."

"Are you sure that's your answer?"

I narrowed my eyes at her face that was devoid of any emotion, but her chin was high and she wasn't trembling anymore.

What was this fucking girl playing at?

"Yes, Emma," I said. "I am not sleeping with you—"

"Even though you already did?"

I raked a hand through my hair. She was impossible. "That was before I knew you were nineteen and Caleb's ex. And now you are my client too. It's not happening."

"I see," she said, her tone even. "Take me to Vixen."

"I already told you—"

"I want to go to the club, Cillian. Take me there. You can drop me outside and leave," Emma said without looking at me and crossed her arms, leaning back on the seat.

Like hell I was going to leave her alone at a sex club.

Neither of us said a single thing for the rest of the ride. There was so much sexual tension hovering in the air that anyone could cut it with a butter knife. I opened the door for her when we reached the club.

We both ignored the long queue outside when the valet took the keys from me.

"I thought you were just dropping me here and leaving," she said when the guard checked our VIP cards and let us inside through the dark door.

"I'm not leaving you alone at a place where you were drugged last time," I said, wrapping my arm around her waist and pulling her closer.

Must and exotic perfume laced the air after the receptionist checked our names and ID. I asked for two masks, one with dark lace trim and the other with feather. Emma raised a brow in question and let me put the white mask on her face, her bright blue eyes dilating when I tied it behind her head, making sure it was secure.

"Don't remove it," I ordered, wearing my black mask, similar to hers, and entered the club.

"Too bad it will be tugged off eventually," she said, smugness dripping from her voice.

I ignored the sultry music playing in the background and everyone's stares as they ogled both of us, and pulled her closer.

"What the fuck does that mean?" I asked, growling in her ear.

Emma blinked up at me innocently. "If you don't want to fuck me, Cillian, I am going to do an exhibitionism show in a private room, and I'm sure I'll get many people—men, women and others—who would want to fuck me."

My arm tightened around her waist as I glared at her small smile. I asked, keeping my voice low, "Are you sure that's your final answer?"

30
TAKE YOUR CLOTHES OFF
EMMA

I tilted my head and raised my brow at his words. "It is, Cillian." I dropped my voice to a sultry tone and whispered, "If you want, you can stay for the show. I won't tell anyone."

Winking, I stepped away from him. I could feel his eyes burning into me, so I smirked and added a little sway to my hips and ordered a glass of sparkling water from Joe. I didn't want a repeat of last time. He raised his brow over my shoulder and slid the drink to me saying teasingly, 'Naughty, naughty, naughty!'

As I looked around, I was surprised to see more people than last time even though it was a weekday. There were lots of older men, women and even younger crowd wearing collars and some even holding leashes walking behind their owners. Dancers in many bodies were dancing in tight clothes in cage-like structures all over, raised by a stage. People were admiring them as different lights fell on their skin. I liked how free they seemed. Anyone could see, but no one could touch.

"Do you like it?"

I turned to a man, somewhere in his late to mid-forties, sitting beside me. He was sipping on auburn liquid and had a wedding band on his left hand. My throat tightened remembering something.

"They're very talented," I replied, drinking all the water.

"So you like to watch?" he asked, keeping his empty glass on the counter and facing me on the stool. He was wearing an expensive suit and had salt and pepper hair. Despite his age, he seemed very handsome.

Too bad I had a thing for tattoos and piercings.

"No," I said, running my nail over his shirt, "I want others to watch me."

"Is that so?" he rumbled, his eyes twinkling with mischief. "If you are alone, I have an offer for you. Join me and my husband in a private suite where others can watch us as we take turns over your gorgeous body."

I blinked at him, surprised by the offer. *His husband?* I looked over his shoulder to see another man, younger than him but definitely older than me, giving me a small smirk.

My gut churned, and I didn't know how to respond. It was overwhelming.

"You are not ready," he said bluntly, but softly.

I frowned. "But I didn't even answer."

"If it's not an enthusiastic consent or approval, it's a no, love," he said, patting my hand. "If you want to be watched, you can have a room with a balcony for others to watch you. I'm sure lots of people would pay to watch you play with yourself. I hope you find what you are looking for." He winked at me and stood up. His husband slid his hand around his waist and they both walked away, leaving me confused and curious.

I exhaled slowly and stood up. I knew what I wanted to do.

* * *

"Whenever you are ready, Miss." One of the employees in their pretty dress said, showing me the way to the private room with a balcony circling it for others to come and watch me.

"I'm ready," I said, raising my chin high, the mask in place on my face.

"Ah, before you go, a gentleman paid a high price to be in the room with you. He won't touch you unless you consent to it, and we have our guards in the audience, so you don't need to worry about your safety."

I frowned, tilting my head. "Then why did he pay a steep price to be in the same room?"

They shrugged, a small smirk on their lips. "Some people like to instruct during the scenes. He could be a Dom or a top. You are free to do whatever you please and use the toys he instructed us to prepare for you at the corner table. Enjoy!"

I straightened my shoulders and tried to relax. I didn't care that there would be another person so close to me while I touched myself. All I cared about was having fun and forgetting about the last few days.

When I entered the room, the first thing I saw were mirrors. So many of them. All around the room. I licked my lips when I felt multiple pairs of eyes on me. A hushed whisper ran through the small crowd when I walked towards the circular bed that was staged higher than the floor. There was an armchair in front of the bed, but I ignored it. I didn't notice the man, but my breathing came to a halt when I found the table full of various toys near the bed.

Moving my hair over my shoulder, I smiled and traced my fingers over them. On it was a huge bottle of lube and cleaning wipes. A sexy pink vibrating egg with a small piece to stimulate the clit, a small wireless wand with different settings and... I took a sharp breath, picking up the cold metal object with a pink rose gemstone on the back.

I had never used a butt plug before, but the curiosity made me want to try it. In front of all these people.

Deciding to be bold, I turned to my audience and smiled when erotic music started playing around the room. The blood red curtains were wide open and even though I could feel all their stares on me, I couldn't see any of them because of the lightning. I could already feel the blood in my veins thrumming with pleasure.

Picking up the vibrating egg, I kneeled on the bed with my dress and heels still on. Spreading my legs and without tucking my dress up, I started the toy on level one and moved it down on my breasts. Even though I was wearing a bra, my nipples stood erect when the vibrations shot tingles of pleasure down my spine and to my pussy.

I had just started and already soaked my panties.

The thrill of being the center of attention of so many people and feeling their lustful gaze on me made me confident and bolder. I lowered the vibe under my dress and sighed, arching my neck as delicious vibrations ran from my inner thighs to the place between my legs.

Now. I need it inside me now.

Tucking my panties to the side, I slid the vibrating egg inside me with a small moan. I was so wet that I didn't even need lube when my tight walls clamped around it, the small stem on my clit keeping me turned on. The toy kept rumbling inside me as I played with my heavy breasts, looking around the balcony through the mask. I wished I could remove it, but I wanted to remain anonymous.

I wondered if he was watching me, jealous and angry that—

"*Oh!*" I moaned loudly when the vibrations of the toy

inside me increased. I clutched the sheets, cheeks red and confused as fuck.

"I knew you'd like this toy, Doll." My eyes widened as I watched Cillian walk from the corner of the room, looking dark and menacing.

His black mask was still on, but there was no mistake it was him. His deep voice, his tattoos and his eyes.

He sat down on the armchair and crossed his legs, his thumb moving on a screen and the vibrations climbed up, making me whimper and so close to orgasm.

"Y-you," I managed to stutter.

He didn't even smile, his face devoid of any emotion when he titled his head. "Are you going to cum?"

"Yes!" Names were not allowed to be spoken, and I wanted both of us to remain anonymous.

"Tsk, that's not how you should address me, Doll." He tutted in disappointment, increasing the vibrations again. "I'll ask again. Are you going to cum?"

"Yes, Sir?" I asked, my eyes hazy from the lust.

"Good girl." He lowered the vibrations when I was about to tip over the edge of orgasm and slowly turned them off. "Take your clothes off."

"W-why?"

I didn't care that he paid to be in the room with me, give me instructions. I just wanted to cum right now.

"Because I bought you for two hours, Doll. I own you and all your pretty holes," Cillian smiled slowly, a sadistic gleam in his dark eyes that terrified and excited me at the same time. This was the man I had met that night who looked like a panther. "I don't want to waste my money or time. Clothes. Off. *Now*."

Oh fuck.

That was the last thing I had expected to happen, and I didn't know whether I regretted teasing him or not.

31
SAY IT

EMMA

I stared back at him, my hands scrunching the sheets tightly as I straightened up and raised my chin. "And what if I don't, Sir?" I asked, my voice full of defiance.

Cillian leaned back on the chair, a small smile on his lips as if he was waiting for me to push back. He looked like a dark king from one of those vampire books Summer reads, his eyes roving over me, already undressing me with them.

"I'll keep teasing you with the vibe, Doll," he said. "And if you try to remove it, I have cuffs that I don't mind using on naughty, spoiled little brats like you." He dangled the metal cuffs at me, and I swallowed the lump in my throat.

Fuck me. He had trapped me.

I knew I could use a safe word and everything would end, but I didn't want it to end. I wanted to play. Especially when so many people were watching me. I could feel the sexual tension thickening in the air and the hushed whispers of the audience disappearing as they waited to see what would happen next.

It made me clench more on the vibe. I had never been so turned on in my life.

I didn't want to test Cillian, so I glared at him, unzipping my dress and pulling it off of me.

"Remove everything," he said, his words sharp and not giving me a moment to breathe as I unhooked the clasps of the lacy white bra and bared my breasts to the world.

My nipples peaked and I could feel my cheeks burning when a hush fell over the crowd. I peered at Cillian, his eyes pinned on my face, not on my bare tits.

"Panties," he reminded me, and I resisted the urge to flip him the bird.

Hooking my fingers through the lace, I removed them, biting my lip when cold air brushed over my wet pussy. I was completely naked on the bed besides the mask. My long blond hair brushed over my nipples, and I took a shuddering deep breath to calm myself down.

"Open your legs, Doll," he rumbled, his voice deep and echoing in my head when he leaned his elbows on his knees.

Laying back on the bed, I spread my legs.

"*Wider*. You can do more—*good fucking girl*." I heard him stand up, walking closer to the bed. "Now remind me, what do I own, Doll?"

I blinked at him in confusion, and the vibe started rumbling inside me. I raised my hips, my hands sliding down.

"No. *Stop*. You will not touch yourself until you tell me," he said harshly, increasing the vibrations and changing the pattern so it kept me turned on, wet and desperate.

Fuck him. He was punishing me for not listening to him earlier and having a blast.

"I'm not going to ask again. What do I own, Doll?"

"*Me*," I replied with a gasp, squirming on the bed. "You own me, C—*Sir*."

"Mhmm, I fucking own you," he growled, his eyes raking over my spread body. Despite feeling the others' stare on me, between my legs, all I cared about was him and his obsidian gaze. "I'm going to touch you. Do you object?"

I shook my head. I wanted him to touch me so bad.

Cillian tilted his head. "Of course you don't. I own you, so I can touch you whenever I want. Isn't that right, Doll?"

I gasped when his fingers brushed over my trembling thighs, "Y-yes, Sir."

My eyes widened when he pulled me on the edge with my feet still on the bed as he spread my legs wider and looked at my face.

"Which holes of yours do I own, pretty Doll?"

My mouth parted at his filthy words, his tattooed fingers brushing over my thighs and hips in light, teasing touches.

"W-what?"

"You know what I meant." He removed the vibe and cupped my pussy in his large, warm hand, squeezing it and making me whimper. "Tell me."

"My pussy."

"And?"

"M-my mouth?" I asked, grinding myself in his hand, his fingers rubbing over my slicked slit, ignoring my sensitive clit.

"Yes, Doll. I own your mouth so I can fuck it whenever I want. This sopping wet cunt too," he groaned, inserting a finger inside me and making me gasp. "You're still missing one thing."

"What?" I panted, rocking my hips against his hand, but he withdrew it when I got close to orgasm, making me whine at the loss of his touch. God, he was fully clothed, and I was already on the brink of orgasm.

He flipped me around, pulling my hips up and squeezing my ass, spanking it lightly. *"This.* What's here, Doll? Your virgin little...?"

I whimpered and shook my head.

"Oh, you're not gonna say it?" he asked, his voice full of mischief. His palm was rubbing circles on my ass, keeping me on all fours. I looked over my shoulder to see what he was doing, and my eyes widened when his palm struck my ass cheek. The scorching pain and burn flowed from my entire body to my sensitive clit.

"Say it, Doll," he said, rubbing the red skin when I gasped in the sheets, holding on to them. His fingers rubbed my clit when he whispered, "Don't make me use a paddle on your pretty ass. Admit it. Tell me which pretty holes I own."

"My mouth, my pussy and ass!" I moaned when he spanked me again, his hand soothing the pain before pulling away.

"Good girl. I own all of you and all your holes." His voice was a little loud as he walked towards the table, as if he wanted everyone in the audience to know that I belonged to him.

Ass.

I trembled when he kept the cuffs and wand near my eye level. He wanted me to see which toys he was going to use on me.

Sexy ass.

"What's your safe word?" he asked, squeezing my cheeks when he moved behind me, still fully dressed.

"Barbie," I exhaled when something cold and smooth landed on my butt. "What are you... *ohmygod.*"

Cillian dropped another dollop of lube on his gloved hand and placed the plug near my feet. He saw the look on my face and said, "Keep your face on the sheet and spread your cheeks for me. I'm going to use you today, Doll."

"W-what?" My eyes went wide as saucers at his words.

"Say it."

I looked from his glistening gloved hands to his handsome face. He was doing everything I wanted and needed. He was perfect. Cillian was fucking perfect.

Licking my lips, I pressed my cheek on the sheet like he ordered me to and spread myself for him. "Use me."

He spanked my other cheek, careful not to hit my hand, and growled, "Beg."

"Please use me, Sir."

"Louder."

Another spank.

"Please use me!"

32
SHE'S MINE

CILLIAN

"That's my good fucking girl," I whispered, kissing her sweet neck and inhaling the rich vanilla scent. "Relax and take deep breaths."

Emma tried to relax, exhaling slowly, and I leaned back to watch the perfect sight of her dripping pussy and the pink star above it. I touched it with my gloved finger, rubbing the lube around and letting her lean into the touch before dipping it inside.

Fuck. She was tight.

"Relax, Doll," I ordered her, her tight ring squeezing on my knuckle as I slowly teased her virgin ass, noting the reaction on her face and body.

I didn't want to hurt her. I'd never hurt her. Especially when it came to pleasure.

"It feels good, doesn't it?" I asked, my voice breathy when she started making sweet, tiny whimpers from her mouth.

"Yes," she trailed off, squeezing her eyes shut when I added another finger and her voice broke off into a moan. *"Oh, fuck!"*

I rubbed her clit with my other hand, her thighs trembling as she reached the peak too soon. I kept fucking her with my fingers, feeling her loosening before I picked up the medium-sized plug. It was four inches long with enough girth that it'd feel comfortable but full. She'd know that she's wearing the little rose gem every time she moves.

"You're doing well, Doll," I said, removing my fingers and adding a dollop of lube on the plug and her ass. "Keep yourself spread for me. Just a little more."

I could feel hundreds of eyes on me, on her and between her spread cheeks. I was going to show all of them who she belonged to.

Me. No one else's. She's mine.

And not just for the two hours.

"Relax," I said, pushing the plug inside her and feeling resistance. She whimpered, and I rubbed her clit with more pressure. "Yes, good girl, just like that."

I bit my lip when I held the plug in place and she pushed herself back on it as if she wanted it inside her. It was hot as fuck to see her enjoying it as moans elicited from her parted mouth, and slowly the widest part of the plug settled inside her and it went all the way in.

"Good fucking girl," I praised her, pushing the plug in and letting her relax as I ditched the glove and marveled at the sight of pink rose twinkling between her cheeks. "You look so fucking sexy with a plug in your ass, Doll."

"Do I?" she asked, her voice small as she looked over her shoulder, her brow furrowed when she clenched and unclenched herself over the plug, accommodating herself with the new feeling.

"Does it feel good, Doll?" I asked, wiping my hands with wipes and caressing her butt, squeezing it lightly.

Her response was a gasp and pushing her ass back into my hands, making me smile. "I knew you'd like it. Now thank me for it, Doll."

I turned her around and held her by her neck as she kneeled on the bed in front of me. She gasped when I tightened my grip on the sides of her neck and pulled her closer.

"Thank me."

Her blue eyes were glazed and pupils dilated, her cheekbones pink as she blew out a shaky breath and held my arm for support. "T-thank you, Sir." Her voice was sweet as honey and I wanted to hear her more. Then her hand dropped to my pants, making me raise my brow. "I want to suck your cock."

"Is that how you want to thank me, Doll?" I asked.

She nodded, licking her plump lips.

I pulled back to get everything I needed. Her eyes were wide, but her pulse was beating wildly, excited and curious. She had loved the plug, and I knew her pussy was desperate for attention.

"Hands," I asked, her wrists lifting, and I cuffed them together.

"You're going to hold this to your clit," I said, laying her down with her head facing the edge of the bed and letting her hold the small wand in her cuffed wrists. "If you cum, I'll stop everything, and this will end."

"Why?" Her voice was frustrated, and rightfully so. I had teased her for so long with no release.

"Because I own you and I want you to cum when I fuck your ass," I said bluntly, starting the wand. "Play with it, make yourself feel good, stop it, do whatever you want. But you're not going to cum until I tell you to. Understood, Doll?"

Her brows were furrowed, but she nodded slowly, moving the vibrating wand over her hips, the sound of clinking cuffs echoing in the air as I watched how perfect she looked. Her pink nipples poking the air, her curves bare for everyone to see, and puffy little sensitive pussy ready to be fucked and used by me.

My slacks were getting uncomfortable, and I quickly got rid of my belt. Her attention snapped to me when I lowered my zipper, her lips parting as I stroked myself in front of her, her eyes pinned on my piercing.

"If you want to stop or take a break, tap the bed twice," I said, telling her about the safe gesture. "You understand, Doll?"

"I do," Emma replied, licking her lips and arching her neck closer, as if she couldn't wait to take me in her sweet mouth.

With gentle hands, I laid her head over the edge of the bed, her legs spreading wide on their own accord. I traced her pouty lips with my thumb. "I'm going to fuck your mouth and you are going to be a good girl and play with your pussy, yeah?"

I didn't wait for her reply. I held my base and slowly slid inside her hot, wet mouth. I sighed when she clamped her lips around me, her cuffed hands moving the wand over her clit as I squeezed her breasts.

"Such a good fucking girl," I groaned, pulling out and slowly sliding back in. "Make yourself feel good, Doll."

33
FILL ME UP

EMMA

My moans were muffled as Cillian's thick cock entered my mouth once again. Erotic sounds of his low groans and the buzzing of wand around my pussy were pushing me into a lust-crazed frenzy with each passing second.

His hand wrapped around my neck, making my hips buck and thighs tremble. "Such a good fucking Doll," he growled, sliding in deeper and making me gag. "Put your wand on your clit."

I didn't listen because I was too overwhelmed by the strong vibrations. I whimpered around his girth when he pinched my nipple with his other hand.

"I'm not asking. Now."

The threat in his voice was real, and a small part of me wanted to disobey and see what he would do. I clenched around the foreign object in my butt, and another moan muffled out of me because the sensation felt so weird yet so fucking good. I moved the wand on my clit and groaned, snapping my legs shut.

"Open your legs," Cillian growled, pulling out of my

mouth and letting me breathe as I blinked hazily at him. His dick was hard with veins around it.

I parted my legs again and leaned up to lick the piercing on the underside of his tip. He pushed inside me again, my throat relaxing around him when he fucked my mouth. I was on the verge of orgasm, slowly rocking my hips over the buzzing wand and clenching the plug that felt way too full inside me.

"Don't cum yet, Doll," he warned me, his voice getting deeper and breathier as his cock grew bigger inside me and I knew he was close.

I relished in the pleasure and moved the wand around my lips, the plug making it more intense. Cillian's fingers twisted on my nipples, tugging them gently as he got close. I gasped loudly when he pulled out of my mouth and spurted his hot cum all over my breasts and stomach.

I melted into the bed when he straightened me up and left my side for a few seconds. I kept the wand beside me, turning it off, and met the blue eyes of a sexy woman in bed from the ceiling. That was me. I licked my lips, my jaw aching a little. Cillian was *big*. I gazed at how unabashedly hot and horny I looked with wetness seeping out of my sensitive pussy and flushed breasts covered in release.

My breathing was still heavy when Cillian came back. He had closed the curtains for the audience, announcing that we both needed more privacy.

"You good, Doll?" he asked, his voice hoarse as he started unbuttoning his shirt and stripping out of his clothes and removing his mask.

I nodded, my tongue too heavy to form any words. I was too busy shamelessly checking his muscular body covered in tattoos. His broad shoulders, piercings on nipples, chiseled abs and thick thighs.

"Drink." He handed me a bottle of water, his fingers

tugging off my mask. I licked my lips when he gently wiped my stomach and chest with wipes. "I would love to keep you covered in my cum, but we are not in the privacy of my suite. Next time." His eyes were burning with promise.

I emptied half of the bottle and peered at him. "Why did you close the curtains?" My voice was sultry and heavy. Every inch of my body was relaxed, yet electrified and curious. Anticipation rolled through me, and I wanted to pull him closer, wanted him to slide inside my wet heat and fuck me.

Cillian caressed my cheek, the pads of his fingers light. His touch was so soft and gentle, I melted into his warm hand. "Because I don't want anyone to see the face you make when your pretty cunt creams on my cock," he whispered, lowering his hand to my neck, my breast, and lightly squeezing it.

I arched into his touch, wanting more.

"How does the plug feel, Doll?" he asked, rolling his fingers around my areola. "Does it hurt?"

I clenched, biting my lip and shook my head. "I-it feels good. I feel full."

His expression changed, pinching my nipple and making me moan. "Yeah? Do you want me to fuck your ass?"

My heavy-lidded eyes blinked at him, his handsome face, his scarred lips. "No," I licked my lips and spread my legs, "Fuck my pussy first."

"Of course, Doll," he said, bringing his lips to mine and kissing me deeply. I was on his lap and moaned when his bulge brushed against my sensitive clit. The pressure of friction sending delicious pleasure all over my body.

"I want you to look at yourself," he demanded, settling me on his thick thighs with my back to him so I faced the mirror in front of us. I squirmed on his lap, his feet on the floor as his large hands spread my legs wider, so I had to lean on him to support myself.

Just like in the car, but we were both naked. My ass was full and there was a large mirror in front of us.

"Look," he grabbed my thigh, spanking me lightly for not listening to him. "Look and tell me how sexy you look, Doll."

My eyes burned, and I shook my head. His fingers brushed over my clit, and I bucked my hips to him, but he slid them lower, dipping them into my wetness.

"See your pretty pussy." His voice was so deep and velvety. I could melt listening to his sexy voice. "Fuck, Doll. Can you see how turned on you are right now? Hm?"

I nodded, my body trembling when he kept rubbing, teasing me with light touches. He kept up his dirty talk, his other hand touching, squeezing, pinching me everywhere until I was grinding on his hard boner. His fingers were drenched in my juices and I was whimpering for more.

"Fuck me, Cillian, please," I cried out when he stopped again, kissing my neck.

"Shh, Doll," he said, gliding his hands over my curves, admiring me and my body. I could see the fiery heat in his dark eyes when I looked at his reflection in the mirror. He was turned on by me. By my body. "Let me get a condom, and then I'll fuck you as much as you want."

He was about to lift me up when I squeezed his forearm, stopping him. "I'm on pills." I looked over my shoulder to meet his gaze. "Fuck me. I don't care if you cum inside me. I want you to fill me up, Cillian."

"I'm sterile but...," he paused, his hands dug into my skin and his gaze darkened. "Are you sure, Emma?"

Not Doll. He was serious.

I nodded, kissing him gently and peered at him from my lashes. "Cum inside me."

His hand tangled into my hair as he kissed me again,

pulling away only when he needed oxygen. "Tell me to breed you, Doll. Tell me to fill your pretty cunt with my cum."

My mouth parted and if I could, I would've cum right then and there, hearing his filthy words. But I had never been so turned on before.

Breeding without the risk of pregnancy and having him… *fuck*.

My nails squeezed his skin, the muscles and tattoos on his forearm clenching when I raised my chin and said, "Fuck me, Cillian. Fill me up and breed me."

34

ONE MORE TIME

CILLIAN

My cock twitched and throbbed hearing her sultry voice, demanding me to breed her. Maybe it was our carnal instinct, but I couldn't help but imagine how perfect she'd look with my cum dripping out of her flushed pussy.

I kissed her, pulling her closer and moaning when the wetness of her heat lubed up my tip. Lowering my hand to rub her clit, I growled in her ear, "Look in the mirror, Doll. Look how your pussy stretches around my thick cock and takes me in."

Her tits were moving with her heavy breathing, and we both watched when my dick slowly slid inside of her. I was not even fully in, and she was gushing around me, her soft moan making me want to push her on the floor and fuck her hard.

But I controlled myself. Slowing down and caressing her trembling body. Emma was definitely getting overwhelmed and overstimulated.

"Does it feel good, Doll?" I asked, feeling her walls clamp

down on me and the plug. It was making her even tighter, and I had to keep myself in control. "Emma, tell me."

I wanted her to only feel good. Not hurt. I wanted to offer her all the pleasures of the world and taint her a little. Just for me. My dirty little Doll.

"Cillian," she whimpered, her nails digging into my arms. "Fuck me. Please. Fill me u—*ooh!*"

We both groaned when I fully slid inside her, my eyes pinned between her legs as her sensitive, swollen clit throbbed as she clenched around me. I bet my piercing was rubbing against all her sensitive spots and keeping her on the brink of orgasm. Her eyes were teary, but she wasn't showing any signs of discomfort or pain. Only pleasure.

"Now," I cupped her throat and growled in her ear, "Look in the mirror and tell me you look hot as fuck with my cock inside you."

"I look hot," she moaned, squeezing her nipples and rocking back and forth on my lap. "Now fuck me!"

"Good girl," I kissed her temple and gently lifted her before slamming her down on me. Emma groaned, her back arching and thighs trembling. "You can cum as much as you want, Doll. You've been so good."

I praised her, whispering filthy sweet things in her ear and kept fucking her slowly until she took the reins and started riding me. Her golden hair was mussed, blue eyes bright with lust and gleaming with tears of pleasure, cheeks flushed pink and lips swollen. There were hickeys all over her neck and body and she looked beautiful, riding me like she owned me and fucking herself until she came, clamping down on me with such warmth that I came inside her.

We both moaned when she finally slumped over me, our orgasm rolling through us and leaving us with aftershocks.

Emma was panting and limp as she kept her head on my shoulder, still trembling with the pleasure. Light sheen of sweat glistened on our body, and I kissed her neck, caressing her soft skin and calming her down.

Gently putting her on the bed, I pulled out, groaning at the sight of my cum dripping out of her pink pussy. She moaned, her heavy-lidded eyes flickering between my face and her legs as I dipped two fingers inside her, fucking it back.

"Cillian…" she moaned, squirming when I pinned her legs back. "I'm sensitive."

"I don't care," I growled, already getting hard again at the sight of her. "I'm making sure I breed you right, Doll. Wouldn't want to disappoint you."

"Ohmygod," she gasped, twisting in the sheets when I moved my fingers inside her, fucking her with our release. "Cillian I—"

I glared at her. "Say the safe word or cum again."

Her blue eyes flashed at me as let out a moan. "M-more!"

"I knew it," I chuckled softly, spanking her thigh lightly and kissing her knee. "My greedy little Doll wants more, doesn't she?"

She nodded, arching her hips as I made her cum on my fingers, holding her down when she tried to squirm away.

"You're going to cum one more time," I said, opening the bottle of lube and settling her on all fours. I could see her flushed face in the mirror as she scrunched the sheets.

"One more time?" Her eyes were wide when I pushed her back down, looming behind her and licking my lips at the sight of the pink rose gem winking at me between her perfect ass cheeks.

"I want you to cum when I fuck your ass, Doll," I said, squeezing her ass. "Can you do that for me, or do you want to stop?"

I would remove the plug, cuddle her, calm her down, and give her a warm bath if she wanted to stop. If not…

She moved her ass and looked at me over her shoulder. "I want you to fuck my ass, Cillian."

Fuck.

"Will you be good and tell me if it hurts?" I asked, my voice hoarse.

"I promise, now please…" She pushed her ass towards me and I had to bite my lip from grinning. Emma was not at all shy about what she wanted when she was horny. Which made her so fucking sexy that I never wanted it to end.

Later. I will think about those thoughts later when I'm alone. Right now, I wanted to make her feel good when I fuck her ass.

"Relax, Doll, I'm going to remove the plug." She stayed still when I took my time to slowly remove it, her ring clamping it as I slowly worked it out. She moaned when it slid out and my cock stirred hearing it.

"Good girl." I poured lube on my hand. "How does it fee—"

Emma looked over her shoulder and I was surprised and in awe when her sharp eyes fell on my face. "I'm fine, Cillian. I want you to fuck me. Now!"

I raised my brow, rubbing the lube over her tight little hole. "Has anyone fucked you here before?" I asked, keeping my voice calm even though I wanted to punish her for not letting me take my time. Anal was meant for slow fuck with lots of foreplay, patience and care. It wasn't something anyone rushed into.

"N-no," her voice stuttered.

"Then let me take my time before I fuck your virgin little ass, you greedy Doll," I growled, spanking her ass. Soft enough to feel the shock of pain and hard enough to see my handprint on her ass.

35
MY GOOD GIRL

EMMA

My stomach was clenched with nerves when I looked at one of the many mirrors in the room to see Cillian tear open a foil with his teeth. Licking my lips, I watched him roll the condom over his glinting piercing and his long shaft.

"Come on, old man," I teased, my voice breathy as I wriggled my ass to him. "Hurry up!"

"This old man is going to take his time." Cillian spanked me, but it was light and playful, making me bite my lip. "Have patience, Doll. I don't want to hurt you."

"You won't." I watched him pour lube on his cock and met his eyes. "And if you do… I'm sure I'll like it. Love it even."

He stopped, giving me a look that I couldn't decipher, and shook his head. "Trouble," he muttered to himself and straightened up, pinning me down with his hand on my arched back and rubbing his tip over my ass.

My eyes went wide when he kept teasing me, never entering.

"Do you see the wand on your left?" he asked, his voice smoky. "Grab it and use it on your clit."

I did what he said because I didn't want him to stop whatever he was doing. I held it between my legs and watched our reflection. I was on all fours on the bed with my butt in the air while his large frame was behind me, his hips rocking, and he gently slid the head of his cock inside me.

"Oh fuck," I gasped at the new sensation of being penetrated and tried to clench and unclench. I could even feel his piercing.

"Relax, Doll," Cillian gritted his clenched teeth and pushed the wand on my clit. "Focus on the pleasure and take deep breaths. I promise I'll make you feel good."

I trusted him. He'd never break his promise.

Cillian stayed still for a while until my breathing became calmer and then slid deeper, my mouth parting at the new sensations that were firing all over my body and rushing to my brain.

"Cillian!" I gasped, struggling to keep the buzzing wand over my sensitive clit when he went all the way in, stretching me around his thick girth and grunting over me. "Oh, God…"

"You are so incredibly tight, Doll," he groaned, squeezing my ass again. "Is it hurting?"

I shook my head, my eyes already rolling over my head. "I feel like… *oh.*"

Orgasm exploded out of me and I whimpered when he pulled out and slowly rocked inside me, making the orgasm last longer and longer. When I came to, I saw Cillian fucking my ass in the mirror. His jaw clenched as he panted over me.

"You just came while I fucked your ass, Doll," he grunted, the sounds of our skin slapping against each other surrounding us. "Does it feel that good, hm?"

"So good," I nodded, my tongue heavy. "I think I'm gonna cum again."

"My Doll cums when she gets fucked in the ass, huh? *Fuck*," he groaned, slamming inside me as I clenched down on him. I felt so full and overwhelmed by all the stimulation. "Increase the level on the wand. I want you to cum again while I fuck your ass."

I pressed a button, and it started buzzing faster, making my entire body tremble. The pleasure of his dick pounding in my ass and the wand on my clit was making my entire body tremble. His fingers dug into my cheeks when he increased his pace, going deeper and harder. His erotic grunts, groans and moans sent me over the edge as I came, feeling him spurt inside the condom.

My eyes squeezed shut at the overpowering orgasm, and I couldn't move when it kept rolling out of me that I had to scrunch the sheets to hold on to something. I mumbled something incoherent when Cillian fell on top of me, his hot breath fanning over my neck as we both stayed like that for a while.

"Cillian."

"Mhm?" He pulled away, his fingers tucking my hair behind my ear so he could look at me.

"I think you broke me again," I whispered. The wand was still buzzing somewhere on the bed.

"Shut up, you're being dramatic," he said, and kissed my cheek. It felt so gentle even after everything we had done that day. The kiss on the cheek and how he caressed my back made my heart hammer. "You good, Doll?"

I gasped when he slid out of me, making me squirm on the bed. "My butt feels weird," I said, looking at him as he stood up, picking up some wipes.

He narrowed his eyes at me, and I glared at his sexy tattooed body. *How dare he look hot as fuck after so much fucking while I looked so mussed up?* It wasn't fair. I already wanted to climb him again. "Is it good weird or bad weird?"

"Good weird?" I asked, blinking up at him as he hummed to himself.

"That's okay. I'll be right back. Stay there," he pointed at me as I sprawled on the bed, watching his firm butt and sexy back disappearing in the bathroom.

I was still on the bed, staring at my reflection in the mirror, when he came back naked—*yay*—with a warm rag. My cheeks turned red when he cleaned me up, his hands gentle as the soft cloth went from my pussy to my butt.

"Do you feel sore?" he asked, holding me up in his arms.

"I can walk. Put me down," I said, snuggling into his broad chest when he walked us to the bathroom. He had already readied the bath with warm water that looked so inviting I wanted to stay in it for hours.

"I'm not letting you go for a few hours. So shut up and answer my question." He looked stern—like he always did—but his tone was soft.

"A bit," I answered truthfully, looking at his tattoo and nipple piercings as he sat us both down in the large tub. "Oh fuck. This feels amazing."

"Just a bit?" he asked, caressing my back and massaging a few sore muscles that made me melt in his strong arms. This was perfect. Having a warm bath with Cillian.

"Yes, just a bit."

I didn't know when my eyes closed and how I drifted to sleep, but I remembered lying down on his chest with his arms around me. His large hand caressing my back as he placed a small kiss on my hair.

"You did so well today," he whispered, his voice soft. "I'm so proud of you, Doll. My good girl."

I knew that he didn't mean just the scene.

36
LITTLE EMMA

UNKNOWN

Oh, she had a huge pair of tits alright. My little Emma. Already allowing herself to feel empowered by showing off her bits—my bits— to everyone. *How dare she...*

It was okay. It was. *Really*. After all, she'd be with me in a few months. Weeks if I make it happen early and get rid of that new nuisance. That piece of shit bodyguard.

Cillian Chang. I had been keeping eyes on him when he ruined my plan for that day. Emma was so willing and pliant and ready for me, mumbling in her sleep when he just had to come back to the suite.

I was furious. He must have used his large body to pin her down and use her. I knew it. Just how he closed the fucking curtains in my damn face just when my sweet little Emma was going to cum. For me. I knew he was torturing her, so I had recorded everything and watched it until my camera battery died when he fucked her.

It's okay. I will prove it to her as soon as I take her away and keep her with me in our home. I will prove how she was being brainwashed by everyone around her and that only I could save her, protect her, and keep her satisfied. No one but me.

Sitting in the car, I waited until dawn arrived. But they still didn't walk out of the stupid sex club of Damon. I wonder how he would react if he knew his sister was being seduced by her own bodyguard. Or how her school would react...

No. I had to think rationally—

A *thump* from the back of my car made me sigh. "Stop it," I said, clenching my teeth. Another *thump*. "Goddamn, stop it!" I yelled, but the shithead kept moving and kicking around.

I glared at the road ahead and started driving to the home that I had purchased for me and Emma. We would live there forever. It had everything she needed and more.

Stopping my car in the garage, I turned on the dim light and opened the trunk.

The man's eyes turned wide and he started shaking his head, trying to get away from me. I chuckled and dragged him out. He was a fat fuck and weighed a ton, so I didn't care when I kept dragging him from the garage to my favorite part of our home—the basement.

I had used duct tape on his mouth and ropes on his wrists and ankles. His muffled screams just made me laugh louder as I dropped his deadweight inside the small little prison I had made with iron bars. It was for my lovely Emma, of course. It had a nice pink bed, a small table so she can do her makeup and a small space from where I could give her a plate.

I didn't like that she had gained so much weight and because I loved her so much, I'd keep her on a proper diet for a few days when she arrives at our home. I was even willing to make love to her on her tiny bed if she wants it, because I was a nice guy. When she looks perfect, like she did before, I'll let her out and show her our special bedroom.

"Look, I don't usually do this, you see," I said to the lawyer, his suit dirty and ripped up at places. I may or may not have been a little rough when I jumped him when he was alone. "But I have to do this."

His muffled shouts became louder with each step I took closer to him. The air was a bit stale in the basement as it didn't have any ventilation, but I was going to keep a cooler for my little Emma when she arrives here. Lincoln, the dirty ass lawyer, bumped into the table I had prepared for my love and dropped a small tray of makeup.

"What the fuck?" I glared at him and picked up the pink palette. "You broke it! Do you fucking know how expensive this shit is?" I screamed at him and pulled off his duct tape.

"Please! Stop! What do you want? I've lots of money, please." The fucker was already sobbing, his face flushed and turning sweaty.

"Jesus Christ, stop fucking crying." I pulled out a knife, and he quickly stopped. "I don't want money."

"T-then? Stocks? Please don't kill me. Let me go. I don't even know you!"

"Stop. Shouting." I pressed the tip of the sharp blade on his lips and made a face. "You're such a disgusting little pig. I have money and stocks. The only thing I want…"

"Please! I'll help you get anything you want. Just let me go."

He looked so pathetic, sobbing and making my lovely Emma's room dirty by being in it. He shouldn't be here.

"What I want is Emma," I said to him and lowered the knife to his stomach. "And I heard her crying today. Saw it. Saw how scared she was when she was around you and how you treated her."

His eyes were wide with fear as he shook his head, "It's not what you think it is—*please!*"

I pushed the knife into him and blood poured out as he screamed. "Shh, it's okay. No one's going to hear you here. It's soundproof." I twisted the knife and continued, "This is why I want to keep her safe and protect her, you know? I mean, if I keep her out there in the world, old creep like you will keep molesting her."

"Please, stop! I didn't—I didn't."

I laughed, "Sure. You didn't molest her. Just touched her shoulder when she was fourteen and said how pretty her pussy would look in your dirty little hands, hm?"

His face turned into horror. "How do you know?"

I leaned in closer and smirked. "Because I was there when you did it, Lincoln. I was watching when she started crying and ran out of the same study room where that bitch's will was announced." I pulled out the knife, making a face when it came out all bloody. "You have guts, I should tell you that, but you're dumb. If you wanted to have her, you should have locked the door. But that would mean you would die afterwards because little Emma belongs to me. *And no one else.*" I said, slitting his throat as he choked, shaking in his tied-up ropes.

I watched the life bleed out of his eyes and smiled. Standing up, I wiped the knife on his suit and took a few pictures of him. This would make good news.

But first... I need to remind little Emma who she belongs to.

37

CHOKE ME HARDER

CILLIAN

"Why did you wake me up so early?" Emma grumbled, meeting me outside her room and rubbing her eyes. "It's the weekend."

I hummed, checking her attire, and nodded in approval. "Good. This will do. Come on, we have a lot to do today."

"What?" she whined, but her footsteps followed me downstairs. It was six in the morning and the sun hadn't risen yet. The weather was cold, so I'd have to train her in her personal gym room. I had been setting it up every evening for the past few weeks between guarding her at school, giving her orgasms at night and wondering why the fuck her stalker hadn't made a move. *Yet.*

It was making me uneasy that he still hadn't showed up. Yes, she was still getting creepy DMs in her social media with lots of fatphobic comments, but none of them were like the stalker who had texted her with a burner phone, giving her a gift that night.

"Why are we here?" Her voice was dull. She crossed her arms and looked at me with narrowed eyes, entering the room with padded floors and all the expensive strength training machines. I had been using the gym every morning before taking Emma to school.

"To make you stronger," I said and pointed at her to stand in front of me in the center of the room. I had asked her to wear gym clothes, but she was grumbling so I readied a legging with a sports bra for her. Along with being her personal bodyguard, I was now working as her personal maid.

"I am strong," Emma said, standing across from me. "What now?"

"Your hair."

"What about it?"

I sighed and walked around her, gathering her soft locks in my hand. "They will get in the way. I'm braiding it."

"Where did you learn to do that?" she asked, her voice soft as I slowly weaved through her hair.

I shrugged. "I used to help my *amma* with her hair when I was a kid."

"Oh, where is she now?"

"Seoul," I said, tying an elastic to secure her braid. "She doesn't like American food, so she stays in South Korea."

"You must miss her."

Her face was sad and eyes were full of emotion when she whispered those words.

"Yes. Sometimes I miss her," I admitted, swallowing the lump in my throat.

Even though her mother wasn't maternal, Emma was close to her. Or else she wouldn't look so sad.

"Anyway, how are you going to make me stronger?" she asked, raising a brow at me.

"I'm going to teach you how to defend yourself," I said evenly. "When the job ends, I want you to be able to protect yourself, okay?"

"When the job ends?" Emma frowned.

"Yes. When we catch the stalker." I cleared my throat and avoided looking into her eyes. "Now stand in this position. Push your weight onto the floor and tighten your core."

She followed my movements, and I asked her to look at the mirror to see her stance and corrected it, lightly touching her back and stomach.

"We will start with punches, kicks, blocks and then end with stretching," I informed her when she raised her arms, her hands in fists.

"Can't I just use a pepper spray or a taser gun?"

I rolled my eyes. Emma shrieked when I took her by surprise and threw her on the padded floor with my hand around her throat and the other pinning her hands. I straddled her waist so her kicking legs were useless.

"Oh, I'm sorry. I was so rude that I didn't wait for you to get your pepper spray out of your bag," I crooned as she glared at me, still trying to fight me and trying to get her hands out of my firm grip. "Stop squirming. If someone wanted to hurt you, they would hit your head or choke you until you were unconscious and take you somewhere else."

Even saying those words made bile rise in my throat.

"Or I can moan and tell them to choke me harder, daddy," she batted her lashes at me even though her face was turning red.

I rolled my eyes and let go of her hands and neck. She gasped for breath and touched her collar. "If someone straddles you like this, there's a way that you can get out. And if you follow my instructions, you can push me off of your tiny body, hurt me and get some time to get away. Got it?"

Emma nodded, her eyes serious. To teach her, I asked her to straddle me and, despite having her on top, I remained in control and slowly got her off me, telling her exactly what I was doing.

After an hour, her eyes were shining brightly as sweat

clung to her flushed skin when we repeated the movements again and again until it was drilled into her skull.

"We will keep doing this for a week and then I'll teach you how to get out of a chokehold, alright?" I panted, wiping sweat from my face with a towel. I had been doing my reps after instructing her to complete her sets of punches and kicks.

She gave me a thumbs up, heaving and sprawled on the floor.

Shaking my head, I offered her a bottle of water. "Drink a bit. We are not done yet."

"What!" Emma cried out, and I bit my lip.

"I'm kidding, Doll. I just wanted to see your reaction," I smirked, winking at her. "But you have to wake up early three times a week so we can keep strengthening you until you can pin me down on the floor, okay?"

She gave me a sly look and said, "I can easily pin you down on the floor, Cillian."

"I'm serious, Emma."

She grumbled and sat up. "Fine. I'll follow all your torturous instructions if you fuck me afterwards."

I stared at her, blond wisps of hair falling out of her braid and replied, "Maybe. If you behave."

"Knew it." She stood up without taking the hand that I had offered and gave me a bright smile that made my heart stutter.

God damn it, Cillian. You barely know this girl for a couple of months and already falling for her.

I swallowed the lump in my throat and turned away. "You can do whatever you want. Let me know if you are going out."

"Oh, I'm not going out."

Thank fuck. I could go back to my home and make sure Caleb hadn't burned it down or worse—Sean hadn't moved in. *I didn't want to be around a certain minx who makes me feel like a teenager—*

"We are going out," Emma said, and before walking out of the gym, she looked back. "Wear something casual, Cillian. You're going to receive your reward."

Fuck me.

38

JEALOUS

EMMA

"We want a similar suit in navy, beige, tan and..." I looked at Cillian and back at the employee. "Light pink."

"Just black. Please," Cillian rumbled at her, but I shushed him, and ignoring his grumpy scowl, I went to the shoes department.

"I don't need more clothes, Doll. I have tons of them," Cillian complained, following me. A few customers were eyeing him, and I saw an old lady tuck a gray lock behind her ear, shamelessly checking him out.

I gaped and held his hand, glaring at her.

"What are you doing?"

"I'm holding your hand. So you don't get lost."

His hand was large, warm, and I liked the soft callouses on the pads of his fingers. He chuckled, and I peered up at him. "What?"

Cillian was smirking now as he leaned down to boop my nose, "You're jealous, Doll."

My cheeks burned, and I cleared my throat and looked away. "I don't get jealous." I dragged him to the private room I had booked, thanking the employee for the suits that were hanging on the rack. It had a suede couch, so I sat on it and pointed to the suits. "Go try them on."

His scowl was back as he went through them. "I don't even know why we were shopping for my clothes."

"Even though you look good in black, I want to see you in different colors. You are my bodyguard, after all," I reminded him, moving my hair behind my shoulders.

He sighed and picked up the beige suit. "Whatever you say, Doll."

I gave him a winning smile when he went into the changing room in the corner and calmed my pounding heart. Looking down at my hand, I traced a finger over it, still feeling the softness of holding his hand.

He makes me cum a million times a night and nothing. Nada. But he holds my hand and suddenly, I've been struck by Cupid.

I'm being so silly.

Leaning back on the couch, I waited for him. And my wait was definitely worth it when he opened the curtain and walked towards me with a frown on his face. The suit was tailormade for him, and the beige color brought out his tattoos, hair and his eyes.

"I don't like it, it's too bright," he grumbled, fixing the cuffs while I gaped at him.

"Shut up. You look handsome as hell." I stood up and fixed the collar of his shirt and took a step back to admire him. "You're dripping with rizz, Cillian. So much rizz." I fanned myself.

"Rizz? What the fuck does that mean?"

"It's like having a game, you know what I mean?" I tilted my head, but he looked grumpier than ever, which made me smile more. I was smiling so much that my cheeks were hurting.

"You and your Gen Z slang. Just say simple words. It's not that hard."

"Okay, Boomer. Sheesh." I picked the light pink suit and pushed it on his chest, "Now go try this on."

Cillian glared at me. "I don't want to play dress up right now."

"You are," I said, crossing my arms and for a flicker of moment, his eyes dipped down my neck to the cleavage of my blouse.

"What will I get in return?" he asked, his voice had gone deeper.

Uh-oh. He was using his seducing voice.

"W-what do you want?"

"Your soaked panties for starters," he said, opening his palm and continued, "Then I want you to spread your legs on the couch, hike your skirt up and touch yourself. If I'm playing dress up with you, then I want to have fun, too."

I glared at him. "You are unfair." Still, I hooked my fingers through the lace and let them pool around my sandal heels before picking them up and handing them to him.

Cillian smirked at the wet spot. Leaning closer, he kissed my cheek, "Your fingers better be dripping when I come out."

* * *

"I CAN'T WALK," I WHINED, SLOUCHING AND WANTING TO SIT. We were still in the mall, and I was tired. Not from shopping. Cillian had made me cum in his mouth wearing the light pink suit and then fucked me in the changing room, pinning me in the mirror and making me watch as we both came together.

My legs were still shaking from the morning workout and… the most recent workout.

"You should've worn sneakers." Cillian kept all the shopping bags on the bench and leaned down. He didn't care there were people around us as he picked up my feet and unbuckled my sandals. He glared at me. "You'll hurt your ankles wearing this shit. Come on, I'll get you a pair of running shoes."

"I don't want shoes."

He stood up and shrugged. "And I didn't want all these suits, shoes and watches. Which you bought for me without my permission."

Oh, so he was still mad about me paying for his clothes.

I wore the heels and followed him. "I'm your boss, so I can buy you clothes, okay? You already live at the manor and attend my classes. Might as well—"

"*Right.*" He gave me a dark look, and for a moment, I feared what he might do and say. "I'm going to buy you shoes and then we are going to every single shop in this mall, and I'm buying you everything I want. Car keys are with me, so you are not getting out of this."

Well, that is definitely the scariest threat if I have ever heard one.

Biting my cheek from smiling, I followed him. Because of his longer legs, his stride was long, too, but whenever he walked with me, he'd slow down so I didn't have to run behind him. It made me want to smile even harder.

Not good, Em. Not good.

I was falling for him.

Unknown

My hands clenched into a fist as I watched my little Emma getting scolded by the jerk. He was rude and mean to her. Looked scary too. With that ugly scar running across his lips.

"Sir, do you want something else?"

"No." I took the bottle of water and walked out of the food court, keeping my eyes on Emma. She had done her hair so well that day with a white bow pinned on the back of her head. Just a few more weeks when that hair is in my hands and I wake up to it.

Oh, I was getting too excited in public.

My smile dropped when her ugly-ass bodyguard held her waist and walked into another clothing store. But what was more horrifying was that she was smiling…

Oh, my poor little Emma. Faking her smiles in front of him.

I needed to save her soon.

And I knew a way to remind her that I was coming to protect her. Opening my phone, I checked the time and finalized my note, sending her a couple of pictures.

Unknown: *Don't worry about your ugly-ass bodyguard. I will take care of him soon enough. Our home is ready! I can't wait to have you here, love.*

39
IT'S OKAY

EMMA

My hands were shaking since morning. I had barely eaten my breakfast and forced myself to swallow a glass of orange juice. I almost shrieked when Summer hugged me from behind, her usual morning routine, telling me a terrible dad joke.

"Emma."

I clutched my skirt and looked at Mia sitting across me. The chair next to me screeched, and I held my breath when Summer sat down.

"Are you okay?" she asked, concern lacing her voice.

I shook my head and pushed my plate away. "I am jumpy and sc—nothing." They didn't know about the stalker, and I didn't want them to worry. If I told Mia, James would know, and that idiot in love would arrange for top security to be everywhere, and Mia would be stuck with a bodyguard as well.

"Oh, come on, you were about to say it," Summer said, her shoulder bumping against mine. "Finish the sentence."

I looked around to find a certain tall, tattooed, and bossy

bodyguard. He was easily noticeable amongst everyone leaning on the wall while raising his brow at me.

I faced my friends and said, "It's a girls' night today. We will have a sleepover at my house, and I'll tell you why I'm so sc—*jumpy*."

They weren't convinced but agreed to meet me at my house.

When I was walking to my next class after the lunch, Cillian stopped me with his hand on my elbow. I followed him when he nodded at the nearby classroom.

"You're not okay, Emma. Let's go home."

I pursed my lips and clenched my books. "I don't want him to win and think that I'm scared of him."

He held my shoulders, worry evident on his face. "This person is delusional who wants to kidnap you and keep you with him," he said, his voice harsh. "He is not fooling around and we both saw what he did to Lincoln."

I swallowed the lump in my throat. A trickle of fear rolled over my spine. "I… I hated him, but I didn't want him to die," I whispered, a tear sliding down my eyes and blurring my vision.

"I know, Doll." Cillian pulled me into his chest and hugged me closer. "I'm afraid that he knows everything about you."

And I'm afraid that he'd do something to you like he did to Lincoln.

That morning, I had woken up to a strange text and puked bile into the toilet while Cillian held my hair. He had heard my scream, helped me, and read the text with pictures of Lincoln tied up, beaten up and all bloody. With a slit throat.

That wasn't the worst part. He had pictures of me and Cillian together at the sex club *after* Cillian had closed the curtains. Thankfully, Cillian's body was covering my naked bits, but he was present and took those pictures. Along with the day at the mall. With Cillian holding my waist and shopping bags on the other arm.

He was fucking everywhere.

"What do I do?" I pulled away, angry that I was letting myself be scared by that piece of shit who had nothing to do but prey on me. "I want it to end!"

"I know, Emma. You don't have to do anything. Just focus on your life and studies, I'll—"

"I can't focus. I'm scared that he's here listening to us talk and taking creepy pictures." My throat burned, and I wanted to snuggle Cillian's chest because I knew he'd protect me. Keep me safe.

His hands caressed my back and wiped my tears. "I won't let him hurt you, Doll. If you remain unbothered or even pretend to, we can find out who he is and arrest him. We are ahead of him."

I clenched my jaw, sniffling as the tears stopped. "Are we? Then why did Lincoln…"

"I don't know. But that means he doesn't want you to be harmed by anyone else."

"But him."

"He won't," he sighed, running a hand through his palm. "We will find him. And until we do, I'm staying with you."

I gazed at his obsidian eyes and nodded. "Okay." Cillian would protect me. Keep me safe. "Okay," I repeated, and hugged the books to myself.

"After school, I want you to meet someone."

I nodded at him and we left the empty classroom. The bell rang, and I hurried to my next class. I was not strong, but I was learning how to defend myself. Cillian was teaching me all the ways I could defend myself lest anyone attacks me, and I was not a helpless girl anymore. I could run, but I could also hurt someone if I had to protect myself.

Taking a deep breath, I raised my chin and entered the biology class.

* * *

"Why are we at your house?" I asked Cillian as he stopped the car. "Do you want to get something?"

"No, I want you to meet my boss."

"Your boss?" I was surprised, following him through the footpath that I had taken for so many years. I spent most of my time at Caleb's house since my mom didn't want any boys in my room. We'd spend time together at his. And yet, I never once met Cillian, just heard of him in little bits and pieces. He was never at home since his wife, Olivia, passed away.

Maybe everyone had their own ways to go through their grief.

"She's not here yet," Cillian said.

"She?" I removed my shoes and wore slippers, walking from the hallway to the kitchen. He offered me water, but I didn't drink it.

"Yes, she. Elena is quicker and faster than me. Can easily take down four of me if we were to ever fight." He spoke of her with respect and awe. It made me happy and... jealous.

I crossed my arms and smiled at baby Caleb's picture. His cheeks were big like apples. "Where is he?"

Cillian sighed. "God knows. He has been waking up early and coming back home late. I wonder what he thinks of all of this."

"What? Us?" I pointed at the space between us.

"He doesn't know about our relationship, Doll," he shook his head. "He'll flip if he did. He knows that someone is stalking you, so that's why he's being so attached at school."

"I figured." I bit my lip. "I just..." Pausing, I shook my head.

"What is it?"

Peering up at him, I leaned on the kitchen island and said, "I just wish he had told me about his sexuality."

"Mhmm." Cillian hummed, crossing his arms, letting me to continue.

I fiddled with my fingers. "I get it he likes everyone, but if he had just talked to me about it, we would have broken up and we'd still be good friends."

"Right."

"I mean, was it so hard to tell your friend-slash-girlfriend that you like boys, girls and everyone, despite their gender?!" I raised my hands and sighed. "I don't mind him kissing boys, but it was a shock to see him kissing Aaron—out of all the guys, on my mom's funeral. Like come on. It made me feel so terrible."

When Cillian didn't offer another monotonous reply, I looked up from my hands to find him shocked. His cheeks were pink and his eyes were wide.

"Why do you look so surprised—wait, he didn't tell you!?" I cupped my mouth, wincing internally.

"He is gay?" he muttered to himself.

I blinked at him and shook my head. "Caleb is pansexual, Cillian. He likes everyone."

"Huh." He scratched his neck and pursed his lips. "He never talked to me about it. Or why you two broke up."

I swallowed and nodded.

"I'm sorry, Emma," he whispered, his eyes soft. "He shouldn't have kissed that boy at your mom's funeral. He should have talked to you, and I'm sorry I couldn't teach him better."

"Please, he is nineteen." I rolled my eyes. "You need to stop apologizing for his actions. Yes, what he did was extremely shitty, but it hurt more that he didn't tell me about his feelings. Anyway, I got to sleep with you because of that."

Cillian raised his brows and tilted his head, "I was your rebound because my son cheated on you with a guy?"

"Of course you were. My ex's hot dad was my rebound." I winked at him.

He let out a soft laugh that made me feel giddy. "That's good to know, Doll."

I bit my lip from laughing and looked around the house. "Do you mind if I go upstairs?"

"We don't have anything upstairs but rooms..."

"You have pictures," I said and climbed the stairs. If I had never seen his house before, I would guess it belonged to Cillian in a second because his taste was very minimalistic yet immaculate. And even then, his home felt cozy with warm, soft lights and lots of picture frames on the walls of the hallway.

"Holy shit!" I neared one photo frame and ogled the man in a dark leather jacket, fitted pants and shoulder length black hair with lots of tattoos and—*fuck me*, a lip piercing. "Was that you?"

"I forgot it was here," he said casually, examining the picture of his young self. "I was a rebel when I was young."

"You look so hot," I breathed and stared at his lips. "You don't have that scar here. Was it because of the lip piercing?"

"Not from the piercing. No." He chuckled and shook his head, "I'll tell you someday, Doll."

"Will you wear a leather jacket for me?" I asked, batting my lashes.

He flicked my forehead without giving me an answer.

Party-pooper. I looked at the other picture and paused.

"She is beautiful," I muttered, seeing Olivia's face holding baby Caleb in her arms. She was American, with dark brown hair and darker eyes. Her cheeks were rosy pink, and a diamond glinted on her left hand.

"She was," Cillian agreed, his voice soft. I glanced at him

and he was watching her with a sad smile. "She loved Caleb more than me. She would have known what to do and talk to him while I can barely hold a minute of conversation with him."

"Why did you avoid him after she…" I shook my head. "Caleb used to vent about you. I'm sorry. I'm being nosy."

"No. It's okay." He took a deep breath and faced me. "I couldn't see his face without remembering her. And how I failed as a husband and a father."

I listened to him, his eyes drifting past my shoulder as he continued. "Olivia had terrible postpartum depression. I did everything I could to help her. Therapists. Medicines. Staying with her for hours while taking care of Caleb. He was a very naughty kid. Then one day…"

He took a deep breath and swallowed. "It was her birthday. I had to leave early in the morning because of a job and wrote a note that I'd be back in an hour. One hour turned into two, then three. I called Sean, my friend, and told him to keep an eye on Caleb since I had promised to bring a huge cake."

His eyes were gleaming. "I bought the cake, went home. I couldn't find her. She was still in bed. I remembered sighing in relief and went to surprise her with flowers and cake." His jaw clenched, and he looked up at the ceiling. "She had taken sleeping pills the night before without my notice and she was… but I didn't notice because I had to rush to work."

My eyes burned, and I reached out to hold his forearm. "I didn't know…"

"I called emergency. Gave her CPR, but it didn't work. She went to bed that night, kissed me on my cheek and never woke up." I wiped my tears when he looked at me. "Caleb hates me because I didn't care to look after him as a parent, as his father, when she passed away. My mom and Sean looked after him while I was away for work, making excuses that I needed to earn more so I could put him in a good school. And now... it's too late."

"It's not," I disagreed, shaking my head. "It's not too late. You are just scared. But he is your son, and he misses you. I know he does because..." I took a deep breath and met his eyes, "I hated my mom. I still do. She was a bully and a terrible mother with no maternal instinct. But... if I got a chance to talk to her about why she hated me so much and still left me with everything, I would take it in a heartbeat. So, talk to Caleb. He is stubborn, but he doesn't hate you. He is just confused."

Tears slid down his face and I tipped on my toes to wipe them away. "Emma—"

"It's okay. You don't have to say anything." I pulled him into a hug and sighed when he squeezed me.

I snuggled deeper into his arms with one thought ringing in my head. *This was going to hurt a lot when it ends.*

40

NOT AN ACCIDENT

CILLIAN

My arms tightened around her body, breathing in her warm vanilla scent. "Emma, I need to ask you about something," I whispered, pulling away to look at her face.

Her eyes were gleaming with tears but she nodded, wanting for me to continue.

"That night," I started, running the pad of my thumb over her jaw, "When we slept together in my suite, I came back because I couldn't find my wedding ring."

Her expression remained passive.

"I wanted to tell you that I was not having an affair and that Olivia is—"

"Shh, I know, Cillian." She offered me a small smile. "I was pretty mad when I found it, but then the drug made me unconscious. I'm sorry I don't have it with me anymore."

I heard the door open downstairs and knew she had arrived. "She's here." I pulled away, squeezing Emma's hand.

"She knows the passcode of your house?" she asked, following me downstairs.

I looked over my shoulder and shrugged. "I trust her."

"And you should." I smiled seeing Elena in my house. She was tall, wearing her long blond hair in a ponytail, shirt, and pants. No one would guess that she was a Princess, Sheikha of Azmia, or my boss. Her sharp green eyes softened as they fell on me and I went to hug her, "You look bigger than the last time I saw you, Cillian."

"You saw me last month on a video meeting, Elena," I deadpanned and introduced her. "Emma, this is Elena, my boss, and Elena, this is Emma."

Emma's chin was high, and she did a little nod at her. I frowned at her silence—

"Hello, hello, hello." My body froze hearing his voice as he strolled in, waving at me, "It's so nice of you to invite me too, Candy."

"Zayed, you know his name is Cillian," Elena rubbed her forehead.

Zayed Al-Fasih was the Sheikh of Azmia, one of the richest and most powerful Mid-Eastern countries, and he was, unfortunately, Elena's husband. Definitely worse than her during a fight, but her total opposite. If Elena was ice, then he was fire. She always complained why she married him despite being childhood friends to lovers turned enemies to lovers (it's complicated), but her voice was soft whenever she talked about him.

And even now, I didn't miss the small glare he shot my way, as if he didn't want anyone near his wife. "You have a great house, Cillian... and you, little doll, must be Emma!"

Emma scowled at him and looked at Elena. "Don't tell me he's your husband."

"Indeed, I am, darling." Zayed winked at her, a dimple poking his annoying cheek as he grinned. "If you were older and had a kink of stabbing me, then I'd have convinced myself to marry you."

Emma raked her eyes over him, and I clenched my hand into a fist. Thankfully, she rolled her eyes and muttered, *"Ew."*

"Ouch!" Zayed covered his heart and looked at us. "She can definitely stab people with that attitude. I think I lost twenty years of my age."

"Behave. Please," Elena said, walking past him, and I followed her, ignoring the Sheikh. I had heard about him, how he helped Elena saving every royal and their friends and family all those years ago when their Golden Palace fell. Even though he seemed goofy and a downright prick in the ass, he was wicked.

"So, let's start from the beginning," I said once all of us were settled around the living room, all my notes scattered on the coffee table. Emma was sitting beside Elena on the couch, Zayed on the chair while I sat across him, in a similar chair. The air was tense because there were pictures of Lincoln's bloody face glaring at all of us.

"You received a message on the day of the funeral," Elena said, flicking her eyes from Emma to me. "And you were with her?"

I nodded. "I told her someone was watching her at the bar. I thought little of it back then, but I think it was him."

Zayed whistled, startling all of us, and straightened up, narrowing his gaze at Emma. "How many exes do you have, kitten?"

"Don't call her that," I snapped.

She answered, "Just one. Caleb. And he wouldn't stalk me."

Zayed chuckled, "Maybe you're right. How about girl-friends?"

I frowned. Mia and Summer would never. Beating up Lincoln would take a lot of manpower, and even though I didn't doubt their strength, they weren't the type to hurt someone for their own benefit.

"I don't think it's a woman. Or women," Elena corrected, showing him the picture of the ruined panties of Emma. I clenched my jaw when Emma looked away.

"This is definitely a sicko," Zayed said, and grinned up at his wife. "I love it."

"If you will not take this matter seriously, leave my house," I said calmly, hoping I could punch him. "You are scaring Emma and you are not helping. I don't care if you are a rich Sheikh. You are not welcome here if you keep—"

"I'd really think about what you are going to say next, Cillian," Zayed said, his demeanor changing as he faced me, a small evil smile playing on his lips. There it was. "I don't want Elena here as much as you don't want Emma to be in this situation. I don't care who gets hurt as long she is safe—"

"Zayed—"

"I'm not done, little witch." He shot a look at Elena and continued, "I'll help you solve this shit, and then we will leave this little town. My wife has already fought enough battles and frankly, I'm tired of killing people."

It was a warning. If someone dares to harm Elena, he was going feral.

None of us said anything. Even Emma's eyes were wide as she stared at Zayed. Elena rolled her eyes and mumbled, 'Dramatic ass', underneath her breath.

"Now, I know it's someone who knows her since she was a kid. Her friend or someone older. My guess was her brother, Damon, but he was at the manor when you met Emma at the bar while the supposed stalker watched her."

"Damon is an asshole, but he wouldn't!" Emma defended and picked up the list of people who had attended the funeral. "Are we sure it's someone who didn't attend the funeral?"

Elena and I agreed, while Zayed didn't.

"He could've attended the funeral and left early—kitten, did you see someone when you rushed out of the house?"

I rolled my eyes at her nickname.

"I don't remember. I was in a rush."

"Did you help a kid, a strange boy, or an old man?" he asked.

"What kind of question is that?" Elena asked, voicing my thoughts.

Zayed looked at her and tapped at the print of all the messages Emma had received. "He is delusional. Stalkers usually have a mental illness that stops them from being social and creates a different world in their own head. She could've helped a kid with an injury and given him a bandage or helped a man cross a road and if they're sick enough, they'd think that Emma loved them and decided to stalk her. Make her feel safe, protect her, and bring the two of them together."

"Is that why he said 'our home'?" Emma whispered.

"Yes. And he killed Lincoln because he…" Zayed paused, looking at Elena. He cleared his throat and softened his voice. "I think he knew what happened and hurt him to protect you."

"But that happened years ago," her voice was harsh, as she couldn't believe it.

I wanted to take her in my lap and cocoon her in my arms. But I stayed put, clenching my hands in fists.

"It did," Elena said, placing her hand on hers. "But he is not thinking rationally or even thinking. He wants you. He has been keeping an eye on you. Sent you gifts, messages and killed someone. He is even more dangerous than we thought."

"What do I do?"

"For now, nothing," Elena said and looked at me. "Cillian will keep you safe. But we can't bide time to see what he'd do next. I will have my entire team to start looking for him. Starting with everyone on your contact list and... your mom's death."

"What about it?" Emma's voice turned pensive, and I straightened up. Her mom was a very sensitive topic. I didn't want them to push her too much that she didn't open up.

Elena and Zayed shared a knowing look before she said, "I don't think it was an accident, Emma."

41
I'M GOING HOME

EMMA

I frowned. Her green eyes were sharp when she told me that my mom was killed. Murdered.

"But it was a stupid plane crash."

"And how often do private planes of huge celebrities crash, kitten?" Zayed asked, his chocolate brown eyes pinned on me.

I shook my head, "No. She couldn't have been murdered. I'm sure—"

"There's a chance that she was."

"Autopsy?" Cillian asked Elena.

She pursed her lips and shook her head. "It seemed a fake, but they cremated her after the funeral ceremony so we can't prove it."

"Who could've killed her?" I asked, looking up from my lap to all of them. Cillian's face was hard to read as always, but Zayed, slowly rubbing his lips, looked like there was something churning in his head.

"My bet is on the stalker… but why would he kill her mother?" He seemed like he was talking to himself.

"Emma, did you know if you were going to inherit everything?" Elena asked me, holding out a few different papers in her hand. "Rich people and royals always die because of their greed and inheritance. Never from weapons."

"I didn't know until Lincoln announced it."

"If the stalker knew Emma since she was a kid, he must have known Dorothy," Cillian said, tilting his head at the picture of Lincoln. I couldn't stomach it, so I looked away. "What if *he* knew she was going to inherit everything?"

"Then why stalk her if he could just kill her?" Zayed asked and leaned back in the chair. He didn't seem like an idiot at all like I thought he was. Sure, he was rich and handsome and maybe a little charming, but he didn't have tattoos or piercings—*shut up. Focus, brain.* "If I was a stalker, I would just drug her and keep her. No offence, kitten."

"None taken." I cleared my throat.

"But if I knew her since the beginning and found out she will inherit everything and I loved her..." Cillian muttered, staring at me. I had the sudden urge to hide my face so they wouldn't see me get so flustered. "I'd ask her mom for marriage and because I'm delusional, I would think she would agree and give me her blessings. Instead—"

"My mom didn't agree and threatened him?" I finished his sentence.

Elena continued, "That is a possibility. And then the stalker got mad, he murdered her, made it look like a plane crash and then it... *wait*. He sent her the text after he was done sneaking into her bedroom and placing the gifts. So he saw her with you, got jealous and went to her room."

"No," Cillian shook her head. "He stayed at the club. He drugged her, planned to kidnap her. She could barely move when I found her."

I remembered it vividly and straightened up. "I think... do we have surveillance for your suite?"

"I do. It is necessary for safety," Cillian said, standing up. I remembered that there were cameras in the private suite if the member wanted to either watch it later or for protecting the submissive. I didn't think Cillian had agreed for the cameras, but it made me feel better.

We watched the entire clip on the television and I held my breath when it ended.

"I think we are all thinking the same thing," Zayed said when no one said anything. "It was the man carrying that champagne."

Cillian was holding his shaking head, his elbows on his knees and hiding his expression. "I watched him walk away after drugging her. He was right there…"

I bit my lip and shook out my nerves. "So, he took my purse but left my phone."

Elena sighed and leaned back on the couch. "He was definitely planning to take more than the purse, but he didn't think Cillian would walk in the room."

He stood up and pulled out his phone, looking anywhere but me. "I'll tell your brother and ask him about the man. We can't see his face, but if someone remembers him from the club, we can have a sketch."

"Keep it low. We don't want him to know we are onto him," Elena suggested before Cillian walked into the kitchen to call my brother.

"I think he already knows, little witch," Zayed commented and glanced at me. "He threatened Cillian in the last text. He knew he was her bodyguard, not her boyfriend. The only reason you received those texts and gifts that night is because of Cillian. You both got along, and it pissed him off that there was someone in his way. If I was a delusional weirdo, that's what I'd think."

"You already are," Elena answered.

He gave her an air kiss. "Too bad you love me."

If Zayed was right, then Cillian was in danger. More than

I was. The creep already killed Lincoln after beating him up, and now he was spying on my relationship with Cillian and threatening him. What if he tries to hurt Cillian? And succeeds? What would I do then?

The trill of my phone snapped me out of my thoughts, and I excused myself from the bickering royal couple. "Hello?"

"Mrs. Karen said you haven't arrived home yet," Summer said in a singsong voice, "Where are you, Em? Are you eating delicious sushi without your best friend...? Hm?"

"Oh, shoot." I bit my lip and looked at the coffee table. "I... I'm out. I'll be back soon!"

"Don't tell me she forgot," I heard Mia's muffled voice before Summer spoke again, "Listen, if you are busy banging your hot bodyguard then say, yes daddy, and I'll end the—"

"Summer. I'll be back soon." I cut the call, my cheeks red.

"What did Damon say?" I asked Cillian who was checking his phone in the kitchen.

He pocketed it and looked at me. His face was stony. "I'll send a few investigators in the early morning once the club closes, so he'll send me any updates if they find something. Who was that?"

"Summer and Mia. I invited them for a sleepover." I leaned on the island and pursing my lips, I said, "I thought I could tell them about the whole stalker thing—"

"No. You're not."

He was already walking out of the kitchen.

"But they are my friends! They need to know—"

Cillian turned back, looming over me like a dark shadow, and glared at me. "No, they fucking don't. You can barely defend yourself and you want to tell your friends about a dangerous stalker who has already killed a man twice as big as you. You will only talk them into danger."

"I won't let anything happen to them," I said, my hands clenching into a fist.

"How? By throwing a punch?" Cillian leaned closer. "You are already a danger to them by being close. You should be glad I haven't locked you up in your room a—"

"*Cillian*." I didn't look away from his burning eyes when Elena said, "That's enough."

"I'm going home," I said, keeping my voice soft, and took a step back. "Once you untwist your fucking panties, you can apologize for being such an asshole."

I walked past him, bumping into his shoulder and keeping my chin high even though it wobbled. I took my backpack and looked at Zayed. "You."

He raised his brow. "Me?"

"Drop me home."

Zayed grinned, a dimple poking his cheek. "What will I get, kitten?"

I glared at him. "Getting to spend time with my charming personality. And maybe sushi if you are good."

"Yes, ma'am. Lets go!" I was surprised when he took my backpack and before we walked out of Cillian's house, he yelled back, "Babe, I'm dropping the kid at home. Don't wait up for me!"

Despite everything that had happened in the kitchen a few minutes ago, I had to stifle my grin when Elena yelled back, 'Go away!' And his grin widened.

"She loves me."

I nodded when he opened the passenger door for me. "She does."

42
I LIKE HIM

EMMA

It was yet another surprise that Zayed stayed quiet while driving. Their car was expensive without a logo and just a golden crest of Azmia country in the front.

"Do you think I should tell my friends? About... everything?" I asked, not knowing if I was really stupid or just brainless to ask his advice. The guy I met a few hours ago.

He glanced at me and let out a small laugh. "You are asking the wrong person, kitten."

"Thought so." I looked out of the window.

"But if you want my opinion, then... go ahead, tell them. They will be hurt if you don't tell them and something happens to you. But they will be disappointed that you were going through so much and didn't seek their support."

I never thought about that. How it would feel if Mia or Summer were in my shoes and never told me they were getting stalked? I'd be furious and feel guilty that my best friends were going through it all alone.

"Wow," I said, shaking my head at him. "You're smart."

"I'm very smart, kitten. I pretend to be a fool, so no one takes me seriously," he winked at me and I believed him. He was a lot more than what he showed to the world. His charming, foolish, golden-retriever type energy was just a front so people can let loose around him.

"So... how did you end up with Elena? She seems very capable, clever and independent."

"I agree. She doesn't need anyone, least of all a man, to support her," he talked about her with an awe in his voice. He was clearly whipped by that woman. "I still don't know why she married me. She was betrothed to someone else."

"Betrothed? It's twenty-first century." I made a face, and he laughed.

"Yes, she's a royal princess."

"Then? What did you do? Don't tell me you killed him."

"No, I did worse." His eyes twinkled with mischief. "I seduced him."

I gaped, "No way!"

"Yes way," he nodded, proud of himself. "I would have done much more—Samir is pretty handsome—but Elena cockblocked us."

"Oh, my..." I cupped my mouth. The tea was bubbling hot. And spicy.

"And yet she loves me even after I betrayed her so many times."

"You betrayed her? How?"

Zayed flickered his eyes at me, "It's a long gory story."

"More gory than what I've been through?"

"*Definitely*. There were a few instances of stabbing as well. Chains and knives were also included. A tiger, too."

I pouted.

"Enough about me. Tell me about Cillian." He raised his brow and took a turn. We were close to home. "Why do you like him?"

"Is it that obvious?"

"Yes, it is. You are turning red like a strawberry."

"He was the first person who didn't treat me like a fragile little doll after my mother's death. Everyone kept saying they were sorry, or poor thing, treating me like a kid."

"You are nineteen," Zayed reminded me.

"But I'm not a kid. I could handle it. I just needed someone to tell me that it'd be okay, you know? And he did. I mean, he didn't tell me that but—"

"He made you forget about the pain. I get it, kitten."

"Even if he is an asshole, I still like him," I mumbled, tucking my hair behind my ear.

"I don't think he was an asshole." His brown eyes were dark when they slid to me. "If someone threatened my Elena, I'd chain her up in my castle and take care of the person before letting her out."

I stared wide eyed at him.

"But... I enjoy having my cock attached to my gorgeous body so I wouldn't exactly chain her up, still, I wouldn't let her fight alone."

I swallowed the lump in my throat and asked, "Aren't you afraid?"

"Afraid of?"

"What if you die?"

He smiled when he looked at me. "You're overthinking, kitten. Even now, I can't bear to be away from her. Of course I'm afraid that I'll lose her. That's why I'd rather die protecting her than live without her."

I blinked at him. "That was sad... and romantic."

"Kids these days," he muttered underneath his breath.

"What? It is awfully sad, but so romantic!"

"That's what sells, right?" He chuckled and glanced at me.

"Maybe it—*Zayed, watch out!*" I screamed, but it was too late. The headlights of the car were off and we slammed straight into it.

After an ear-piercing ringing, everything went dark.

PART IV

"Sit on my fucking face and suffocate me with your cunt."

43
MY FAULT

EMMA

My head hammered as I struggled to push my heavy lids open. There was a constant ringing in my ears and my face felt warm. Something burning made me cough, and I forced my eyes to blink.

I could see shattered glass and the tight belt around me, holding me to the seat. I looked beside me and let out a whimper. Zayed was bleeding from the temple and his eyes were closed. The car was burning. We had to get out.

"Z-Zayed," I coughed out. I winced, pushing the button to unlock my seatbelt and fell on the ground. My legs were bleeding, but I could move despite the soreness in my body. I did not know what happened, but I was scared and needed Zayed to wake up.

"Zayed, wake up!" I tried to yell, but my voice was hoarse. Leaning up, I undid his seatbelt, his unconscious body falling on the roof of the car. I needed to get him out.

Crawling out of the small window, I stood up on my shaky legs and held his shoulders. "Zayed, wake up, please," I gasped out, dragging his heavy body. I kept pulling, using all my strength. Elena will kill me if anything happened to him.

Oh god, he was a royal. So not just Elena, but entire Azmia would kill me.

"Elena?" he sputtered, blinking his eyes open.

"Finally!" I kept dragging, and he was almost out of the car. "You need to wake up and call—"

"Now, that's alright, little Emma."

I froze hearing another person and turned around. My mouth parted into a scream, but the man in the black ski mask rushed closer and put a cloth on my mouth and nose, forcing me to inhale the burning chemical.

Groaning, I squirmed in his tight hold while he tried to quiet me. I tried to kick him, but my legs were still shaky from the accident. My head swirled, and I dug my nails into his forearms and tried to scratch him anywhere I could. Clawing his neck, his face, I heard a satisfying scream when he pulled back.

I fell on the ground, coughing as tears slid out of my eyes, and held a shard of glass when he tried to come closer.

"Stop fighting, little Emma, we are going home," he cooed, and I couldn't see his eyes through the tears and slashed at him.

"G-go away!" I tried to shout, wishing Cillian was there.

The smell of metal hung in the air and I noticed that the fire was slowly licking away at the car, its scorching heat making me sweat.

A yelp of pain coming from the man made me snap my eyes at Zayed. He was standing—no, barely standing and holding a dagger-like knife in his hand against the man who was possibly my stalker. My vision was getting hazy, my limbs shaking when I tried to stand up.

"I'm protecting you, little Emma!" the man yelled, pulling out a little pocket knife. It made Zayed grin, his lips bloody. It made me shudder to see him like that. "Don't worry, I'll take care of him."

How dare he call me little. Hurting me for months, the mental toll of looking out of the windows and closed curtains, the distressing feeling of always being watched just because he had some sick fantasy of me in his rotten head.

I tightened the broken glass in my hand, not caring that it cut my skin made me bleed.

I hated him. He had made my life a living hell, and I hated him for it. Killing my mother, my self-esteem, and making me live with fear day and night.

"Stop speaking to her, you delusional fuck," Zayed wavered, but swung his arm out when the stalker tried to kick his leg.

They both fell. I didn't care what happened to me as I let out a cry and forced the shard of glass onto him. He turned away, but I felt it gave way and sink into his skin when he yelled, pushing me off him with a tug on my hair.

"Emma, kitten, come on," Zayed held my shoulders and dragged me away, lifting me up as the car burned, and I cried out.

"Let me kill him! Let me!" Even though I tried to scream, my voice was small, and my head was throbbing. Maybe I had inhaled enough chemical that it was making me unconscious.

"Sh, it's okay. Calm down."

Those were the last words I heard before darkness took me again.

Cillian

I walked the same hallway again and again. Pacing from one end to another. My black polished shoes—the ones she bought for me a week ago—padded against the marble white floor. The bright white lights were adding to the headache that the grim scent of medicine, cleaner and scrubs were giving me.

"Will she be okay?" Mia asked for the umpteenth time, sitting beside Summer, whose knees couldn't stop shaking.

"The doctor will let us know soon, Princess," James, her rich old boyfriend, said, then looked at me. "But it won't help if you keep pacing like that."

I shot him a glare, his piercing blue eyes matching it as he crossed his arms. "Where were you, anyway? You are her bodyguard, aren't you?" he asked, tilting his head. "Why was she alone with a Sheikh of Azmia out of all people?"

"It's none of your business," I gritted out of my teeth and kept pacing, raking a hand through my hair.

The call from Zayed had been devastating, and I was already driving when Elena ended the call. Seeing Emma unconscious and hurt had made my heart stop until Zayed promised that she was breathing and well, just fainted. I had stayed in the back seat, holding her while Elena drove us to the nearest hospital.

My hands were red even though I had scrubbed off all the blood. Her blood. That was still clinging to my clothes.

What have I done?

"Security from Azmia will arrive soon," Elena said, her green eyes weary as she looked at Emma's friends and pulled me aside. "Her brother?"

"On his way." I had to ask her. "Will they find him?"

She shook her head, pinching the bridge of her nose. "Zayed cut his stomach and Emma stabbed his thigh with a piece of glass. But he still escaped."

"*Fuck.*" I ran a hand across my face and sighed, "She shouldn't have to stab someone... it's my fault."

"We will talk about the blame later. For now, stay calm."

"I can't stay calm, Elena. This is the first time someone got hurt—"

Her eyes sharpened, "My husband is lying on a hospital bed. Don't you think I want to maul and skin that piece of shit alive? Because trust me, I want to hurt him. More than you do. But right now, the only thing we have in our control is our patience." Everyone was staring at her, nurses, doctors, Mia, Summer—and a narrowed but calculating gaze from James. She lowered her voice and said, "Focus on Emma. Tell her friends the truth and no one else."

"I will." I swallowed the lump in my throat, my jaw clenching. "I have to."

"The crash will be reported everywhere."

"Why?" I gaped at her.

"*Zayed*. He is a Sheikh, and I don't think Zain or Khalid would listen to me on this. The stalker, whoever he is, has made a huge mistake trying to make Azmia his enemy." She rubbed her forehead, and we both leaned on the wall. "Cops will track him and maybe even CBI will try to find out if he went to any of the nearest hospitals."

"But this would mean Emma will have more eyes on her than ever before."

"Yes. Unfortunately." She looked at me, her face stern. "That's why I hired you. To look after her. Don't disappoint me."

"Yes, ma'am."

44

A FAVOR

EMMA

I woke up to a brooding brother, worried friends, and a cold Cillian standing in the corner of the hospital room.

"Why didn't you text me that you met Zayed Al Fasih? Do you know he has met the Queen?" Summer asked, her brows furrowed as she looked over at me.

"Summer," Mia elbowed her and turned to me. "She means to say that we were worried when we heard the news about this... and found that you were in a car with the Sheikh of Azmia."

"He was dropping me off," I mumbled, a dull ache forming in my head.

"What was that?" Summer asked, leaning closer.

"Girls," Damon said, shooting my friends a look. "Do you mind if I talk to my sister? Alone?"

Mia squeezed my left hand and whispered, "We are outside."

"Cillian, don't let Damon scold our friend again," Summer said to Cillian, shooting daggers at my brother before leaving the room. It would have been comical if I wasn't strapped with an IV on a hospital bed.

"How are you feeling?" Damon asked, not even meeting my eyes.

I scoffed, but it hurt my lungs, making me wince. Out of the corner of my eyes, I saw Cillian take a step and retreat when I straightened up. "I'm great. As you can see."

"Cillian," Damon looked at him. "Give us a few minutes."

He stared at him for a few moments. It was a weird man-to-man telepathic connection, and then he walked out of the room without saying a word or looking at me.

Jesus, did I look that horrible?

"I'm sorry."

My eyes widened when I looked at my brother. His gray eyes were on me and without the small glimmer of sadness in them, he looked cold as ice. "You're what?"

"I..." He took a sharp breath and looked at me. "I'm sorry."

"For?"

"For these past few months. No... not just months. For everything."

I swallowed, but my mouth was dry. I turned to pick up a glass of water and winced at the sudden burst of pain from my legs and right hand. Damon stood up, poured me water, and handed the glass to me.

"Doctor said you're fine. Your hand will heal in a few days, and you have a few bruises on your legs from the window, but they will also heal."

"Okay." I emptied the glass of water, licking my lips, and kept it on the nightstand. Tension and an air of confusion hovered between us, our silence stretching.

"What is everything?"

"Hm?" He raised his head to look at me once again.

I repeated. "What 'everything' are you apologizing for?"

"Do I have to say it?"

I glared at him. "Yes, you fucking do."

"*Emma.*"

"Don't you dare *Emma* me right now," I pursed my lips, my headache getting worse, and took a deep breath. "I have had enough, okay? I'm tired of your constant bullying and scolding and do this, do that, you're young, you're an adult and whatnot. I'm tired. So please leave."

"Look, I was stupid. I was an arrogant idiot who was angry when our parents split up," Damon said, meeting my eyes. "I was a kid and blamed it on you. I grew up and kept blaming it on you because at least mother gave you attention. Dad left me on my own—kicked me out and told me to make my own life. I didn't..." He took a deep breath and looked down. "I never thought that you were hurting, too. I stopped caring and—I'm sorry, Emma. For not being there when you needed me and for being a terrible brother."

My lips parted, but I couldn't say anything. I watched him with gleaming eyes as he raked his hand over his dirty blond hair and stood up. "Even now. I can't protect you from a fucking stalker."

"Damon..." I bit my lip. "If you want me to forgive you, you have to do something."

His stormy gray eyes were clear for the first time in many years. It reminded me of the brother I had who'd play hide and seek with me and stick gum in my hair. "Anything," he said, his hands clenched at his sides.

Taking a deep breath, I said, "I want you to take over the makeup business. I still have school to finish and need to focus on my studies. Maybe I can help more once I've graduated, but for now, I don't think I can handle both responsibilities. Do you think you could do that?"

His eyes widened, taking in what I had just said. Damon nodded, "Absolutely. I don't know much about cosmetics, but

I do know how to run a business." He sat on the edge of the bed to discuss the plan in a bit more detail.

I could feel him relaxing and the bond between us restoring as we spoke.

* * *

IT HAD BEEN TWO DAYS SINCE THE ACCIDENT AND CILLIAN WAS acting weird. He wouldn't look at me for over five seconds (yes, I counted) and answered one-word replies in a monotonous voice. He was acting like a wall of brick and kept his face poker whenever I was around, despite catching him smiling at one of Zayed's lame jokes.

"When can I go to school?" I asked Mrs. Karen when she helped me put on the bandage on my right palm. The doctor had discharged me and Zayed since neither of us had any serious injuries. Zayed was living with Elena in one of their penthouses and they both had strict securities with over twenty guards surrounding them since the accident.

I felt bad that he got hurt because of me, but he said, and I quote, *"It felt good to use the dagger after so long."* Yep. He was still a weirdo.

"Not for a week at least, Emma," Mrs. Karen replied, frowning at the bandage and slowly patted my other hand. She had wrinkles around her eyes, and her hair was completely gray. "Why do people keep hurting you, child?"

"What do you mean?" I raised my chin and waved my injured hand around. "This is a battle scar, not an injury."

"Foolish girl," she said playfully and stood up from my bed. "Go to sleep. Call if you need help."

"I won't. I'm a big girl now."

"Sure you are."

I narrowed my eyes at her and shook my head. I wondered what my mother would think of the scar on my palm. She'd probably book an appointment with an esthetician to help me heal the scar faster.

Tracing my finger over the minor cuts on my legs, I drifted back to the time when the stalker had attacked me and Zayed. He rammed his car into ours, tried to kidnap me, hurt Zayed and still ran away with a wounded thigh.

His face was covered, but I had seen his eyes. Heard his voice and knew his body build. Tall, lean, with muscles and a groggy voice. As if he wasn't used to speaking. Did I know someone like that?

He had hurt Zayed… what if it was Cillian instead of him? What if he had a gun?

My skin crawled with fear and uncertainty. I didn't want anything to happen to him…

Shaking my head, I stood up from the bed and patted down my hair. Straightening the night dress I had worn to bed, I took a deep breath and walked out of the bedroom. His room was closest to mine, just six paces away.

"D-don't!"

My body froze, hearing the low groan from inside his room. A sob. "Please don't!" Another sob. My heart stuttered hearing breathless cries. Was he…?

I knocked on the door. "Cillian? Can I come in?"

Nothing.

Then a sharp cry. The small hair on the back of my neck rose in attention and my limbs moved before I could think. Opening the door, which was already unlocked, I walked into his dark room.

45
SHOW ME

CILLIAN

It was a nightmare. I knew that much.

I had been reliving the same dreams of my past, of my sins, for years. But that time... it was different and horrifying.

My feet floated into the house that looked like mine. My brain was a victim of its trauma, and I couldn't stop myself when I started climbing the stairs with flowers and a cake box in my hands. It was happening again.

"D-don't!" I tried to warn myself. To stop. To turn away. But my brain wasn't listening to me, and I kept floating.

I opened the door and found a woman lying on my bed. "Please don't!" I cried out, moving closer and instead of dark brown hair, wavy golden locks splayed on the pillow.

My body froze, something like fear and raw terror creeping through my bones.

I moved closer, my breath in my throat, and found her blue eyes staring at me. Red blood sliding from the side of her head as she slowly sat up. Her school uniform ripped at various places, cuts all over her legs with a deep wound on her palm. The white sheets of the bed were turning dark red as she bled.

"What did you do, Cillian?" she whispered, her eyes watering, and I couldn't make myself speak when the bouquet of wilted flowers fell from my hand, the box of cake dropping on the rug.

"I'm sorry," I said, my voice barely audible as I kept watching her. My Doll getting hurt while I couldn't do anything.

Her warm, pale skin turned white, her plump pink lips turned colorless, and her eyes lost their shine.

"You did this," she said, a dark figure looming behind her, and a low sound elicited from my throat when that shadow grabbed her shoulder. I tried to move, but my limbs were tightened by an invisible rope, and I could not use them. Just watch as the shadow used a knife and cut her.

My lips parted. My Emma was getting hurt and I couldn't do anything.

"Cillian," she whispered, her lids falling close—

"Cillian!" I heard her voice from somewhere else. "Cillian, wake up!"

My eyes snapped open, and I became alert. There was someone on my bed. Without thinking, I pushed them down, ignoring a yelp and held onto their neck. I pinned her down, glaring at her in the darkness.

Her?

"C-Cillian," she gasped, her hand clawing at my wrist that tightened on her neck. "It's me—Emma."

I looked closer at her face and hair in the dark and quickly pulled away. It was Doll. My Emma. Oh fuck. "I'm sorry," I said, my voice hoarse from the sleep. I sat on the edge of the bed, my back to her as she wheezed.

"Oh god," she gasped, and I felt guilt bubble in my stomach. I poured her a glass of water and handed it to her without looking.

"Thank you," Emma mumbled softly, sipping on the water. "Were you having a nightmare?"

I ignored her question and covered my face. Why the fuck had Elena ignored my resignation? I shouldn't be here. I wasn't capable enough to be her bodyguard. I just fucking choked her and almost killed her. Someone else was better suited to protect her when I couldn't save her from myself.

"Cillian if—"

"Get out," I snapped. "You need to rest."

I felt the bed dip behind me and tensed when a soft hand touched my shoulder. "I'm not going anywhere until you talk to me," she said, her voice firm.

"Emma, there's nothing to talk about." Her hand felt gentle when it glided over my back, caressing me. "I'm sorry I choked you. It won't happen again."

"Well, that's a pity," she said, making me more tense. She was so close that I could feel her body heat and warm breath on my shoulder. "What if I want you to choke me?"

"This is…" I shook my head and tried to stand up, get away from her touch and siren-like voice, but she wrapped her hands around my torso. "Emma."

"Shh. I know you just had a nightmare and you are sorry for choking me. I forgive you, Cillian," she mumbled into my skin and kissed me. "You don't have to talk if you don't want to, but please don't leave me."

My throat went dry, and I held her left hand, my jaw ticking at the sight of the bandage on her right palm. "I won't," I promised.

"Do you mind if I sleep here?" she asked, her blue eyes flickering up at me through her lashes. I touched her cheek, relieved to see that her skin still had color. Her lips were pink and her body was warm. She was okay.

"Why?" I asked, trailing my fingers down her cheek to her neck, the flimsy straps of her nightdress that did nothing to hide her beautiful, heavy breasts. I twirled a lock of golden hair around my finger and gently tugged, seeing her pupils dilate. "Answer me, Doll. Why do you want to sleep in your bodyguard's bed?"

Her breathing got heavier and lids fluttered when my exploring fingers moved from her hair to her arm, feeling the goosebumps skitter on her soft skin that smelled like vanilla. So fucking good.

"Because I…"

"Because?" I pushed, moving my thumb on the pulse of her wrist, feeling it beat wildly underneath my fingers. Such dainty wrist and nimble fingers.

"Because I'm not scared when I'm with you, Cillian."

My exploring stopped and eyes averted to the small healing scars splattered over her thighs and legs. Instead of lust, a raging fire bubbled inside me. Anger overpowered the guilt, and I grabbed her wrist, pulling her closer.

"I choked you a minute ago. You were going to faint. Could've died and yet you are still here, letting me touch you and grab you." I gripped her jaw, a small gasp parting from her pouty lips. "Either you are really not scared of me when you should be, or you're stupid. Which one is it, Doll?"

Her eyes burned, and she struggled, trying to squirm away. "Is it so bad for me to like you? To want to be with you?"

My grip loosened. My voice was sharp and deep. "Yes. It is. You should go to sleep in your—"

"No," she said harshly. Her hands cupped my face, her soft fingers grazing over my stubble. "Look at me and tell me you don't want me and I'll go away."

"I don't want you to leave, Emma," I said, her soft body

pressing against mine. Warm. She was warm and alive. "But we can't be together. It's dangerous."

She swallowed, her hand lowering to my chest, feeling my hammering heart. "I get hurt when you're not around. Even if it's dangerous, I want you near me all the time because I'm selfish." Emma raised her chin and said, "I am a spoiled brat and I want you. I like you and I won't stop until you tell me to fu—"

Holding the back of her neck, I pressed my lips against hers. Her lids fluttered when I kissed her again. There. There it was. The softness of her lush pillowy lips that calmed the raging anger and guilt that burned through me. I needed her more than she needed me.

"I like you too, Doll," I whispered, pulling away, her swollen lips parting to pant for air. I rubbed her bottom lip and gazed at her pretty face.

"Show me," she said, her voice sultry.

I waited, her eyes roving over my bare skin, my tattoos and piercings. Licking her lips, she met my eyes and said, "Show me how much you like me, Cillian."

46

SIT ON MY FACE

EMMA

His features looked sharper in the room's darkness. Moonlight fell over the floor and white sheets as I stayed put, his large hands touching me.

"Do what I say, Doll," he commanded and kissed me again. I sighed, melting into his arms and giving away my control over him.

His confession kept echoing in my head, butterflies fluttering in my belly. Small gasps and moans escaped my lips when his kisses feathered down the arch of my neck, my collarbones, and lowered. I tugged at his hair, kissing him in between and moaning when I felt his stiffened member through his boxers.

"Is this the one that I bought?" he asked, his voice hoarse and so deep that it made me squirm. His finger ran through the thin strap of the lilac-pink satin night dress. It was short, ending on my inner thighs, with a lace hem, but it was very comfortable to sleep in.

"Yes, one of the many," I replied, my voice breathy. He had bought me a lot of expensive lingerie and clothes on our shopping day. Even when female employees came for help, he listened with his usual stoic expression and asked me as if there was no question for whom he was buying. He exuded confidence even when he bought me lace bras and made sure they were comfortable and the underwires weren't digging under my boobs.

"I like it," Cillian said, his hands gliding over my thighs. "I want you to wear a new one each day for me. I'll buy you more."

My cheeks burned, and I shook my head. "I don't need them. I have enough—"

He tilted my chin, his face calm and onyx eyes burning with lust. "I wasn't asking, Doll."

"Yes, Sir."

I didn't know how, but it just spewed out of my mouth and I saw how it affected him. His pupils dilating and fingers digging into my skin.

"You like me, Doll?" he asked, his hand still on my chin. Even if I wanted to cover my face, he wouldn't let me.

"Yes, I like you," I answered, my voice soft.

"Good girl. You're going to sit on my face and tell me again how much you like me, hm?"

My lips parted and Cillian didn't wait for an answer before stripping me, throwing the expensive lingerie on the floor and rolling us over. I straddled him, his thick boner pressing against my wet folds while he waited.

"Come on, sit on my face."

"I…" I shook my head, eyes wide. "I can't."

"I wasn't asking, Doll."

"I can't do it, Cillian."

"Why not?" He glared at me as if he wanted to get squished between my thighs.

"Do I have to tell you why?"

"Yes, Doll, you do," he said, his hands holding me down on his hips. "Tell me."

I glared at his sexy abs and said, "I'll... suffocate you."

"What was that?" he asked. "Say it louder."

I clenched my hands and looked at him. "I'll suffocate you. I'm—what are you doing?" I squeaked when he tugged me closer to his face.

"I don't care. I want your pretty pussy in my mouth. So sit the fuck down," he ordered, my knees on either side of his face.

"Cillian, I can't!"

"Doll," he said slowly, his hands squeezing my thighs, "Sit on my fucking face and suffocate me with your cunt."

I bit my lip, still worried.

Cillian kissed my inner thigh, his hands caressing my skin. "You asked me to show you how much I like you, Emma. I want to show you just how much when you grind your clit on my tongue, okay?"

My mouth parted, and I lowered myself slowly on his face. But Cillian was impatient. He let out a low growl and pulled me on top of him, my eyes widening when he kissed my pussy, his strong hands firm on my hips so I wouldn't pull away.

"Cillian—*fuck!*" I moaned, writhing on his expert tongue, and grabbed the headboard to hold on to something. I looked down at his face between my thighs and held his dark, thick hair when obsidian eyes stared at me. I tried to pull back, but his grip was firm.

"Delicious," he groaned, its reverberations going straight to my clit when he licked his wet lips. "Be a good girl and stay on my mouth. Or I'll tie you up."

"Y-yes, Sir," I gasped when he sucked my slicked lips, his mouth, tongue and teeth sending rolls of pleasure out of me while I held onto his thick hair and headboard.

I threw my head back, squeezing my eyes shut and grinded on his tongue like he had ordered me to. I could feel him increase his pace when I reached closer and closer to release. His hand squeezed my breasts, pinching a nipple. I came, exploding in his mouth as white light blinded me.

"Such a good girl," I heard him growl from somewhere, holding me upright while I melted in his arms, my lids heavy. "You taste so fucking good, Doll."

I mumbled something incoherent and when I opened my eyes, I was lying on my back. The sheets smelled like Cillian, his spicy male cologne overpowering my senses and making me dizzy.

"I want to make you cum again on my mouth, Doll," he whispered, and I found him between my thighs, his broad shoulders keeping my legs spread as I let out a whimper when his fingers touched my sensitive clit.

"Cillian, I'm sensitive," I said in a meek voice, his lips peppering soft kisses all over my legs and thighs where my tiny scars were healing.

"I'm showing you how much I like you," he said, his lips and chin wet with my orgasm, and licked his lips. "I want to eat you out again."

"I'm sleepy!" I protested, even though my hips bucked against him.

Bad body! Betraying me for a handsome face.

He smirked, his scarred lips making him look sexier with his tousled dark hair. "You can sleep after I make you cum."

Before I could argue, his mouth inched closer, his tongue slowly lapping over my wetness. I couldn't hold back my moans when he inserted two fingers inside me.

He kept his promise, eating me out until I came again and again until I passed out with a silly smile on my face, in Cillian's bed with his body wrapped around me.

47
TOUCH SOME GRASS

EMMA

"Shouldn't you be in bed and resting?" Mia asked, crossing her arms and trying to intimidate me.

"No. I got bored." I closed my locker and looked over her shoulder. "Who's that?"

The man was tall, dark-skinned, with broad shoulders. And he was glaring at Cillian, who was standing across him with his arms crossed.

Mia sighed and rolled her eyes. "That's Jacob, my bodyguard. James hired him because of... you know. How's your hand?"

Swallowing the lump in my throat, I replied, "It's okay. It will heal soon."

"When will my time come?" Summer drawled, walking beside us to our first class. There were lots of stares and whispers from students, their eyes pinned on our guards.

Cillian had warned me that everyone would know what had happened. About the accident, Zayed, and the stalker. That was one of the reasons he wanted me to stay at home for a week, but I would not sit in my room all day and sulk.

"Time for what?" I asked, eyeing her soft chocolate brown eyes.

"To get shagged by a billionaire or ex's dad. Heck, I'm open to both at the same time."

Mia patted her shoulder, pursing her lips. "You need to get laid, love."

"For an asexual, you sure as hell are kinky," I said with a smile.

"Asexuals can be kinky and besides, my libido is off the charts these days. The only wet dreams I have include six vampires—"

"We get it, Summer," Mia stopped her when we entered our first class. She leaned in and I huddled closer when she whispered, "I know a sex toy shop where you can explore very interesting toys."

I smirked. "Did James take you there?"

Her cheeks reddened, and I knew the answer. We stopped talking when Miss Laxmi entered the class. I could feel stares on me, but I didn't let it bother me because all I could think about was a certain tattooed man who was scorching me with his gaze.

Before the next class, I needed to use the washroom and forced Cillian to stay in the hallways. I didn't want other students to get scared to use the loo because of him.

Just as I was done with my business, I heard the door open and three pairs of shoes entering. I held my breath and stayed in the stall. The girls were laughing and my ears perked up when I realized that one voice belonged to Claire.

"I swear to god, Emma doesn't deserve the pity looks," one of her friends said.

I rolled my eyes, hoping they'd leave soon and I wouldn't have to listen to their gossip.

"Or Caleb's dad. He's too hot for her," Claire said. "I have a theory that she banged Caleb just to get to his dad and then dumped him on her mom's funeral so she could have sympathy points to fuck his dad."

I clenched my hands into a fist and calmed my breathing.

"Girl, that's too much of a mean girl shit, don't you think?" her other friend said.

"It's just a theory. For now." Claire continued, "I think she's doing all this for attention. We get it, your mom died and you're sad, but walking around so close with your bodyguard is too much. Not to mention the entire stalker thing sounds fake as hell! The marketing team for the Sheikh of Azmia could have been more creative than someone stalking Emma Moore out of all people."

Okay, that was enough.

I opened the door and walked out of the stall. I didn't look at them when they scattered around as I washed my hands. I checked my makeup and flipped my hair over my shoulder.

"You need to grow up, Claire," I said in a bored tone, eyeing her clothes and face. "I don't care if you believe that I'm being stalked or not, but gossiping about my life when you hate my guts seems out of character. And you two should stop hanging around her. She's bad news."

"You're just jealous," Claire said, crossing her arms.

I laughed at her. "Me? Jealous of you?" I leaned closer to her. "I didn't know you were delusional as well. Stop spreading rumors and touch some grass."

I didn't wait for whatever bullshit she wanted to spew to get attention from me and walked out of the washroom. If others think that I'm faking having a stalker, then let it be. They weren't the ones dealing with the inner turmoil I was going through.

Cillian walked beside me to my next glass and brushed his knuckles with my hand. Tingles shot up my spine as I looked up at him and saw a small smile tugging at the corner of his lips.

"Good job."

"What for?"

"For standing up to bullies."

I looked away, biting my cheek when warmth spread over my body.

"Emma?"

I met his eyes. "Yes?"

"What does touching grass mean?" he asked, his face serious.

A soft laugh bubbled out of me and I took my notes from him. I patted his hand and wiped a tear from my eyes. He looked adorable when he was confused.

"I forgot you're old, boomer," I teased him and walked into class. I didn't miss his glare and knew he would later 'punish' me for calling him that.

Maybe the stalker won't interrupt my life again and I'll be able to keep Cillian by my side forever.

Just maybe.

48
DEMONSTRATION
CILLIAN

"So I was thinking..." Emma drawled after finishing her plate of pasta and keeping the fork down. Her right palm was completely healed after two months of care.

"Here we go," I sighed, leaning back on the chair and taking a sip of sweet white wine.

There was no news of the stalker. No creepy gifts or messages. Elena and Zayed were in New York, and after having private meetings with Damon without Emma's knowing, we had a list of suspects that fit the descriptions of the stalker. But we had kept her in the dark because I didn't want to burden her with the information, despite how carefree she pretended to be. I knew that the incident had scarred her, physically and mentally. No nineteen-year-old should have to go through something like that.

"I'm serious," she snapped, her sapphire eyes blazing.

"Go ahead, Doll," I said. I had booked a private room for our dinner date for a special reason.

"You know how CBT therapy is working well for me," she started, her eyes on the empty plate. I sat straight and leaned my elbows on the table. She had been going to therapy since the incident after getting a recommendation from Mia's neighbors, Ivy and Aiden. I had met them a few times and Aiden seemed like a good therapist despite looking cold as ice. Emma's therapist was a woman, as per Aiden's recommendation, and slowly I could see how much it had helped her over the period. She wasn't self-conscious anymore when we had sex. She was confident as ever and I loved it.

"I thought that maybe you should try it, too?"

I frowned, tilting my head. "Try CBT?"

Emma licked her lips and my eyes averted to them for a flicker of a moment. "Yes. Your nightmares are rare, but... it could help you."

Her eyes were wary, and she was holding her breath, waiting patiently for my answer. I had been to therapy when Olivia passed away. Caleb, too. But I had never thought about revisiting my dark thoughts with a professional.

"Okay, Doll. I'll book an appointment with Aiden," I replied, my heart pounding in my ears when she smiled at me, her cheeks turning pink and blue eyes softening. She looked so fucking beautiful. I wanted to push off the plates and have her as my desert.

"I knew you would consider it—" She excitedly stood up, her heel pressing on her dress and the sharp sound of fabric tearing interrupting her.

My eyes were wide when she looked down in horror at her dress. "Did I just—?"

I stood up slowly and examined the damage. There was a small rip on the side of her dress, baring her soft skin and side boob to the world. But it was salvageable.

"It's okay, Doll, stop panicking." I kissed her temple and sat her down on her chair. Handing her a glass of wine, I said, "Drink this. I'll be right back."

"Do they have a tee shirt? Or a shirt?" Emma asked when

I came back to our private dinner room with a thread and needle in my hand. I locked the door before eyeing her in the pretty navy dress that matched my suit. There was much more to do before the night ended.

"No, but I have this." I removed my suit and rolled up the sleeves of my shirt to my elbows. "Strip out of the dress and get comfortable."

"Cillian, we can't have sex here—"

I smirked. "We are not having sex, Doll. Give me the dress and sit down."

She looked down at her dress then at me. "I'm not wearing a bra."

"I know."

"You're unbelievable," she muttered underneath her breath before turning around and letting me unzip her.

"I've seen every naked inch of you, Doll. You don't have to get shy around me," I whispered, kissing her neck when the dress pooled around her heels. I groaned at the sight of her bare tits when she sat down on the plush chair, her face red. She was wearing nothing but a tiny lace thong.

"Stop staring," she grumbled, trying to hide her face with her long hair.

"I wish I could keep you naked all the time," I confessed before picking up the dress and sitting across from her. It was a tad bit difficult to sew when I had a raging boner pressing against my pants with the marvelous view of Emma and her heavy breasts.

But I sewed back the torn side of the dress and helped her back in it. "Good?" I asked, making sure nothing was digging into her skin and making her uncomfortable.

She smiled at me, and tipping on her toes, and pressing her lips on my cheek. "Thank you! I didn't know you could sew."

"Why not? Don't you know how well I am with my hands?" I teased, wrapping my arm around her waist as we walked out of the restaurant into the chilly night.

"I think I forgot. I need a demonstration, Cillian," she whispered, pressing closer to me when the valet brought my car.

I had never driven so fast in my life. We had decided to spend the night at my house since it was a weekend and Caleb would be busy partying. We got little privacy besides her room or my guest room at her manor, so we would spend days at my house when it was empty.

"I thought we were going slow tonight?" she asked, her voice sultry when I pinned her on the door, my mouth on her neck.

"No, I want my cock inside you right now, Doll," I whispered, pulling away to remove my suit.

Emma gasped when I picked her up in my arms, her legs wrapping around my waist. I was planning to take her to the bedroom, but I couldn't climb the stairs when she was grinding on my hardening length and making such lewd noises.

I placed her on the kitchen island, swallowing her moans and sighs, kissing her. Her hands fumbled, unbuttoning my shirt and hastily removing the belt and palming me from my boxers. I humped into her hand, groaning her name and turning her around.

"I'm going to fill you up and cum inside you, Doll," I growled, yanking her hair and flipping her dress over her ass to spank it. I watched it jiggle and pressed her down on the cold marble, stroking myself and lining against her soaking entrance. "And you're going to take it like a good girl, hm?"

"Y-yes," she gasped, pushing her hips back. "Fuck me, Cillian."

Before I could thrust inside her wet heat, I heard footsteps padding downstairs.

"Oh my fucking god," I heard a small gasp and looked over my shoulder to find Caleb looking at us with wide eyes, his mouth agape.

Oh well.

49
I SLEPT WITH YOUR DAD

EMMA

I shrieked in surprised and quickly covered myself, straightening my dress and hiding behind Cillian when he buttoned his shirt, his face emotionless.

"Caleb," he started.

My heart hammered in my ribs when Caleb kept staring at us both. The last time I talked to him, he was sorry that my hand got hurt while fighting the stalker. We didn't even bump into each other at school very often, and if we did, we acknowledged each other before moving on. But now... he had seen me bent over his kitchen island with his dad behind me.

"No... I—Do we have bleach?" he asked Cillian, making me frown. "I need to bleach my eyes after what I just saw—Emma, really?"

"Calm down, Caleb," Cillian said, and I really admired how he could remain stoic even in this situation.

"I just saw you... my ex—What the fuck?" he said to himself, running a hand through his hair and pacing around the living room.

Yep, he was losing it.

"Caleb, we are in a relationship," I blurted, holding Cillian's hand and squeezing it.

He stopped, looked at us, our entwined hands, and laughed. "That's hilarious."

"She is serious," Cillian said in his stern voice.

"You're telling me..." he pointed to himself, his eyes still wide with a flush on his cheeks, "that my dad is not only protecting you from that creepy stalker, but..." He made a circle with one hand and rocked the index finger of the other in and out of that circle repeatedly.

I stared blankly at him and crossed my arms. "Yes, I slept with your dad."

"Oh my fucking god," Caleb whimpered, kneeling on the ground and covering his face.

Cillian glared at me. "Did you have to be so blunt?"

I raised my brow. "He is acting like a dramatic little bitch. It's not like we were hiding it from him."

"He is sensitive," Cillian whispered in my ear.

"I'm not sensitive!" Caleb yelled, staring at both of us with tears gleaming in his eyes.

"I know he is," I whispered back. I couldn't stand seeing him on his knees like that and helped him up. "I think you should have this conversation alone with your dad—"

"I don't want to talk—" He tried to leave, but I held his arm.

"*No.* You're not leaving again. You're going to talk to Cillian like an adult."

He made a face and looked at both of us. "Please don't tell me you are going to get married, and I'd have to call you my step-mommy or some shit."

"Are you high?" Cillian asked, narrowed his eyes at his son.

"No, but I wish I was so I could be saved from this—"

"Caleb, you owe me big time for what you did," I snapped, and pointed at the couch. "Go sit down and calm your ass."

He glared back, but shut his mouth and sat down. Cillian was staring at me with an amused look. "I can definitely see who wore the pants in your past relationship."

"Talk to him and apologize," I whispered to Cillian, squeezing his hand. "I'll be upstairs and if I hear shouting or something breaking, I'm going to be disappointed."

His eyes softened, and he was going to kiss my hair, but stopped. "Yes, ma'am."

Cillian

The silence between Caleb and me stretched. Neither of us were willing to look at each other. Emma would definitely be disappointed.

"I didn't know you were home," I said quietly.

His jaw was clenched as he kept staring at the rug. "I was planning to watch a football match with you."

"Oh." I blinked at him, confused and guilty. "You could've told me. I would have bought some beer—"

"Tell you when, Dad?" he asked, his voice rising. "You are at Emma's house all day."

"It's my last job, Caleb."

He sighed, running a hand down his face. "I know you are keeping her safe, but…"

"Before you say anything, I am sorry." I clenched my hand, my stomach tightening. "I didn't take care of you when you needed me. I kept wallowing in self-pity. I know you hate me, and our relationship will never be okay, but I want you to know that I care about you, son. I apologize for not showing it to you."

Neither of us said anything and I couldn't bring myself to look at him as shame creeped over me.

"I don't."

"What?" I glanced at him.

His face was red when he scratched his neck and cleared his throat. "I don't hate you, Dad. I never did. I was just upset that you were never around to see my games or have dinner with me."

"O-okay, good." I swallowed the lump in my throat, my eyes burning.

"Do you really like her?" he asked, finally looking at me.

"Of course, I do."

"Good." Caleb nodded and shook his head. "I mean, not good. Fuck. It's weird."

"It is."

"Out of all the people in this world, you had to fall for Emma?" he asked.

I shrugged, leaning back on the couch. "I didn't ask for it, Caleb. It just happened."

"Right," he said softly, staring at his hands and I knew he had someone special like that, too. "I... I need to tell you something."

I straightened up.

"I-I think... I don't know for sure, but I like men too," he stuttered, blinking at me and the rug. I let him continue and listened closely. "I like women, though. And everyone. Despite their gender. So... yeah."

"Okay," I said slowly. "You're pansexual?"

His face snapped at me. "You know what it means?"

"I touch grass."

He made a face and shook his head. "You're hanging around Emma too much. Stop speaking Gen Z. It feels weird hearing it from you."

"Deadass?"

"Jesus Christ." He groaned audibly, covering his face. "Please don't."

God, I loved being a dad sometimes.

I slapped his shoulder and stood up. "You're not matching my vibe, son."

"Please leave me alone." He sounded like he was in pain.

I smiled proudly. "I don't care about your sexuality, Caleb. Date whoever you want to… just take care of yourself and call me when you need me."

He met my eyes, his dark eyes softening as he nodded. "Okay, cool, Dad."

"Yeet," I made a peace sign and made my way towards the stairs, hearing a groan that made my grin widen.

But it was short-lived when I heard it… the sound of thud coming from upstairs.

"Caleb," I whispered, grabbing a gun from the drawer and checking if it was loaded and planting my back on the wall.

"What are you doing?" He asked, his eyes wide.

"Someone's upstairs," I mouthed. "Follow me."

My heart was pounding in my ears when I slowly crept upstairs, with Caleb following me and holding a baseball bat in his hands. He was trembling, but I would not let anything happen to him. I was worried about Emma. If she was okay.

The hallway looked clear, and I quickly made my way to my room, taking a deep breath before opening the door and pointing the muzzle in front of me, my finger on the trigger.

"Emma?" I called out, noticing the room was empty, with an open window and a lamp on the floor. "Emma!" I rushed into the en-suite washroom finding it empty with the lights on. There was a sharp sound of something hitting—

"Dad!"

I turned back and stormed into the hallway, seeing Caleb clutching his stomach.

"Cillian, don't!" I heard her scream and turned back around. My hand didn't move fast enough to block the baseball bat that struck me on the side of my head, pain reverberating over my entire body as I fell on the floor, warm blood slicking my face.

I could hear Emma scream and scramble for me, but he held her by her hair, yelling in her face, "Shut the fuck up!"

I glared at him, pushing my palms on the ground, and stood up when he kicked my ribs, making me groan.

"I'll take care of her, don't worry," the man said, his voice raspy and dark gray eyes gleaming with something evil when he took Emma over his shoulder and climbed downstairs.

No, no, no. I can't...

Blood poured out of my mouth and dripped onto the floor when I used all my strength to sit up. Caleb was clutching his stomach, and I knew the fucker had attacked him first. I took my gun and tucked it on my back, calling emergency care at my home.

"I'm sorry."

I patted his shoulder and stood up. "Stay. I'll bring her back."

50

OUR HOME

EMMA

My mouth was as dry as Sahara when I woke up with a throbbing headache. I was getting really sick of waking up like that. My lids felt heavy when I looked around me. Dread seeped into my veins when I found myself on a small twin size bed with pink blankets, a soft dim light from the gray ceiling, and an old, small desk in the corner. There was a heart-shaped pink mirror and some stuff lying on top of it.

I forced myself to remember what had happened, but my memories were hazy. Cillian and Caleb were talking downstairs while I was getting ready to take a relaxing bath in Cillian's washroom. I remember turning around and being pushed into the cold tile with a chemical handkerchief covering my nose and mouth. I had panicked seeing the black ski mask and struggled to fight. Even though I had tried to smack his face with the bottle of conditioner, he had overpowered me. Tying my wrists together and dragging me into Caleb's room when I heard Cillian and Caleb climb upstairs. I had whimpered and begged the man not to hurt them, but he didn't listen to me.

They both were on the ground and Cillian was bleeding from his head when the stalker picked me up. And the last thing I remembered was being forced into a trunk of a car—

Oh my God.

I sat up, my head pounding as I tried to shake off the dizziness and looked around. I was in a fucking prison with bars covering me from three sides with a wall on my back.

"Finally, you're awake, little Emma."

I clenched my hands behind me, my legs wobbling in the heels that I was still wearing. "W-who are you?" I asked, my voice hoarse.

The tall shadow leaned closer, and I saw his face. He was average looking with dark gray eyes and darker hair. I didn't remember him. I had never met him.

"I'm disappointed that you don't remember me, love, but it's okay." He smiled creepily and opened the door, the snick of a key unlocking it. He kept the key around his neck and entered the cell, my feet stumbling back until my back pressed against the icy wall. "We have a lot of time to spend together, so you'll remember me soon enough."

"I don't know who you are," I said, my body shaking with terror, but I willed myself to stay calm. If Cillian was here, he'd keep his breath in control and handle the situation calmly. I couldn't overpower the man in front of me, especially when I still felt drugged.

He pouted, standing across me and touched my cheek. I looked away, but he grabbed my chin, an evil look in his eyes. "Don't look away when I'm touching you, little Emma."

I swallowed the urge to spit on him and stayed calm.

"We spent so much time together, don't you remember?" he asked, his voice gentle when I kept looking at him.

I shook my head and sighed in relief when he pulled away his hand. "That's sad. But I know once you remember, you'd never want to leave me, little Emma." He smiled, and there was nothing sweet or loving about it.

"Really?" I asked, reining in my anger. I licked my lips. "Then I want to remember. Please, help me?"

His eyes widened, and he looked like he was in awe. "You want to know me?"

I nodded quickly. Cillian was right. He was delusional. "I want to know s-so we can stay in our home together," I stuttered. I wanted to throw up, but I needed to escape and get away before he completely lost it. "That's what you said in the message, right? Our home?"

He smiled and nodded, cupping my cheek. "You don't know how happy it makes me to hear you say that, little Em. Say it again for me?"

Fuck you.

"Our home."

I squeezed my eyes shut when he leaned closer and kissed my forehead. He smelled like chemical and garlic. My body wanted to push him away.

"I can help you, but I prepared all of this for you," he said, waving around the prison cell with gray floors and—my breath hitched in my throat when I found a puddle near the desk. I remembered it. *Lincoln.* The picture of Lincoln was taken there. *Then that means...*

My knees wobbled when I peered up at the man, my heart threatening to burst out of my ribs. *Run.* I needed to run away from him. He was a murderer. He had killed him *here.*

"Are you fucking listening to me?" he asked, his voice rising as he came closer. "I did all of this for you!"

"I-it's great!" I said, my eyes burning. "I love the pink blankets and... and this makeup." I touched the lipstick, my eyes fixed on the heart-shaped mirror as a tear slid down my face. "I can't believe you prepared so much for me."

My throat burned with the lies and fear.

Cillian. Help me, please.

"Right? I knew you'd love it." It seemed he was in awe. "After seeing your bedroom and all the makeup stuff, I knew you'd get sad if I didn't have it, so I bought all this for you."

My bedroom. He had snuck into it and…

"Really?" I asked brightly, smiling at him and clutching the lipstick in my hand.

"Yes! So you can dress up for me."

This pervert.

"I also bought this ring for you." Something shuffled and I turned around to see a familiar golden band. "I'll buy one for you tomorrow so we can say our vows and get married."

A lump formed in my throat. It was Cillian's wedding ring which he had stolen after drugging me.

I need to get out. Now.

"What's your name?" I asked, batting my lashes. "You know my name and I don't know yours. It's unfair."

"It is?" he asked, blinking at me.

"Yes."

"But if I tell you, then… you'd know."

This was my chance. I took a deep breath and kept the soft smile on my lips. "How about you tell me your name when we go upstairs?"

He frowned and nodded. "I like that you are accepting this faster than I thought, little Emma. This way, we can live our happy life together!"

"I can't wait!" *To fucking punch you.*

He held my hand, and I looked down when steel handcuffs cinched around my wrists. A shudder rolled over my body.

"W-what's this for?"

"So you don't do anything silly," he smiled, dragging me

out of the cell, holding my arm. "If you do, I'll have to punish you and lock you back here until you learn your lesson."

My hope diminished, and I let him drag me upstairs.

51
STOP

CILLIAN

I winced, wiping the blood from my head, and sped my car. My cellphone was in my other hand as I noted her location and shared it to Elena's team. I had called her, ignoring her order to stay back, and got in my car.

My vision was blurry, but I kept driving, my hand clutching the steering wheel. He lived so fucking near her house, and all that time was wasted because we did not get search warrants.

I prayed that Emma kept her heels on by some miracle. I had inserted a tracking device in each pair she owned, hoping that I'd never have to use them

We shouldn't have underestimated the stalker. Look what he fucking did.

My jaw clenched, and I cut the engine, parking blocks away from the house. It was a quiet suburban street with huge bungalows on each side of the road. No wonder no one suspected him, even though he seemed fucking weird. If he was loaded, no one would bat an eye.

I checked the time on my watch and took a deep breath. The normal protocol was to wait for the team, surround the house, enter and seize the stalker and bring the hostage to safety. But I didn't give a fuck about it when Emma was the hostage.

Checking my gun, I pulled off the safety and marched towards the house. I was going to save her, no matter what. I promised her.

And that's when I heard her scream.

* * *

Emma

MY LIPS PARTED WHEN I LOOKED AROUND THE VAST CEILING and golden chandelier. The house was empty, with just a small dining table and two chairs, barely anything else. But it was enormous.

"It's very... luxurious," I said, our steps echoing on the floor when he sat me down on the chair. He pulled the other one closer and patted my bare shoulder. I held back my wince and kept smiling.

"I'm glad that you think so. I wanted you to decorate it so I haven't done anything yet since I got it."

"Got it?" I tilted my head, and he chuckled.

"Right, my name." His dark gray eyes seemed familiar under the light and I held my breath when he said, "I'm Drake."

Drake? Where have I heard that name before? Why does it seem familiar?

I looked at him once again and swallowed. "Drake... N-no."

"Yes, I'm Drake Grant, little Emma," he grinned, his hand squeezing my shoulder. "Do you remember me now? How we used to play hide and seek all the time and promised to live together?"

What the fuck? I stared at him. My head swirling with all the memories of my childhood. I remembered playing with Damon... and yes, I remembered bits and pieces of it.

My mother married a famous director, Miles Grant, who made cringey young adult movies with young girls. He already had a son, Drake, from his previous marriage, where his wife died mysteriously. When mom got married to him, they both had Damon and me. I was a kid when they split up, so I didn't remember him, but Damon went to live with him, keeping his last name.

How the fuck was I supposed to remember Drake when I had been four at the time?

"I was a kid, Drake," I said slowly and gently.

"So?" he chuckled, touching my hair and petting me as if I was his fucking dog. "You were such a cute little kid back then. I always called you little Emma when we played together."

"With Damon?"

He scoffed, pulling away and rolling his eyes. "Damon was stupid. Never understood anything and always cried when I told him not to play with you."

"Why?" I asked, even though I wasn't sure I wanted to know his answer.

"Because you're mine, little Emma," he said, his eyes gleaming with lust when they roved over my body and I remembered I was still in that dress. The one which Cillian helped me zip up after sewing it so carefully. Cillian. I wanted Cillian.

"I'm yours?" I asked, still playing dumb, trying to unlock the cuffs underneath the table. But the damn thing wouldn't budge.

"Yes, you're mine. I claimed you when you were a kid. But you were so wild that I let you experiment with that Caleb boy." My hands froze, and I kept my eyes on him when his face twisted into an evil laugh. "Did you hear how he fucking whimpered like a girl when I kicked him? And that ugly bodyguard, too! Both are so fucking weak. And ugly." He leaned closer and kissed my nose. "They can't protect you like I can, little Emma. I'm your half-brother after all."

I hummed, clenching my hands into a fist. I tried to change the subject. "Can I remove the heels? They're hurting my feet—"

"No," he said sharply. "I like how you look in heels. Keep them on."

I watched him walk towards the kitchen and looked around to find something blunt or hard, but the entire place was empty.

"Honestly, I should've just kept you in the fucking cell until you learned some manners," he said angrily when he slammed a plate on the kitchen counter, making me jump. "First, you ignore my messages and then got a bodyguard, and slept with him like a fucking whore! When I tried to save you from that creep, you hurt me!"

He was screaming, banging the drawers shut when he poured something on a plate and walked back to the dining area. I stayed frozen, keeping my lips shut because the asshole had lost it.

"Are you even going to fucking apologize, you little bitch!" he shouted, leaning close and trying to intimidate me.

It hurt that it was working. I said in a meek voice, "I'm sorry."

"Are you?!" he asked, sitting down on the chair, his nose flaring when he ate the gross-looking puddle of mush that looked like badly cooked mashed potatoes. "You hurt me! Your love!"

I licked my lips and said, "I'm sorry I didn't remember you and... your face was covered, so I didn't know."

His jaw was working as he put down his fork and spoon. "Do you mean that, little Emma?"

I smiled and placed my hand on his, the clink of the cuffs dragging against the table. "Of course, I do, Drake."

He nodded, looking down at my hand. "Okay, I believe you." He continued eating while I stared at the fork. "I don't like what you've done to yourself."

"Sorry?"

"You've gotten fat. Very chubby too," he said, a scowl on his face as he pushed his plate away and leaned back. "You've got to get in shape, so I'm going to give you one meal a day until you get your sexy little body again."

My throat went dry. I didn't know what to utter. All the fear that I had for the arrogant, delusional man sitting near me evaporated into anger. I was about to snatch the fork and stab his eyes when he pushed his chair from the table and patted his thigh.

"Come on, you can start apologizing to your dear stepbrother by sucking me off." He unzipped his pants, lowering them to his ankles as I stared at him. The scar on his thigh. "And make it good and sloppy. I've seen you give a blowie to that ugly muck of your bodyguard."

"What else have you seen, dear Drake?"

"What haven't I done and seen for you, my little Emma!" He said it like he was proud of it. "You know, I tried to be nice and talk to your bitch of a mother and get her blessings, but she wouldn't listen to me."

My heart stopped and I stared at him. "You talked to m-my mom?"

"Of course, I did. For you, little Emma," he crooned. "But she insulted me, called securities on me and told me to stay away from you. She insulted me so I killed her."

My eyes burned, looking down at the floor. They were

right, mom's death wasn't an accident. It was murder. He killed her because she tried to protect me.

"I killed Lincoln for you," he smiled as if reminiscing about it. "Remember that dirty old lawyer?"

I nodded, wanting him to continue.

"I was there, hiding in the study when he touched your shoulder and said those things to you, little Emma," he said, his smile widening as if he loved telling me how he watched me get harassed and did nothing. "I let it go because you were young."

"So you killed him recently."

"Yes, I needed to get revenge on him." He was serious. "I'll bring you that Caleb and that bodyguard's head, too, so you are not scared anymore, okay?"

My throat burned, my hand shaking with anger when he kept spouting bullshit.

"Don't worry about the silly stuff. Come on, suck me off!" He was whining, begging me to suck his dick.

I kneeled on the floor and looked at him. "Can you keep your hands on the chair? I want to try a new thing. You will love it, Drake."

He instantly got hard, bile rising in my mouth when I gave him a tight-lipped smile as he kept his hand on the arms of the chair.

"Hurry!"

"Yes, Drake."

I calmed my heart. Taking a deep breath, I exhaled slowly when I got closer between his legs. His ankles were still in his pants. I could do it. Cillian had taught me how to defend myself. I could do it.

With my eyes laser focused, I grabbed the fork and slammed it down on the scar that was on his left thigh. The fork dug into his skin and he yelped in surprise and pain. I pulled it away and stabbed him with it again, glaring at him.

"You like that, you piece of shit!" I cried out and pulled away when he tried to grab my hair. I was still wearing the damn heels when I crawled away from him.

"I trusted you!" he groaned, his thigh bleeding as he limped towards me. "You are a bitch and a whore! I'll treat you like one!"

I tried to stand up, but he slapped me, making me yelp when pain rang on my cheek through my body.

"Stop!" I screamed when he pushed me down, pinning my hands over my head and tugging at my dress. "Get off me!"

"Shut the fuck up. I'm going to breed you with my babies, you fucking whore!" His hands were harsh. Tears spilled out of my eyes and I tried to get ahold of something, anything.

"Stop!" I begged, pushing him, but he was too strong—Cillian was also strong, but he sprawled on the mat when I had tried it.

Using my hands, I jabbed his throat and when his grip loosened, I pushed him off of me with all my strength and stood up. Scrambling away, I picked up the bloody fork in my shaking hands.

"You're dead to me, little Emma," he spit out, rubbing his throat when he stood up. "I'm going to fuck you and kill you."

"I dare you to touch me again, you asshole!" I shouted at him, tears sliding down my face, when I looked over his shoulder and started sobbing.

Finally.

Drake yelled, ready to pounce on me when he jumped in. I slumped on the floor, covering myself.

52 JUST THREE?

CILLIAN

TW: A bit of violence.

I tackled him down before he could touch my Emma again. He groaned when I held the back of his hair and slammed him down on the floor. Again, and again and again until I saw a pool of blood.

My eyes were seeing burning red. Emma was crying and her screams were echoing in my head.

I held him upon his feet before throwing him on the floor. I covered Emma with my suit and said, "Cover your ears, Doll. Keep your eyes closed until I tell you otherwise, okay?"

She nodded, her bloody hand clutching my jacket and covering her ear. I stood up, glaring at the piece of shit who was trying to crawl away from me.

"Stay the fuck away from us, you ugly fuck! She's *my* bitch and *my* whore!" he said, his eyes swollen and beaten up when I loomed over him.

"Say it again," I said calmly. "I dare you."

He opened his mouth, and I kicked him, shoving my

polished shoe—the one Emma bought for me—into his mouth. His eyes widened when I pushed hard until I heard a satisfying crack. I removed my shoe from his mouth and kneeled on the ground. Holding the collar of his bloody shirt, I punched him.

I kept punching him until my knuckles were as red as his face. I only stopped when I heard a small sigh. I turned to find Emma standing, her eyes on the barely breathing shit that was lying beneath me.

"Emma," I said softly and stood up, her eyes pinned on the other man. "Look at me, Doll."

She didn't avert her eyes until I blocked her view and cupped her face, blood smearing on her cheeks. "You're safe now. I got you. I'm here," I said, pulling her face against my chest and kissed her hair. I was reassuring both of us that she was safe and in my arms. "I'm not going anywhere. You're safe."

Emma didn't hug me back, but I knew she needed to hold on to something, so I stayed still. There was a tug on my hip and I quickly turned around to find the bastard holding my gun.

"Drop it and I won't kill you," I warned him, standing in front of Emma, whose hands tightened over my shirt.

He chuckled, and it was weak and pathetic. "Do you think I care? I'm going to kill you both."

The safety was off but I kept my eyes on him when he pressed the trigger and fired a shot.

I released my breath and looked down my body to find... nothing. There were no bullet holes and no pain.

Drake slumped and fell to the ground, my gun still in his hand. I looked at the side door of the dining room and found Elena, still aiming the nozzle at him as she slowly stepped towards him and kicked the gun he held away from his hand before looking at me.

"Are you hurt?" she asked, turning the safety on her gun off before holstering it.

I looked behind me and found Emma peering over my shoulder. "She is," I said, pressing her closer.

"Thank you," I said to Elena when her team covered the entire house.

She gave me a dark look before facing Emma, who was still shaking in my arms. "There's an ambulance outside. She should get checked."

I swallowed the lump in my throat and nodded. "Come on, Doll," I whispered, holding her in my arms and letting her bury her face in my chest.

She didn't want me to leave, but I needed to talk to Elena. As the nurse and the doctor treated her in the ambulance, and the other officers hustled around us, I stayed rooted in place with a clear view of Emma.

"I gave you one order," Elena started, her arms crossed. "One order, Cillian. Stay back until the team arrives."

"I heard her scream," I lied. I had just arrived at the location when I heard it. "I couldn't wait."

"You broke—"

"If you had heard Zayed's scream, you wouldn't wait."

Her jaw ticked. "Then explain to me why Drake Grant has a broken jaw, black eyes, three teeth on the floor in the puddle of his blood, several ribs broken and an open wound on his thigh."

I stared hard at her then at Emma, who was talking to the nurse, her face devoid of emotion. I met Elena's eyes and asked, "Just three?"

"Cillian," she hissed and leaned closer. "I can't protect you from this."

"I don't need protection. You should thank me that he's not dead."

"What the fuck am I supposed to say, that you hurt him in defense?"

"Yes." My jaw clenched, and I looked down at my knuckles. "I need to be with Emma right now."

She sighed, pinching the bridge of her nose. "Go ahead."

I paused and looked at her. "How did you end up here? I thought you were in New York."

"You should be lucky Zayed wanted to meet you both before we left for Azmia," she said and nodded at the ambulance. "Oh, great."

I marched towards the Sheikh of Azmia, who was grinning with Emma. My steps slowed when I saw the light in her eyes and a small smile on her face. Even though I didn't like the man, he had a good heart.

"And we are—mostly I am—awarding you with a golden ticket," Zayed grinned. "You can come visit me in Azmia anytime you want and you will get a royal treatment."

"Like a princess?" Emma asked, raising a brow.

"Like a queen, kitten. You saved my life."

Emma smiled at him and I was relieved to find that it reached her blue eyes. I tensed when they flickered to me.

"Ah, the man and the hero of the hour!" Zayed stood up and slapped me on the back. "Only three?" he whispered in my ear. He tsked. "*Amateur.*"

I hid my smirk when he walked towards his wife, leaving me alone with Emma.

"How are you?" I asked her, getting into the ambulance and sitting beside her on the bed. They had offered her a blanket, but it was on her lap, my suit covered her bare arms.

"My head is hurting. Cheek, too. But…" Her eyes softened when she leaned her head on my shoulder. "I feel relieved. Oh and… this belongs to you."

My eyes widened when she gave me the familiar wedding band. "How did you…? I thought I'd never find it."

"He had it." She swallowed before giving me a small smile, "I think he took it when I was unconscious. I snatched it from him before anyone found it."

"Thank you, Emma," I whispered, pulling her close and kissing her hair. She didn't know how much it meant to me.

"Do you want to sleep?" I asked, keeping my voice low and playing with her nimble fingers. She was so strong. I had witnessed it with my own eyes. If I hadn't reached her in time, she would have run away and she'd have saved herself.

"No," she replied. "I want to go home. Sleep in your bed."

I smiled, kissing her hair. "Whatever you want, Doll."

"Cillian?"

"Hm?"

Emma leaned up and looked at my face with a small frown. "How did you find me so quickly?"

"I inserted a tracking device in your heels," I said, pointing at the blue heels. They were bloody, but I was sure she could clean them off if she kept them. "All of your shoes."

"All of them?" she gasped.

"All of them."

"I think..." She licked her lips, her sapphire eyes flickering from my eyes to my lips. "I think I love you, Cillian."

My heart stuttered to a stop.

"I love you, too, Emma," I said, cupping her bloody cheek and pressing my lips against hers in a soft kiss.

The End

EPILOGUE

EMMA

I giggled, running in the woods as grass tickled my bare legs.

"Emma!" Cillian shouted behind me. Birds and leaves of trees whispered against each other as my laugh echoed in the small clearing. "Emma, slow down!"

Golden hair flew in my face as I looked over my shoulder and shouted, "Hurry up, grandpa!"

"Oh, you wait."

More laughter bubbled out of me. I was definitely getting punished for that. The sun glared down my bare limbs, the soft fabric of my summer dress flowing around me when I reached the edge of the spring. Perspiration slid down my neck as I panted, gazing at the beautiful scenery of sparkling fresh water and the waterfall.

It had been months since Drake had been murdered in his own prison cell. It was a mysterious murder that even Elena wasn't able to solve, but it was a relief that he'd never hurt anyone else.

"Got you." I giggled when his strong arms wrapped around me, lifting me in the air before putting me down and caging me against a rock. "Now where will you run, Doll?"

I licked my lips when dark eyes gazed at me with admiration and so much love. His tattoos and piercings peeked from the white loose shirt he was wearing, his dark hair with bits of gray was tousled. He made me blush even after a year of seeing the same love-struck look.

I cupped his face and kissed him. "Have you ever skinny-dipped before?" I asked, pulling away from him and tugging off my dress.

His eyes lowered to my bare breasts, and he shook his head.

"Come on," I urged him, removing my underwear and unbuttoning his shirt. "Let's skinny-dip."

"In a spring?" he asked, removing his shirt. I stared at his chest, my mouth going dry. No matter how many times I had seen him naked, it always made me blush and wet.

"You have stayed in Coral Springs for years and never skinny-dipped in a spring?" I tutted at him, walking towards the water. "Come on, old man. Loosen up."

"Call me that again and I'll show you who has more stamina between the two of us."

I smirked and looked over my shoulder to find him naked and hard. "Old man," I whispered, diving into the cold water.

When I swam up back to the surface, I didn't find Cillian. Just our clothes on the edge and—

A squeal escaped my lips when a hand wrapped around my ankle, dragging me underwater, and I saw him, his dark eyes pinned on me like a predator when I struggled to get away from him. But I wasn't really struggling, I was laughing.

"You are trouble, Doll," he said when we gasped for air, the cold water surrounding us.

I poked my tongue out at him. "Too bad you're stuck with me."

"Too bad indeed," he said, closing the distance between us and gripping my chin. He kissed me. Despite his firm hold, the kiss was soft and playful. I loved that about him, how gentle and rough he was. How large and scarred he looked, but from the inside he was a soft bear.

"Cillian," I whispered, running my hand through his hair. "Fuck me here."

His eyes darkened, and he pulled me closer. I gasped, feeling his hardened member pressing against my stomach. "I'll fuck you wherever you want me to, Doll. But you have to promise me something."

"What?"

"Scream my name when you cum," he rumbled, swimming us to a rock, pinning me on it, my hands over my head. "Can you do that for me, Doll?"

"Yes, Cillian. Fuck me. Now," I demanded, arching my back and moaning when he rewarded me by squeezing my breasts and taking my nipple into his hot mouth.

Water lapped against our naked bodies when he parted my legs and lined his cock against my entrance. I held him close, my arms around his neck when he surged inside me, filling me up with one thrust and making me whimper at the small stretch of my walls around his thick cock.

"Emma," he groaned, slamming inside me again and again.

"Yes," I gasped and moaned when he bit my nipple, drawing it in his mouth and squeezing my ass as his pace increased. Pleasure shot through my clit to my spine when he made me cum and I shook around him, screaming his name like he wanted me to.

Cillian swore and, keeping his head between my breasts, he came inside me, filling me up with his warm release. We stayed like that, catching our breath and caressing each other in the postcoital bliss.

I held onto him when he walked us out of the spring and sat down on his shirt with me on his lap.

"Cillian," I whispered into his skin.

"Yes, Doll?"

My cheeks flustered when he caressed my back and looked down at me. "I love you," I said, kissing his cheek.

He smiled down at me and said, "Say it again."

I raised my chin. "I love you, old man."

Cillian chuckled, slapping my ass lightly. I smiled too, watching the corner of his eyes crinkle when he held my chin and kissed me. "I love you, too."

UNKNOWN

TW: VIOLENCE

"Boss."

I grumbled underneath my breath and pulled away from a marvelous pair of tits. I pouted when I found her sleeping so comfortably on the small bed.

"Boss." Another sharp knock on the metal door of my prison cell.

I rolled my eyes and pulled away from Lilliana's warm body. We had fucked all night until she tapped out, too exhausted to put her uniform and get out. I kissed her cheek, tucking a blanket on her shoulders and wore my Hugo Boss boxers.

The good thing about having a vacation in prison as a mafia boss was that you live like royalty.

"What is it this time?" I said, opening the cell door from inside and leaning on the stone wall. I glared at the tall, bald monster in front of me and scowled, "Your hand better be precious to you that you decided to knock on my VIP suite. Do you know how much I'm paying for this shit?"

I waved around at the grim looking room. A tiny window for ventilation, open toilet, basin and a small bed. And a rack for my Tom Ford suit, shoes, perfume, boxers and a box of condoms. Right, it was empty so I have to add that to my grocery list.

"Boss, it's about the new inmate."

That perked my attention. A cop in uniform walked past him, his eyes flitting toward me and the woman in my bed before he quickly looked away and kept walking.

"Keep talking. Eyes on me." I warned him, pulling on the usual garbage orange clothes and hiding my tattoos.

"He stalked a teen, kidnapped her and—"

I looked at him, "And?"

Poor guy was too sweet to say it out loud so he kept his eyes on the floor and shrugged. "Tried to assault her."

"But he didn't?"

He shook his head. "She was saved."

I released the breath I was holding. "How old was she?"

"Nineteen."

My jaw ticked. "Where is he?"

He snapped his face at me. "Boss, no."

I raised my brow at him, "Oh, I'm sorry, are you the boss or me?"

"Where are you going?" a soft feminine voice said from the bed and I nodded at him to wait outside.

"I'll be right back, peaches," I whispered to her, eyeing the blue uniform on the floor. "We can roleplay again if you'd like. Maybe I'll use cuffs on you if you don't behave."

She rolled her eyes and pushed me away making me chuckle. "You're a horny ass, Dominick."

"You weren't complaining about it last night when this horny ass fuck—"

"Yeah, yeah, I get it," she sat up, my eyes averting to her bare tits. I licked my lips. "Shit, I've to get ready for my shift."

"Or you can agree to my deal," I said, standing up and watching her put on her sexy uniform. Ever since I enrolled (yes, I paid for it) in the VIP prison cell, she couldn't keep her eyes to herself and I had to take her to bed. I can't resist smart-mouthed women.

"I'm never becoming your mistress or side-chick, Dominick," she wore a bra making me pout. "This is a one-time thing."

"Uh-huh, that's what you said yesterday. The day before that and before that."

"I've to—"

I held her arm, bringing her close to me and smiled. "I'm sorry but you have to wait here. I'll be right back."

Lilliana frowned when I pulled away and opened the door. She yelled my name, "Uncuff me right now you piece of shit!"

I smirked and pocketed the little key, closing the door behind me. I waved my fingers at her, "Tootles, darling!"

"I hate you!"

I smiled and followed my guy to meet the stalker.

"Who the fuck are you?" the guy said as soon as I stepped into his cell. I ignored him and looked around, three of my people were waiting outside as other inmates pressed against the metal bars to see what was happening.

"I heard you stalked someone," I said, finally looking at his face and chuckled. "Someone got to you before I did, huh?"

He was beaten up badly. Two black eyes, broken nose, lips and cheeks. Shit. Whoever beat him to pulp must have been furious. *Who wouldn't be?*

"What do you want?" he snapped, his eyes wide and angry as I pulled a small stool and sat on it crossing my legs and watching him pace around.

"I want to know if you stalked a nineteen-year-old, kidnapped her and tried to assault her," I asked calmy. He was new so he didn't have any personal belongings but there was a thick encyclopedia about space on top of his bed.

"That's bullshit!" he yelled. Three teeth were missing. He leaned closer, my guys straightening up and looking at me for a signal when he said, "I didn't stalk her. She was my whore! She still is! She promised me we'd be together so I was just fulfilling it."

"Is that so?" I asked and stood up, easily towering over him. "She promised you?" I said, taking a step closer.

He chuckled and I could see nothing but greedy lust in his eyes. I had seen men like him before. Killed them with my own hands and yet the disgust that crept up my body made me want to strangle him with my fucking shoelace.

"She did! But we were young so I even let her fuck other guys—"

I interrupted him with a punch on the ribs. He wheezed, falling on the floor and looking up at me, "What was that for?"

"Keep talking," I said, tutting at him when he held my leg, trying to push me down. "I want to hear your last words."

Before he could stand up, I grabbed the book, bashing it on his head. He fell on the floor again, coughing out blood. I knelt down and grabbed his hair. "Your first mistake was to harass a fucking teen and proudly telling me about it. You won't get any mercy at all."

I chuckled when he spit at me and ran a hand across my face before pouncing on him. By the time I was done, my orange shirt was covered in blood and the jerk was no longer breathing.

With a deep breath, I stood up and called in my guys. I stared at the dead man lying on the floor and then at them. "Cut off his dick and show it to everyone. If they have assaulted anyone, I want them begging for mercy for a quick death."

"On it, Boss."

I took the napkin from the man and wiped my knuckles.

"Is Lilliana mad?" I asked, ignoring all the inmates' stares when I walked back to my cell.

"I... Good luck, Boss."

I let out a soft chuckle and slapped him on the back ignoring the way he shuddered as if I'd ever hit him. He had taken an omertà to me. I'd never hurt my own men and women. They were my family.

"It's good that my tongue game is good," I muttered to myself and entered my cell.

PREVIEW OF DON'T DATE YOUR BEST FRIEND

KIARA

"If you don't want to kiss me then... let's swim."

"Yeah, sure."

"Naked."

"*What?*"

"I always wanted to try skinny dipping." I pursed my lips and said, "And I really want to get out of these clothes."

When I thought about it, I wasn't feeling self-conscious about my body when it came to him. Yes, he had seen in me in bikinis and accidentally walking in when I was busy writing something on my Post-it in my underwear and bra. But I was never self-conscious about what he would think of me or my body. I did have stretch marks, but I wasn't uncomfortable about them. What I was most worried about was *myself*. If he got naked and my hormones spiked up, I didn't know if I would control myself and not jump on him.

Gosh, I sounded so bad in my head. Not to mention, my best friend would be the first guy I would ever see naked. *Way to go, Kiara.*

His voice was strained when he said, "What if someone catches *you* ... me, both?"

I moved my damp hair over my shoulder. "We will be in the pool, Ethan. And no one can see us from the living room." I smirked when I said, "Unless you want to watch me while I swim, you can stay here."

The thought of Ethan watching me with his intense green-blue eyes while I was swimming naked in the pool sent a delicious shiver down my core.

His eyes darkened and he looked away, probably thinking the same when I noticed red blush creeping up his neck and making his ears and cheeks flush. *Cute.*

I prodded, "Come on, Ethan. Don't be a chicken . . ."

"*Fine.*"

He stood up, his tall frame towering me. I forgot how to breathe when his dark eyes seared me, slowly trailing down my body as if he had all the time in the world. His voice was rough when he said, "Remove that sweater first."

I raised my eyebrow at the sudden change in his demeanour.

Ethan said, "You have an extra piece of clothing than me."

I grinned. "Who said I was wearing any underwear?"

I loved the way his pupils widened in shock, surprise and then they were clouded by scorching desire. Biting my lips, I whispered, "I was messing with you."

Holding the hem of the sweater, I tugged it up and removed it. I straightened my damp hair and shivered. But it wasn't because of the cold air.

His eyes averted down my breasts, which were barely covered by the ivory lace bralette. As it was wet, he could easily notice my hardened nubs, which were begging for his attention.

We were crossing a dangerous line right now. And I knew neither one of us wanted to step back.

"Your turn," I managed to whisper.

EXCLUSIVE CONTENT

Want more exclusive content? You can sign up for Mahi's Patreon to read steamy one shots every Saturday!

As a supporter, you get access to early drafts, exclusive VIP content, deleted scenes, deleted chapters, cat pictures and YOUR NAME in the Acknowledgements of my books.

www.patreon.com/mahimistry

ALSO BY MAHI MISTRY

Have you read them all?

Alluring Rulers of Azmia Series

Dirty Wild Sultan

Filthy Hot Prince

Tempting Rebel Princess

Charming Handsome Sheikh

Alluring Rulers of Azmia Complete Series Books 1-4

The Unfolding Duet

Don't Date Your Best Friend: Best Friends to Lovers

Don't Date Your Ex Best Friend: Second Chance Best Friends to Lovers

The Unfolding Duet Books 1-2

Dominating Desires Series

Twisted Therapist: Brother's Best Friend Age Gap Romance

Tempting Teacher: Student Teacher/Dad's Best Friend Age Gap Romance

Bossy Bodyguard: Bodyguard/ Ex's Dad Age Gap Romance

Billionaire Boss: Sister's Best Friend Age Gap Romance

Scan to easily access all of my books:

ACKNOWLEDGMENTS

Thank you so much for reading Bossy Bodyguard!

Thank you to my lovely editor, Jeanie and brilliant friend and proofreader, Edresa. This book wouldn't have been written without you and there aren't enough words to convey my gratitude.

Thank you to everyone who accepted the ARC edition of this book and helped me share this book with the world. To all the bloggers and book lovers, bookstragramers.

If you enjoyed reading this book, please don't forget to leave a review. I would really appreciate it. It helps find more readers like you and they are very important for authors!

Special thanks to the backers who supported my first ever Kickstarter campaign:

> Jeanie Creech
> Christina-Joy Derrick
> Edresa Ramos
> Charlene.

I adore you all!

ABOUT THE AUTHOR

Mahi Mistry has been writing since she was in middle school. Soon, she fell in love with writing passionate, steamy romances. Her stories have elements of humor, suspense and character development. Mahi's main purpose in her life is to make one person happy every day, even if that is a stranger reading her book and rooting for the main couple or her cats by giving them extra treats.

She enjoys simple things in life, like spending time with her family and friends, cuddling with her cats, reading and writing drool-worthy characters while sipping on hot chocolate from the wineglass to validate herself that she is actually an adult. She is an avid reader of fantasy, romance and thriller books and thinks writing about yourself in third person is atrocious. She firmly believes that cats rule the world.

www.mahimistry.com

www.ingramcontent.com/pod-product-compliance
Lightning Source LLC
LaVergne TN
LVHW091719070526
838199LV00050B/2458